A Land Remembered

Volume One

a novel by

Patrick D. Smith

A Land Remembered

Volume One
Student Edition

PINEAPPLE PRESS, INC.
Sarasota, Florida

Inquiries should be addressed to:

Pineapple Press, Inc.
P.O. Box 3889
Sarasota, Florida 34230

www.pineapplepress.com

Library of Congress Cataloging-in-Publication Data

Smith, Patrick D., 1927–
      A land remembered.— Student ed., 1st ed.
cm.
      Summary: Traces the story of the MacIvey family of Florida from 1858 to 1968.
            Volume 1 : ISBN 978-1-56164-223-6 (pb : alk. paper) ISBN 978-1-56164-230-4 (hb : alk. paper)
      Volume 2 : ISBN 978-1-56164-224-3 (pb : alk. paper) ISBN 978-1-56164-231-1 (hb : alk. paper)
      [1. Family life—Florida—Fiction. 2. Florida—Fiction.] I. Title.

PZ7.S65748 Lan 2001
[Fic]—dc21

                                                                00-053749

First Edition

Hb: 10 9 8 7 6 5 4 3 2

Pb: 15 14 13 12 11 10 9

Design by Carol Tornatore Creative Design
Printed in the United States of America

To the grandchildren —
Dan, Kimberly, Joshua, Matthew, and Alex
with love from "Grampy"

Acknowledgments

This student edition was the idea of Mary Lee Powell and Tillie Newhart, who labored on the preparation of the text. They, like many other Florida teachers, often read this favorite Florida historical novel to their classes, abridging as they read to a level appropriate for younger students. Now, with the help of a Martha Robertson Harris Scholarship through Delta Kappa Gamma Society International, they have made it available to all teachers and students in this abridged edition in two volumes.

Mary Lee Powell recently retired after teaching for thirty years in Osceola County, Florida. She has won numerous awards, including Osceola District Teacher of the Year and Disney's Teacher Merit Award. Tillie Newhart has taught for ten years in Osceola County. She was recently named Elementary Social Studies Teacher of the Year for the Osceola School District. Together they initiated a community-wide effort to involve students in developing a museum of Florida history. The Cannery Museum, located at 901 Virginia Avenue, St. Cloud, Florida, is recognized nationally as the only student-run museum in the country. The students' exhibits display many of the scenes of Florida history they learned about in *A Land Remembered*.

Foreword

It is a great pleasure to introduce a new generation of readers to one of my favorite books, given to me years ago by my grandfather, who also loved it. It tells an authentic and exciting story set amidst Florida's unique historical and cultural heritage. As you follow this family through several generations, you will see our state as it was then and understand better how it came to be as we know it today. The landscapes and people you will meet in *A Land Remembered* have changed over time. Many of you will recognize the places described here; others will be encouraged to seek them out.

The compelling tale of this family, enduring hardship, poverty, and the forces of nature, will imprint itself on each of you. You will share their tragedies and triumphs, while learning how the choices they made still impact us today. It is as enthralling a tale as it is inspiring, one that will change the way you see our state and your place in it.

A Land Remembered brings to life some fascinating cultures that are woven into the fabric of our state. Beginning with the Indian peoples who lived here for over 12,000 years, and the Spanish, French, and English settlers who followed them, Florida is a blend of many societies. The story of Tobias, Emma, Zech, and Solomon that you are about to read is just one of many exciting tales of Florida's past. Today's Florida is an exciting cultural mix of Caribbean, Latin American, Asian, and European traditions. Each has a colorful and exciting history that they bring to our state. Your family will have as great an impact on Florida history as the fictional MacIvey clan.

As you read and enjoy *A Land Remembered*, think about how the characters in this book adopted Florida and made it their real home. Each of us leaves an indelible mark on this pristine land for future generations to revere or decry. This marvelous story helped me to see our state in a new light. I hope it will help you, too, to think of Florida as your precious land, illuminate our exciting history, and inspire you to be a thoughtful steward of our environment.

You are about to enter *A Land Remembered*, a land which still can be experienced if you venture off the interstate. Enjoy the adventure!

Katherine Harris
Florida Secretary of State

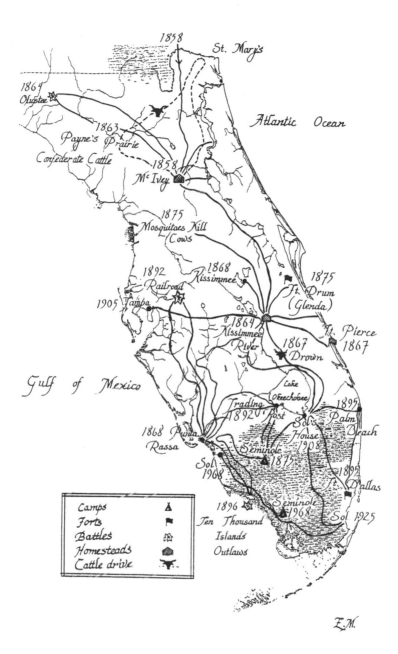

1858
St. Mary's

1864
Olustee

Atlantic Ocean

1863
Payne's Prairie
Confederate Cattle

1858
Mc Ivey

1875
Mosquitoes Kill
Cows

1892
Railroad

1868
Kissimmee

1875
Ft. Drum
(Glenda)

1905 Tampa

1864
Kissimmee
River

1867
Drown

Ft. Pierce
1867

Gulf of Mexico

Lake
Okeechobee

Trading
1892 Post

1895
Sol's Palm
House Beach
1908

1868 Punta
Rassa

Seminole
1875

1895
Ft. Dallas

Sol
1968

1896
Ten Thousand
Islands
Outlaws

Seminole
1968

Sol 1925

Camps	⛺
Forts	🚩
Battles	✵
Homesteads	▨
Cattle drive	🐂

E.M.

✝

La Florida

1863

"Not again!"

The sound of it boomed across the small clearing and seemed to rattle the palmetto trees just beyond. A startled rabbit jumped straight upward and then bounded off into the brush.

"They done it again!"

This second outburst caused a flight of crows to change course and shriek loudly in protest.

Tobias MacIvey kicked at the dry dirt with his worn brogan shoe. His black-bearded face showed sweat beneath the protection of a wide-brimmed felt hat, and his slim six-foot frame was dressed in a pair of badly faded overalls.

Just then Zechariah MacIvey came out of the brush, running as fast as his six-year old legs would carry him. He scurried through the split-rail fence and shouted, "What's the matter, Pappa? What is it?"

"Them wild hogs done pushed through the fence again and got in the garden. Just look at that! Everything I planted is rooted up, and I ain't got no more seeds. Guess we'll have to eat acorns this winter right alongside the squirrels. From the looks of this mess them hogs ain't been gone from here more than a half hour.

1

Maybe we can at least get some meat out of it. Run fetch my shotgun while I fix the fence and see if I can save anything."

"Yessir, Pappa. I'll run fetch it and be back real soon."

Tobias was on his knees, trying to straighten a collard plant, when the boy returned. He staggered as he half-carried and half-dragged a double barrel ten-gauge shotgun that looked to be as long as the trunk of a cabbage palm. He also had a shell sack around his neck.

Tobias took the shotgun and lifted it to his right shoulder, and then Zech followed as the thin man left the garden and followed a trail southward into thick woods. Tobias studied the tracks carefully, and then he said, "Looks to be about six or seven of them. They're heading for the creek to wash down my vegetables. You be careful of snakes. In this heat they'll be laying up under bushes. I wish them hogs would eat snakes like they're supposed to and leave the garden alone."

They moved silently past a thick stand of hickory trees; then the man motioned for the boy to stop. "You be real quiet from here on," he cautioned. "They're just up ahead. We don't want to come on them sudden like and have 'em turn on us. Then you'd really learn how to shinny up a tree in a hurry."

Once again they moved forward slowly, the shotgun now pointing to the ground. Tobias suddenly stopped and lifted the gun to his shoulder. Fifty feet ahead the seven hogs came out of a clump of palmetto and faced him. All were boars and each had tusks that formed a complete circle. The hogs looked ready to charge when Tobias pulled the trigger, sending forth a tremendous boom followed by a thick cloud of smoke and fire.

For a moment neither man nor boy could see through the smoke, and the sound of animals running frantically overwhelmed the echo of the shotgun. Then the wind whisked the gray cloud away, and before them one boar ran in a close circle, the entire top of its head missing, blood spewing over the ground in a flood. Then the boar fell to the ground, kicked wildly for a moment, and lay still.

Tobias said, "You see where I shot him, Zech? Right in the head. You gut shoot a wild boar, he'll run a hundred yards after he's hit, and tear your leg off with them tusks. Always shoot him in the head so he can't see you and come after you. You best take note of this."

"Yessir, Pappa," the boy said, his voice quivering. The sight of so much blood was making him sick. He forced himself to watch as his father slit the boar's throat to make sure it was dead.

Tobias then ran the knife blade down the hog's stomach, dumping the entrails onto the ground. He said, "There's my collards, right in his belly. He won't eat nothing of ours no more. He's a big one, over two hundred pounds, and he's sure too heavy for me to tote back to the house. You wait here while I go and get one of the oxen. Then we'll drag him back."

The boy sat down reluctantly beside the bloody carcass as the man walked away quickly.

Tobias MacIvey was thirty years old and had been in the Florida scrub for five years. He had come south out of Georgia in 1858. In his horse-drawn wagon there was a sack of corn and a sack of sweet potatoes, a few packets of seeds, a shotgun and a few shells, a frying pan, several pewter dishes and forks, and a cast-iron pot. There were also the tools he would need to clear the land and build a house: two chopping axes, a broadaxe foot adz, crosscut saw, auger bite, a fro and drawing knife.

His wife, Emma, five years younger than he, held the baby as gently as possible as the wagon bounced over an old Indian trail that skirted to the east of the Okefenokee Swamp and then turned due south.

Tobias had owned forty acres of red Georgia clay which he tried to farm and failed. When he sold the cabin and land he had enough money to buy only what was in the wagon.

When they crossed into Florida and reached Fernandina,

Tobias traded his horses for a pair of oxen which Zech named Tuck and Buck. Included in the trade was a guinea cow, a strange-looking little Spanish animal with a small body that stood only one foot from the ground. But she would provide milk for all of them.

The rumble of a coming civil war had already been felt in Georgia when Tobias left the clay hills and headed south to seek a new life in an unknown land. He knew it was just a matter of time. He also thought the war would not affect Florida as it would Georgia, and if he went into the eastern scrub area, he would be left alone for a long time, perhaps forever. There was nothing in the Florida wilderness worth fighting over. And his guess had been right. The war thus far touched only the coastal areas of the state, and because his homestead was so isolated, he knew little of what was happening. Occasionally a stranger would drift by and give him the news. He would also hear of the war when he made trips to a small settlement on the St. Johns River to trade animal hides for supplies.

The first two years in Florida had been a time of near starvation. He cleared a garden and planted his precious seeds, but the poor sandy soil offered little in return. And the wild animals were a constant problem when plants did break through into the sunlight. Deer, turkey, and hogs were plentiful in the woods, but shells were so hard to come by that he could kill only when he had to. Also during the first year, panthers killed the guinea cow and left only a pile of shattered bones.

During this time they lived in a lean-to made of pine limbs and palmetto thatch. There was nothing to ward off the summer mosquitoes and the roaming rattlesnakes and the rain and the biting winter cold. Emma feared for the safety of the baby, and they finally made a crude hammock so that she could at least keep him off the ground.

In the second year, Tobias started building the house, cutting the logs in a nearby hammock and dragging them to the site with the oxen, shaping the logs and lumber by hand, building a wall

4

one torturous foot at a time. The roof was of cypress shingles, and devoting what time he could to produce them, he made twenty-five each day. It took more than five hundred to build the roof. More than a year of sweat and pain went into the rugged structure before it was complete enough for them to move inside. Yet ahead of him was the task of building beds and tables and chairs and completing the mud and stone fireplace.

There were many times when Tobias thought otherwise, but they did survive. He learned many things by trial and error, and passing strangers told him of others. He learned that he could plant a wide-grained rice in rows on sandy ridges and that it would grow without irrigation, depending solely on the natural elements. Some of the seed had been given to him by a family heading south in an oxen caravan. When the first crop came in they whisked off the stalks by hand and then beat them inside a wooden barrel, catching the grains in a cloth sack.

He also found that nothing would grow on pine ridges but many food plants would survive in hammock ground, and after the second year he moved his garden away from the house area and into a nearby hammock.

A man in the St. Johns settlement told him that twenty miles to the west there was a herd of wild cows. They were too wild for anyone to ever catch without dogs and horse, but in one grazing area they had littered the ground with manure. Tobias went there with his wagon and brought back a load of manure for the garden, and each spring he would return for another load of the life-giving fertilizer.

Gradually, he made chairs from sturdy oak and wove cane bottoms onto them, and he fashioned a table from cypress. He trapped enough raccoons to trade their furs for a coal oil lamp so they could have light at night. Brooms were made from sage straw, soap from animal fat and lye; meat was preserved by smoking, and what few vegetables they did harvest were canned or dried for the winter. Emma learned to make flour from cattail roots and they used wild honey as a substitute for sugar. What they all missed most were milk and butter, and there was no substitute for them. He vowed someday that he would own another milk cow, and this time he would protect her better.

The one thing Tobias feared most was the abundance of predators that roamed the land: bears, panthers, and wolves. Nothing was safe from them, and he dared not go into the woods without the shotgun. Darkness was when the predators roamed freely, and he kept the oxen locked inside the small barn each night, even during the hottest part of summer.

Tobias came into the clearing leading the ox with the hog tied behind with a rope. Zech was riding the lumbering animal, kicking his feet into its sides and whooping loudly. The ox paid no heed to the boy as it ambled to the side of the house. Emma came outside at the sound of the commotion.

She was a robust woman dressed in an ankle-length gingham dress and high-topped laced shoes patched with deer hide. Almost as tall as Tobias, she was big-boned and brawny, and her raven-black hair was tied in a bun. Before marrying Tobias she spent her youthful days in cotton fields where her father worked as a share-cropper, and she knew work from the moment she was strong enough to carry a water bucket from well to kitchen. She was the personification of strength, and it affected all those around her.

Emma looked at the hog and said, "He's big, but he sure is scrawny. Not an ounce of fat for lard. I'll have to boil him down good before I can do anything with him, else he'll be tough as shoe leather. Maybe we can grind up some for sausage. Slice off a few thin strips of the loin and I'll fry it for supper."

Emma turned and went back inside the house as Tobias said, "Put ole Tuck back in the barn, son, and I'll start the fire." First, he would scald the hog in the huge black pot, then he would scrape the hide and cut the meat into sections. What they could not eat before it spoiled would be cured in the smokehouse Tobias had built beside the barn. The skin Emma would make into cracklins.

Soon the clearing was filled with smoke as a fire came to life beneath the cast-iron pot. Then the smell of seared flesh permeated the surroundings.

*L*ate that afternoon, they sat down to a meal of fried pork and a pot of boiled poke Emma gathered in the woods behind the barn. There was also a loaf of flat bread made from cattail flour.

Tobias said, "Lord, thank Ye for the vittles. Amen." Then he said, "Ain't much to be thankful for, is it?"

"It's food," Emma said. "But I sure wish we could get some cornmeal. A pone of cornbread would go good with some fresh swamp cabbage."

"What I hanker for is beef," Tobias said, chewing hard on the tough pork. "A roast as big as a saddle blanket. Zech's done growed up without tasting beef, and a boy like him needs beef to make him strong."

"Hog is fine for me, Pappa," Zech said, helping himself to another spoonful of poke greens.

"That's because you ain't had nothing better. If I had knowed it would be so hard here I might have stayed in Georgia. We got to get us a catch dog. If I just had a catch dog, I could round up some wild cows and start a herd. I need a horse too. A horse ain't worth nothing in pulling a wagon through this sandy soil, but you sure can't catch cows without a horse and a dog. And a dog would help keep the varmints away from here at night."

They ate in silence for a moment, and then Emma said, "It will all come in time, Tobias. We're not that bad off. We can make do till times get better for us. The Lord will look over us."

"Well, I don't believe the Lord would like to live all winter on

7

nothing but coon meat and swamp cabbage. I got to have a horse and a dog. And some more powder and shot to make shells. I can trap coons and trade the hides, but I can't trap a 'gator. You got to shoot him. And the man at the trading post told me he would pay a dollar fifty for alligator hides. I bet there's a thousand of them in the creek just waiting to be shot and skinned."

"Maybe we could kill them with an axe," Zech said, becoming excited at the thought of hunting alligators.

"Son, you hit a 'gator on the head with an axe, he'd just grab the handle and eat the whole thing. Then he'd finish up his meal with both your legs. You got to shoot a 'gator to kill him. So for now we'll have to make do with coon hides. Maybe I've got enough of them tacked to the barn to get us some real flour and some cornmeal too. And also a pound of coffee. I done forgot how it tastes. I'll go over to the trading post the end of the week and swap all I have. Tomorrow I'll cut some cypress poles and start building a pen for the cows. Somehow or other I'm going to get me a dog and horse."

🐂

CHAPTER TWO

Tobias was at the edge of the swamp just after dawn the next morning, cutting pond cypress to be used as fence rails. As each thin pole was cut he stacked it on a sled tied behind the oxen.

He heard no sound but the thud of the axe, and was unaware that someone was standing behind him. When he turned and faced the two men and the woman, he was startled. His first reaction was to run for his shotgun propped against a tree, but then he noticed that none of the strangers was armed.

The two men stared at him, as if undecided as to what they should do. The woman moved close behind the men. They were Indians, and all of them looked exhausted. The woman was dressed in a tattered deerskin robe, and the men in clothes that had a thick covering of dirt.

Tobias said cautiously, "My name is Tobias MacIvey, and I have a homestead nearby. I mean you no harm."

These were the first Seminoles Tobias had seen since coming to Florida although he had heard many tales of the Indian wars. He wondered why they were here now since there were supposed to be no more Indians in this part of the state.

One of the men said, "I am Keith Tiger, and this is Bird Jumper." He made no mention of the woman's name. "We also mean no harm. We need rest and food. Do you have food?"

"There's nothing here," Tobias responded, becoming less uneasy. "We have hog meat back at the house. We can feed you something if you'll go back there with me."

"There is not much time," Keith Tiger said, acting as spokesman for all of them. "They have horses and dogs, and they will be here soon."

9

"Who?" Tobias asked curiously.

The Indian didn't respond to the question. He said instead, "We do not mean to bring you trouble. We will eat quickly and leave. But we must have food."

Tobias picked up the shotgun and started leading the oxen into the woods. The three Indians followed in silence. They had gone but a short distance when the faint barking of dogs could be heard. Tobias stopped the oxen and said, "What's this all about? Who is it that's coming with those dogs?"

All of the Indians looked frightened. Keith Tiger said, "We killed a calf for food. It had no marking on it, and we thought it to be wild. We were seen by a man on foot, and now riders are coming for us. We have been running since noon yesterday. If they find us with you it might cause you trouble, so we will leave now."

"No," Tobias said firmly. "You will eat first. No one will harm you at my place, I'll see to that. The woods is full of wild cows, and you have as much right to an unmarked calf as anyone."

The Indians followed Tobias reluctantly as the sound of the dogs grew nearer. Just as they entered the clearing the dogs bounded out of the woods and began circling them, growling.

There were six of them, all curs, part hound and part bulldog. The two oxen bucked away from Tobias and ran for the nearby woods, pulling the loaded sled behind them. Emma and Zech came out the kitchen door, puzzled and frightened by the sight of the circling dogs and Indians.

Tobias shouted, "Go back in the house and bolt the doors! Do it quickly! And don't come back outside no matter what happens!"

They both went back inside and then peeped out a window to watch the strange happening.

Three men on horses came into the clearing at full gallop, and then reined up just short of the dogs. Two jumped from their horses while the third made a loud whistling sound, causing the dogs to back away. All of the men had muskets attached to their saddles, and all carried cowhide whips.

Tobias started backing away from the dogs. He said loudly, "What is going on here? You're invading my private property!"

One of the men said, "They stole a calf and butchered it, so we're going to teach them a lesson about rustling. And besides that, it's against the law for an Indian to be in Florida now. They're all criminals and ought to be in Oklahoma. That's the law."

"You'll do nothing to them here!" Tobias responded. "They told me the calf had no markings, and what's one puny calf to anyone?"

Two of the men suddenly unfurled their whips and started lashing the huddled Indians, making popping sounds as loud as musket fire. Each time the cowhide hit flesh, little plugs of shattered cloth and skin sprayed the air. The Indians doubled up and grunted as the whips slashed back and forth.

Tobias shouted, "Stop! I say stop!"

The two men idled the whips as the third made the whistling sound again, causing the dogs to rush forward and swarm over the Indians, growling viciously with snapping teeth as they covered the two men and the woman. The Indians tried vainly to beat the dogs away with their arms.

Tobias waited until one dog ran outside the flaying circle and then crouched, ready to spring back into the fray. He aimed quickly and fired, sending forth a cloud of gray smoke. The two unmounted horses broke and ran for the woods, and the startled dogs backed away. One of the dogs was blown in half.

The three men stared in disbelief as the long barrel came their way. One said, "What you mean, fellow? That dog was worth as much as a horse!"

"I told you to stop it!" Tobias said, his voice filled with anger. "I told you, and you wouldn't listen! Now you catch them horses and get away from here, and don't come back!"

"You taking up for them Indians? They're criminals! This ain't the end of this! We'll be back for sure!"

Tobias pointed the shotgun directly in the man's face, the barrel almost touching his nose. "You do, and it'll be the worst mistake you'll ever make! I'll be hiding behind a bush, just waiting for you! You better leave right now before I do it anyway!"

The three men backed away sullenly. Tobias continued pointing the gun as they disappeared into the woods in the direction of the horses.

Emma and Zech ran outside, and Emma said, "What in the world was that all about, Tobias? Who were those men?"

"Never mind," Tobias answered. "Just go inside and cook up some hog for these people. They're hungry. They ain't et nothing since noon yesterday. And while you're doing that I'll go fetch some swamp cabbage and some poke greens."

As Tobias started towards the woods with an axe, he turned to Zech and said, "You best go find Tuck and Buck and bring them back to the barn. We probably scared the life outen them."

*L*ater that afternoon Tobias and Zech sat on the ground outside the kitchen, watching as the Indians ate ravenously, even cracking the hog bones with their teeth and sucking out the marrow. They did not stop until nothing was left of meat or greens. Zech was facinated by them and watched each move they made.

Keith Tiger drank the last drop of liquid in the poke bowl and said, "We thank you for this, Tobias MacIvey. We could have gone no further without food. And I know of no other white man who would have risked what you did for an Indian."

"I'm just sorry we don't have more to offer. Them men had no right to do what they did, and if they come back after you I'll make it plenty hot for them." Then he asked curiously, "If it ain't asking too much, how come you folks being here? You're the first Indians I've seen around these parts."

Tiger said, "We have been walking for more than a year now,

making our way from Oklahoma, traveling mostly at night. Bird and I were with Billy Bowlegs at the start of the last war, and we went with him to Oklahoma when it ended in eighteen fifty-seven. My wife here, Lillie, went also. We stayed there until one year ago but we did not like it, and we are making our way back to join our people who are hiding out in Pay-Hay-Okee, a land far to the south that is yet unknown to the white man. There are still Seminoles hiding in swamps elsewhere, but most are in Pay-Hay-Okee."

"Well, I'm sorry I can't offer food for your journey," Tobias said, "but we just don't have much in the way of vittles. I don't have a dog or a horse and ain't got money to buy them, so I can't round up any cows. We've been having to make do mostly on coon and greens."

"What you need is a marshtackie," Tiger said. "It is a horse left behind by the Spanish soldiers. It is small and runty but very strong and big of heart. It can run all day, and it can take you to places in the swamps where no other horse can go. My people used the marshtackie back in the days before the white men told us we could no longer herd cattle. There are some of them still left in the swamps and woods. Perhaps you can catch one for yourself."

"I don't know how I could do it without a dog to help me. But I'll be on the lookout for one of them. I tried a few times to catch a wild cow with a rope, but ever time I got close enough to throw the rope, that ole cow would just run off a piece and laugh at me."

"There are ways to catch cows without dogs and horses," Tiger said. "Maybe someday we can show you. But we must go now. We have a long journey yet ahead of us."

"Ain't a bit of use in the world to do that," Tobias said. "You can stay the night here and rest, and then go in the morning. If you don't mind sleeping on the floor, you can stay in the kitchen."

"The rest would be good for us," Tiger responded, "but we will sleep in the shed. We are not used to a house."

"You're plumb welcome to do so. And in the morning, we'll

scrape up something for you to eat, even if it ain't nothing more than coon stew."

Keith Tiger said, "We thank you again, Tobias MacIvey. We will not forget you for this."

The next morning, just before dawn, Tobias went out to the shed to awaken the Indians to eat coon stew Emma had prepared for them. There was no one there.

✝

CHAPTER THREE

The wheels creaked loudly as the wagon moved slowly along the old Indian trail that was just wide enough for it to pass. Both sides of the trail were bordered thickly with scrub pine and hickory and giant oaks, whose limbs were entwined with muscadine vines and Spanish moss. Occasionally a palmetto frond blocked the way and Tobias had to duck under it as the wagon passed.

Dawn was just breaking when the wagon left the woods and entered the flat expanse of marsh leading to the west bank of the St. Johns River. Fog lay low over the land, forming a cloud through which Tobias could not see, so he watched the ground ahead of him carefully as he pointed the oxen and wagon in the direction of the settlement.

As the sun rose higher, the fog burned away quickly , exposing huge flights of egrets and herons and wood ibis, winging their way both north and south to favorite feeding grounds.

Tobias could now see a thin spiral of black smoke drifting straight upward from the trading post chimney. This was a good sign, for it meant no rain, and Tobias feared the low-lying river flats when they were muddy or flooded. If the smoke drifted downward, it meant morning rain.

In addition to the trading post, there were three shacks built along the river bank, and all were the homes of mullet fishermen. Tobias guided the oxen to a hitching rail in front of the weathered old building and stopped. The trading post and the shacks were built on pilings ten feet off the ground to protect them from spring floods.

When Tobias climbed the cypress steps and entered, the

proprietor, Silas Jenkins, was sitting by a pot-bellied stove. He looked up and said, "Morning, Tobias. It gets chilly on the river in early morning, and a fire feels good." He was a thin man in his fifties, with skin burned black by the Florida sun, his hair solid white and rumpled.

Tobias said, "It's always cooler here than in the scrub. Sometimes I wish I'd settled by the river, but here again we don't have skeeters as bad as you do."

"That's a fact for sure. What can I do for you?"

"I've got twenty coon skins in the wagon I'd like to trade for supplies."

Jenkins shook his head negatively and said, "I got bad news, Tobias. Some Reb soldiers with wagons come in here three weeks ago and took everything I had. Flour, sugar, coffee, cornmeal, bacon, salt. Everything. Paid me just enough to cover my cost. I ain't got one blessed thing left to trade."

This news frightened Tobias. "Lordy, that is bad, Silas. I'm out of everything. I don't know what I'll do."

"It's bad on everyone along the river, including me. I ain't et nothing for three weeks now but mullet. And I won't have nothing else at all to trade unless a boat comes down from Jacksonville, and that ain't likely with them Federal troops taking the city one day and then leaving and coming back the next. They done took it now three times. One of the Reb soldiers told me that the Feds took it again about two months ago, and when they pulled out to go fight up around Savannah, they set fire to the city and burned about seven or eight blocks, including the church and the courthouse."

"How is the war going?" Tobias asked.

"Real bad, they say. The Feds have got every port blockaded, and ain't hardly nothing getting through from Cuba. Even the Reb soldiers ain't got uniforms to wear, much less anything to eat. Women are sewing socks and pants and making bandages from anything they can get their hands on. Them soldiers told me that if it wasn't for the scrawny Florida cattle they wouldn't have no meat at all or no tallow and hides. Even their salt is coming from St. Andrews Bay over on the Gulf. He said they were making coffee from parched meal and sweet potatoes. And it's going to get a lot worse before it gets better."

Tobias felt a deep sinking feeling as Jenkins spoke. "What about powder and shot?" he asked anxiously. "Did they take all that too? There ain't no way I can make it in the scrub without some more powder and shot."

"With that I can help you a mite," Jenkins said, getting up. "I hid some under a plank in the floor. I knowed there would be people around here in deep trouble without it. In even more trouble than the Reb soldiers. They can always surrender if they have to, but there ain't no way a man can surrender to a bear or a panther or a pack of wolves. I'll let you have what I can."

Tobias felt relief as Jenkins removed a box from beneath a loose plank and measured out a sack of lead shot and a sack of black powder. At least he could make more shells for protection and to kill for food when he had to. He said, "I don't know how to thank you, Silas. I'll bring in the skins."

"Just throw them on the porch when you leave. And Tobias, keep a good watch out. Them Feds has got raiding parties out everywhere now. They done hit Palatka and Gainesville, and they're roaming the countryside. What cattle they can't steal, they shoot. They're taking anything that ain't nailed down, and they've burned a lot of homesteads. The Rebs have formed a Cow Cavalry of local men to help fight off the raids and guard the cattle. If they come your way, you best be careful."

"They ain't likely to come into the scrub, unless they get a hankering for coon meat. But I'll keep an eye out, and I rightly thank you for the warning. I'll be back afore long."

"Take care," Jenkins said, sitting again by the stove.

17

On the way back Tobias decided not to tell Emma and Zech just how severe things were. He would say only that the trading post was temporarily sold out of the things they needed. Maybe a supply boat would get through before winter, and there was no need to cause them unnecessary anxiety.

He was also thinking of the news Jenkins gave him of the Federal raiding parties, the blockades, and the burning of Jacksonville. Thus far the war was not real to him. It was something happening elsewhere, but now it was getting closer and becoming very real. The scrub was no longer a sure sanctuary, and he dreaded the thought of what would happen if Federal troops fired the woods. Fire was the most feared killer in scrub land. It could race over the land as quickly as the wind, destroying man and animal before they had any chance of escape.

Before he reached the clearing, he stopped in a low hammock area and allowed the oxen to graze. There was nothing for them to eat on the pine ridge, and since he had no corn or other feed to give them, he had to take them each day to wherever grass could be found.

The sun was setting when he finally unhitched the animals and locked them inside the barn. Layers of red and orange meshed all across the sky and caused the tops of trees to glow a somber yellow. He looked up momentarily as a flight of crows passed over the clearing, cawing loudly, heading for some unknown haven for the night.

When he came into the kitchen with only the small sacks of powder and shot, Emma looked at this and said, "Where are the supplies, Tobias? Do you need help bringing them in?"

Tobias sat at the table and said, "There are none. They were sold out of everything, but a supply boat will come soon from Jacksonville. I'll go back then and get the things we need. I did trade for a small amount of powder and shot."

Emma made no comment as she stirred a pot of poke greens.

18

She dumped them into a bowl, set it on the table and then said, "The Indians ate up the rest of the hog meat, and this is all we have for supper. I'm sorry. Maybe you can trap a coon tonight."

Zech came to the table and sat down, and he and Tobias helped themselves to the greens. Tobias said, "Trapping coons is something that's beginning to worry me. I got nothing left to bait the traps, and ain't no coon or nothing else going to walk into a trap for nothing and then shut the door on himself. Maybe I can build some bird traps. I could bait them with grass seeds or berries or something. They's plenty of birds in the woods just waiting to be et."

Emma joined them, and for several minutes they ate in silence. Then she said, "Did Mister Jenkins say anything about the war? Did he have news?"

"Not too much. He said the Feds took Jacksonville about two months ago, but they're gone now, up to Savannah. He also said there are Federal raiding parties up to the north of us, but they won't come here. The Rebs have formed a Cow Cavalry of local men to keep the raiders away from the herds."

Emma looked up anxiously. "What if they come for you, Tobias? What if they make you join this Cow Cavalry?"

"They don't even know we're here," Tobias responded, noticing her sudden fear. "I don't think they'll ever come into the scrub."

Emma had never complained about her isolated and lonely existence. Sometimes she ached for female companionship, for just someone to talk to, for a church social or a quilting bee. But she kept these yearnings to herself. Tobias and Zech would never know. But the fear of being left alone in the scrub without Tobias was overwhelming.

Tobias watched her closely, and then he said reassuringly, "They'll never come here, Emma. There's nothing to fear."

"I hope so. It would be hard for me and Zech to be out here alone."

Changing the subject, Tobias said, "Since I have powder and shot, I can make shells tonight. Maybe tomorrow morning I can kill a deer. I know a place on the other side of the creek where there's a patch of wild rye grass, and the deer are feeding there. The last time I took the oxen there to graze, I seen deer tracks everywhere."

"Can I go with you, Pappa?" Zech asked quickly. He had never been further from the clearing than the south hammock or the east bank of the creek where they killed the boar.

"Yes, you can go. It's about time you learned something about the woods over there."

Zech became even more excited. "Can I shoot the gun, Pappa? Will you teach me how to shoot it?"

Tobias laughed. "We better not do that just yet. You fire that big ole cannon, it would probably knock you slam from here to the St. Johns. You ain't growed up enough for that yet."

🐂

Tobias waited until dawn for them to leave the clearing and enter the woods. The pine ridges and bottom lands were filled with rattlesnakes. He knew he could probably avoid them, and instantly hear their warning, but Zech could be hit before he knew what was happening. And this would be even more likely in the dark.

Mist seeped through the woods like smoke, and the ground was damp with a thin covering of dew. Squirrels barked constantly as they scurried from their nests and bounded off through tree limbs, jumping from tree to tree, starting a daily circus which would continue until they went back to the nests in mid-morning to rest. Then it would begin once more in late afternoon.

Zech became more and more excited as they penetrated the thick woods and went past the spot where Tobias had shot the hog. They soon entered bottom land, and here there were thick canebrakes and huckleberry bushes and rotted logs and clumps of palmetto and Spanish bayonet.

They turned south and followed the east bank of the shallow creek. Its water was crystal clear, and green moss on the bottom waved gently with the slow-moving current. Bass could be seen darting in and out of the foliage, chasing small perch and minnows.

Suddenly they heard a series of harsh, loud screams come from somewhere above them. It sounded like quarrelsome old men fussing at each other. Tobias put his hand on Zech's shoulder and cautioned him to be very quiet.

A flock of ten birds lit in an oak tree just ahead of them. Zech's eyes widened in wonderment as he stared at them. They were a foot long and six inches tall, with long pointed tails and yellow heads that became rich orange around their bills.

Zech whispered, "What are they, Pappa? I've never seen birds like that." He was afraid they would fly away too soon, and he felt that he could stare at them forever.

"They're Carolina parakeets. I come on them down here ever once in a while, but not often. They stay mostly along bottom land. They used to be in swamps up in Georgia in the summer, but they're gone now. Folks killed them for the meat and the tail feathers. The cold kills them too, and that's why they'd always fly south in winter. If it ever comes a hard enough freeze down here and stays that way long enough, it will probably wipe them out if they ain't all been shot and et by then."

"I wouldn't kill them," Zech said, his eyes still wide. "They're too purty to kill. I'd rather shoot a ugly ole crow and let the parakeets alone just to look at."

"Some folks don't care," Tobias said. "When I was about your age I followed some men on a hunt, and they come on some of these birds in a swamp. They shot one, and when it fell to the ground, the other flew off into the trees. In a few seconds one of them came back to the dead one, and then they all started coming back, one by one. They are the only birds I have known to do this. They kept coming back to the dead till the men just sat there and killed every one of them. Maybe they were coming back to grieve over the dead. I don't rightly know. But when them men found out that if you kill one Carolina, then the others will keep coming back to the dead, they hunted them and shot every one in the county. Wiped them out clean. Let's let the birds be and move on now and see can we find us a deer."

As they started forward, the birds flew away, again screaming loudly. Zech wondered if he would see them again. He stared after them until the sound could no longer be heard.

Tobias said, "We best cross the creek here. The meadow is just over yonder."

They waded through the cool water and skirted the south end

of a canebrake. Just past this there were more dense woods; then the trees thinned out along the edge of the meadow.

As they approached the opening, they got down on hands and knees and crawled. The clearing was covered by a slightly swaying carpet of deep green rye, but it was empty. No deer were to be seen.

Tobias eased out into the meadow cautiously, searching each path that led back into the woods. Then he stopped and dropped to his knees. There was pile of manure on the ground, and when he touched it, it was warm. He said, "We must of just missed them. They ain't been gone two minutes. Maybe they heard us coming and took off. Let's ease back to the edge of the woods and wait. They might come back if we'll be real quiet."

They hid behind a bush and waited. Crows flew by and cawed, and squirrels barked in the trees above them, but no deer came. Tobias was just about ready to give up when he heard a sound in the woods across the meadow. It was a thrashing sound, not like a deer, more like a bear or a pack of bears.

The sound grew louder, and then the bushes shook as the animal suddenly broke through them and ambled into the clearing. Tobias exclaimed, "Great day, Zech, it's a Andalusian bull!"

Zech was too fascinated to say anything. And he was also frightened. The bull was bluish roan in color, with huge horns that came upward out of its head and then turned outward, spanning three feet each.

Tobias had seen wild cattle in the woods before, but they had been the smaller, runty yellowhammers, some not much larger than deer. He knew there were also Andalusians, but this was the first time one had come this close to the homestead. They usually stayed on open prairies where they could band together to fight off predators. One lone bull this size would stand no chance if attacked in thick woods by a band of wolves.

As the bull started grazing, Tobias eased up the shotgun and cocked one hammer. He was awed by the bull's majesty and sleek strength, knowing that this animal and its kind had survived in the wilderness over the centuries since it was brought here by the Spanish, overcoming tremendous odds. He hated to kill it, but he knew he was seeing enough beef on the hoof to keep his family alive for a long time to come. He hesitated for a moment more, and then he aimed and fired.

At first the bull just stood there, and then it bellowed loudly and fell on its left side. It was dead instantly, its heart having caught the full load of shot. Blood rushed from a huge hole in its side and from its mouth. Its eyes rolled upward and then inward, as if trying to see inside its own body and determine what had happened.

Tobias trembled as he walked across the meadow to the downed animal. A huge spot of the green grass was now stained red. He put his foot on the bull's back and shoved, to see if there was any life left. His brogan pushed only dead weight. Then he turned to Zech and said, "There ain't no way we can get this critter out of here by ourselves. You think you know the way back to the house?"

"I know, Pappa. What you want me to do?"

"Go and get both Tuck and Buck and bring them back here. And bring an axe. I can cut some poles and make a sled, and we can haul it out of here on that. While you're gone I'll go on and gut it. Can you do this, Zech? If you ain't sure, I can go back with you. I just don't want the buzzards to get at all this meat."

"I can do it, Pappa. Don't you worry none at all. I'll be back before you know it." He turned and ran quickly into the woods.

It was dark when Tobias hung the last section of meat in the smokehouse and stoked the fire. Every ounce of the bull would be used. The tail was skinned and chopped into sections for stew, and the leg bones and ribs would go into soup. The brains would be scooped out and fried, the hooves boiled into jelly. Tobias would take the hide and the horns to the settlement. He thought he would get at least two dollars in trade for the hide.

Emma was taking a roast from the pot and putting it on the table when Tobias came into the kitchen. He said, "Thank the Lord for all blessings and for making that bull come out of the woods just when he did. Now we can keep old man hunger away for a while longer."

Emma smiled and said, "In the morning I'll boil the heart and liver for breakfast. It will be good for Zech. Beef liver makes a boy grow strong."

Tobias sniffed deeply. "Lordy, Lordy, that meat smells good. I don't know if my belly can still handle a beef roast. It's so used to coon and poke. But I'm sure willing to try."

They all sat at the table and relished the meal in silence. Afterwards, Emma cleaned the plates and then they sat on the stoop outside the kitchen. Tobias patted his stomach and said, "I wish I had a pipe and some tobacco. A man needs a smoke after a meal like that."

Zech groaned, "I et too much, and I'm kind of tired after all we done today. Is it all right if I go on to bed now?"

"We're all tired," Tobias replied, "and we'll all go on to bed. I'll have to get up around midnight and see to the fire in the smokehouse."

As soon as they were inside, Zech climbed the ladder to the loft where he slept. Almost instantly they could hear the sound of snoring.

From far in the distance Tobias heard the lone cry of a wolf. Then it was answered with another cry, and then another, a mournful, menacing sound. He wished he had a dog, or better still, a pack of them. If he had at least one, it would help keep the varmints away. And maybe with it, he could catch a cow.

🐂

CHAPTER FIVE

Summer passed slowly into early fall as Tobias finally finished building the fence where he hoped to someday pen his wild cattle. One row of corn in the garden had been made to grow again, and there was a patch of collards. But there were no beans or potatoes. The hogs had taken care of that. The family had eaten as little as possible of the beef and were saving it for the coming winter months when things would be even more lean than they were now.

He also made another trip to the trading post on the banks of the St. Johns. No supply boat came south out of Jacksonville, and there would be no flour or cornmeal or sugar or salt and no oil to light the lamp. Jenkins gave him the last few ounces of the hoarded powder and shot, and each precious shell would have to be used wisely.

Tobias was out by the shed, chopping firewood, when he heard the sound of a rider coming through the woods. He put down the axe and picked up the shotgun, which he always kept nearby.

The man was riding a tall black stallion. He wore a huge brown hat and boots that came up to his knees. His face was completely covered by a red beard. A pistol was strapped to his side, and there was a rifle in his saddle holster. He rode directly to Tobias and dismounted.

"Howdy," Tobias said cautiously, holding the shotgun with his right hand on the hammer, relieved that the rider was not wearing an army uniform.

"Howdy," the man responded, "Name's Henry Addler."

"Tobias MacIvey."

"You can put that down. You don't need it with me."

Tobias leaned the shotgun against the shed wall. "It pays to be cautious these days," he said.

"That it do."

The man looked around for a moment, and then he said, "Some place you got here, but it's sure isolated. I ain't seen nothing for two days but woods. How long you been here?"

"Going on six years. Came down out of Georgia in fifty-eight. Built the house myself and cleared the garden."

"Don't see how you folks make it out here in the scrub."

"It ain't easy. Times has been hard."

"You ever herded cattle?" Addler asked.

"All I ever done is farmed."

"Don't matter. You'll learn fast."

This statement puzzled Tobias. He said, "What you mean by that?"

"I'm a state marshal, commissioned by the governor, and I'm rounding up drivers to move a herd up to Georgia. Most ever ablebodied man who's not in the army is riding patrol with the Cow Cavalry. You the first one I found who ain't, so I'm recruiting you as a driver. I got the authority to do so."

Tobias felt a deep sinking feeling. He said, "How do I know you're what you say you are? You got proof?"

The man pulled a piece of paper from his pocket and handed it to Tobias. "Read this. It's my commission from the governor."

Tobias took the paper, glanced at it briefly and handed it back. "I can't read. I'll just have to take your word for it. But I got a wife and a boy out here. It would be hard on them if I left them alone."

"Ever man's got a wife and boy. It's hard on all of us. This war ain't no church social. If we don't get them cows to the army, our soldiers won't have nothin' to eat. And if they don't eat, they can't fight. It's as simple as that."

"Just what is it I'm supposed to do?"

"The herd is up north of here, on the Alachua savanna. We got to move them to Trader Hill on the St. Marys River. From there an army squad will take them over the state line and up to Atlanta."

"How long will it take?"

"I can't rightly say. We'll have to let them walk at their own pace, and graze along the way, else time we get them there they wouldn't be nothing but hide and bones, not even fittin' for soup. I'd say we'll cover eight or nine miles a day at best. You ought to be back home in a few weeks. You got a horse?" Addler asked.

"No. I only got oxen."

"They's horses up at the savanna. And you don't need to bring along that cannon. That's the biggest shotgun I ever seen. You try to take that thing on a horse, there wouldn't be no room for the saddle."

"It hits what you aim at."

"I'll wait here while you go tell your woman, but get a move on. Them cows should 'a been in Georgia two weeks ago."

Tobias turned and walked slowly to the house, feeling as if the weight of an ox had suddenly been dropped on his shoulders. Emma was standing outside the kitchen door, watching. She too had heard the approach of the rider. She could tell by the expression on Tobias' face that it was something serious.

Before Tobias could speak she said, "You've got to go, haven't you?"

"Yes. He's a state marshal. I got to help move a herd of cattle up to the Georgia border. It's for the army. Soon as we get them there I'm done with it and can come on back home. It ought not take too long."

"We'll make do all right," she said, trying hard to conceal the fear that would cause Tobias additional worry. "We got meat, and there's greens enough. We'll make do fine."

Zech was standing nearby, listening. He didn't understand what was happening, only that his father must go away. He said, "I'll take care of the garden, Pappa. And I can chop wood too."

Tobias put his hand on the boy's shoulder. "You ain't hardly big enough to pick up an axe, much less chop logs. But do the best you can by your mamma, and give her all the help you can. You hear?"

"I hear, Pappa."

Tobias then turned to Emma. "The shotgun is loaded, and there's more shells in the kitchen cabinet. I should have taught you how to shoot it, but I didn't think this time would come. Use it if you have to. And don't let no strangers come in the house."

"I know how to point a gun," she responded. "Just don't you worry. We'll be fine."

"There's one thing you'll have to do, Zech," Tobias then said. "Take ole Tuck and Buck down to the hammock ever morning and let them graze awhile. And don't ever leave them outside the barn at night. Not ever! And be sure the barn door is locked."

"I'll do it, Pappa. I can look after them."

Tobias took Emma's hand and said, "I'm sorry. He's a state marshal, and I've got to go. I'll be back just as soon as I can."

With that he turned and walked away quickly, following the mounted rider into the woods.

Emma stood on the stoop and watched him disappear. Then she looked around the empty clearing and at the wood shed. She said to Zech, "I best cut some more firewood. Tobias didn't get to finish the chopping."

By the time they reached the Alachua savanna three days later, Addler had recruited five more men to act as drivers. All of them were older than Tobias, and one had a left arm missing. Another wore a patch over his right eye.

Addler opened a box and handed each driver a rawhide whip. Then he took one himself and swished it back and forth, making it pop. He said, "After you learn to use this thing, you can pop off a rattler's head at twenty feet. And there ain't no cow alive you can't turn with it. So best you learn how to use it real fast."

Tobias and three of the other men selected horses and mounted. All of the horses had McClellan military saddles without horns. Addler then motioned them into a circle and said, "We'll move 'em along an old military road as far as we can and try to keep 'em out of the woods. If one goes off into the woods, go after him right away. And don't try to push them. Just let 'em walk along as slow as they want, and eat. Last time we pushed a herd too fast the cows lost a hundred and fifty pounds apiece time we got to Georgia. An extra hundred and fifty pounds per cow will feed a lot of men. So let 'em go slow. And just remember one thing. These are wild swamp cows. They didn't come out of somebody's barn. They ain't used to being drove, and they spook easy. If one goes, they all go. They can take off like thunder and stomp a man and a horse as flat as a pancake before you know what's happening. So be careful."

Addler then furled the whip and said, "O.K., that's it. Let's go to Georgia. They's a lot of hungry soldiers waiting on us."

It was on the fifth night after Tobias left that Emma was awakened by the sound of the oxen kicking the barn wall. Zech heard it too, and they both went to a window and looked out. Zech said, "What is it, Mamma? The oxen are trying to tear down the barn."

"I don't know, but something is sure frightening them."

A full moon bathed the clearing with light, revealing the barn and the shed and the woods beyond. From behind the barn there suddenly appeared a black form, and then another. Then came the sound of growling.

"Bears!" Emma said. "They're trying to get in the barn. Oh Lord, Tobias! I don't know what to do!"

"Pappa always said fire," Zech said. "He said they're afraid of fire."

"We can't go out there, Zech. There's nothing we can do but

hope they don't break into the house. I best get the shotgun ready in case we need it."

Zech grabbed his mother's arm and said, "We got to do something, Mamma! Pappa put me in charge of Tuck and Buck! We got to do something!"

His insistence calmed her. She said, "We'll light two pine torches and go outside. But if they come after us, run back in the house as fast as you can. Do you understand me, Zech? Don't try anything foolish!"

Emma lit the torches and handed one to Zech; then they went into the yard just outside the kitchen. The bears were circling the barn and scratching at the door, causing the oxen to shriek like screech owls and kick the walls violently. One bear turned and ran directly at them. When Zech thrust his torch forward, the bear stopped and reared, looming over both of them. Emma and Zech started backing toward the stoop.

Emma said, "They're not afraid of the fire, Zech. We'll never drive them away. We best go back in the house."

"They're hungry, Mamma, and they're after something to eat," Zech said. "Maybe if we open the smokehouse they'll smell the meat and go after it and leave the barn alone."

"Maybe so, and maybe not," Emma replied doubtfully. "But I guess it's worth a try. You stay here and I'll go open the smokehouse door."

Zech watched as his mother made her way slowly to the smokehouse, undetected thus far. The bears were still clawing at the barn, and the sound of kicking hooves became louder. She unlatched the door and propped it open with a stick, and then she started backing toward the stoop.

Emma was halfway across the yard when both of the bears rushed over and circled her, blocking her escape route. She whirled around and around, terrified, pushing her torch at them. Fear gripped Zech as he watched; then he threw down his torch, ran inside and returned, dragging the shotgun.

The bears circled and growled as Zech tried vainly to lift the heavy gun and point it. Then he went to the side of the house and picked up a piece of firewood. He sat on the ground, propped the long barrel on top of the split wood, and took aim at the nearest bear. When he pulled the trigger, the shotgun flew out of his hands and he was knocked backward, tumbling over and over in the dirt.

The load of shot hit the bear with such force that it knocked him into the wall of the woodshed ten feet away. The tremendous boom caused the other bear to scurry off into the edge of the woods. Emma dropped her torch and ran for the house, knowing that the retreat was only temporary.

Zech was stunned senseless for a moment, and then he pushed himself up and crawled to the shotgun. He picked it up as Emma shouted frantically, "Go in the house, Zech! Go in the house!"

They both rushed inside and looked out a window as the other bear came back and invaded the smokehouse, growling as it slashed into chunks of meat. For more than an hour the fierce sounds broke the stillness of the night, and then the bear ran into the woods and did not return.

When she felt sure the bear was gone for good, Emma lit more torches and they went outside cautiously, watching the edge of the woods for any sign of activity. Zech noticed now that his shoulder hurt badly. He unlocked the barn door, went inside and patted the oxen, saying gently, "Don't you worry none. It's all over. They ain't going to hurt you. Pappa put me in charge, and I'll see to it."

Emma was by the woodshed, holding the torch over the lifeless form. Zech came back out, locked the barn door and went over to his mother. The bear was covered with blood and its eyes were wide open, staring at them, its mouth peeled back in a snarl.

Emma shuddered, and then she said, "I don't want to look any-more. I'll have nightmares all night as it is. Let's go back inside and bolt the doors. I wish that thing would just get up and go away. We'll have to do something with it in the morning."

As they started toward the house Zech said, "Pappa put me in charge of the oxen. That bear better not come back here no more. He better not!"

Emma put her arm around him. She thought that perhaps he had missed his childhood, that he had been forced to grow up too soon. She said gently, "I love you, Zech. And Tobias will be real proud of you. Real proud."

The drive went well and on the fourteenth day they reached the banks of the St. Marys where Confederate soldiers waited to take over the herd and cross the river into Georgia.

Addler said to them, "Any man who wants to can ride back with me to the savanna, but some of you might want to take a more direct route home. It's up to you."

"I'll turn straight south," Tobias said. "Ain't no use in me going back that far north. Can I take the horse?"

"No way!" Addler said firmly, surprised that Tobias had even asked. "You ought to know better than that. We got to have them horses for the next drive."

"Without a horse, how am I supposed to get all the way from here back to my place?"

"Same way you got from your place to the savanna. Walk. You know I can't give you a horse. But you got some pay coming. Every man gets a dollar a day for the drive."

This surprised Tobias, for he had not expected pay. As he took the coins he said, "I sure thank you for this, Mister Addler. It's the first cash money I've had in a long time. But can I at least keep the whip? It would be a great help to me in the scrub."

"Yes, you can have the whip. We can replace it but not a horse."

Tobias put the money in his pocket. "I'm glad we made it with the cattle," he said. "But Mister Addler, please don't come after me again. I fear for the safety of my wife and boy."

"Maybe I will and maybe I won't," Addler said. "I try to spread the job around as best I can. So maybe I won't. I know how you feel about your family so far out in the woods. But let me tell you one thing for sure, MacIvey. If soldiers come to recruit you into the army, tell them you're a driver just home between trips. If they think you're one of my men they'll leave you alone. We need drivers right now a lot worse than we need soldiers."

"I'll do that," Tobias said gratefully. "And I thank you for telling me. It's best I start now. I've got a long walk ahead of me."

Addler watched him for a moment, and then he called after him, "Good luck, MacIvey! And be careful! Maybe I won't see you no more!"

It took Tobias eight days to make his way down the west bank of the St. Johns to the trading post and then through the woods to his homestead. Along the way he scrounged whatever he could find to eat. One night he slipped into a barnyard and stole a chicken, gripping its throat tightly so it would not cackle and give him away. This lasted for two days. He also caught frogs along the riverbank and cooked their legs on sticks.

When finally he walked into the clearing he was even more skinny than he had always been. No one was in sight as he came around the side of the house to the kitchen door.

The moment she saw him Emma rushed to him and said, "Tobias! I'm so glad you're home! I'm so glad!"

Zech heard her and came running from the direction of the barn, shouting, "I killed a bear, Pappa! They tried to get Tuck and Buck and we wouldn't let 'em! I killed one, Pappa!"

"You killed a bear?" Tobias questioned.

"I shot him, Pappa! Blowed him clear across the yard and into the woodshed. That old gun knocked me all the way back to the stoop. It got a real kick, ain't it?"

"I guess it has." He then looked at Emma. "What's Zech talking about?"

"They came one night, Tobias, two of them, trying to get in the barn. They was in a real frenzy, and we didn't know what to do. We tried to run them off with torches, but they wouldn't go away. I finally opened the smokehouse so they would leave the barn and go after the meat. They hemmed me up, and Zech shot one of them. Hadn't been for Zech I don't know what would have happened to me."

"Goodness!" Tobias exclaimed. "They could have kilt you as easy as nothing. But it's good you opened the smokehouse. All the meat in the world ain't worth one of you getting hurt or kilt. You're a good boy, Zech! You done real good. I couldn't have handled it better myself."

"Where'd you get the whip, Pappa?" Zech asked. "Can I see it?"

Tobias handed it to him. "They gave it to me after the drive. It's what you use to herd cattle. And it will kill, too, if you want it to. It's rawhide."

"Did you fight a battle, Pappa?" Zech then asked, unfurling the whip.

"Yes, we had a real ruckus one night."

"With soldiers?"

"No. With wolves. We had as bad a time with them as you did with the bears."

"Can I try the whip, Pappa?"

"Yes. You can try all you want. But be careful. That thing can strip the hide off a bull at twenty feet. It ain't no plaything. Drivers kill rattlers with them."

Zech slashed the whip back and forth as Tobias and Emma went into the kitchen and sat at the table. Emma said, "I'm really glad you're back, Tobias. It was a bad night when the bears came. But Zech did you proud. If he was afraid he never showed it. The next morning he tried to skin out the bear by himself, but he just couldn't cut through the hide. I helped him, and we got out some meat. One of the bears shredded everything in the smokehouse, and there was nothing left that was fit to eat."

"It don't matter none at all, Emma. I'll get more meat somehow

35

before winter sets in. I'm just glad you were done no harm. I don't want to go away again and leave you here by yourself."

"Was the drive bad?"

"Not too much. It was rough at first, me sitting in a saddle all day and not used to it. I could hardly squat down at night to take a meal. At the end of the drive Mister Addler gave me fourteen dollars, a dollar a day in pay. It ought to be a big help to us if Jenkins ever gets in more supplies. I come by there yesterday and he still didn't have anything."

"We'll make do somehow. We always have."

Tobias said, "It must be real bad up in Georgia now. Real bad. Folks is likely starving. And it's going to get worse. Sometimes I wish we'd never stopped here but kept going south, as far away from the war as we could go. I hope they don't come after me again."

"Did the man say he would?"

"No. He wouldn't say for sure. He said he'd try not to, but he's got a job to do, and he has to do it any way he can. I'll just have to wait and see."

Emma then said, "Are you hungry? I clear forgot to ask."

"I'm about to starve. I didn't have much along the way."

"You sit right here and rest while I go pick some collards. I'll make you a big pot of greens. And I'll fry the bear meat that's left in the smokehouse. It won't take me but a few minutes."

As he sat alone at the table he could hear the whip popping. He got up and looked outside, watching as Zech cracked it almost as well as Addler could.

🐂

CHAPTER SIX

A sharp February wind stung his face as Tobias stood beneath the bare hickory tree, watching the squirrel come closer. The leaves were gone now, as were the patches of wild poke, and only the palmetto and the cabbage palm looked the same as it did in summer.

The squirrel flicked its tail nervously; then it came further down the limb. When the whip cracked, it knocked the small animal senseless. As soon as it hit the ground Tobias grabbed it and broke its neck. Then he put it in the hunting sack with the others.

Zech had also become expert with the whip and had killed several rabbits with it. It was the only thing keeping meat on the table.

Tobias folded the whip and started back along the path to the clearing. His feet made crunching sounds as he walked over thick beds of brown leaves. He thought that tomorrow he would go down to the creek bottom and gather cattail roots which Emma would roast and then pound into flour.

When he reached the garden he paused for a moment and looked at the bare ground. He said to himself, "Next spring I'll make the fence stronger and add a few rails. There's bound to be a way to keep the critters out."

When he came around the side of the barn he noticed the horse immediately. No rider was in sight, and he thought that perhaps Addler had returned for him. He had really been expecting it but hoped it would not happen.

Then a man in a uniform came from the kitchen, followed by

Emma and Zech. The uniform was Confederate gray. The soldier was the same age as Tobias, and he too wore a black beard.

Tobias approached the house with dread, remembering what Addler told him to say if an army recruiter came. He said "Howdy." Then he threw the sack of squirrels onto the stoop floor.

The soldier returned the greeting, and then he said, "I'm Captain Graham. We need your help."

"I can't go in the army," Tobias said quickly. "I'm a driver."

"Who do you work for?"

"Addler. Henry Addler. We run from the Alachua savanna over to the St. Marys. I'm just home between drives."

"I'm not here to put you in the army, so it don't matter if you're a driver or not."

"If you don't want me to soldier, what is it you want me to do?" Tobias asked, puzzled.

"Cut logs for forts. The Federals have sent thirty-five troop ships out of Hilton Head. They'll land at the mouth of the St. Johns. Then they'll try to cut the state in two and stop the supply lines. If they do that, there won't be no more cows heading north for you to drive, and there won't be nothing more for our men to eat. We've got to stop them or it'll be all over. We've got two thousand troops ready now and three thousand more on the way. We're making our stand at Olustee, a few miles east of Lake City. And we're in bad need of log cutters."

"And what if I don't want to go?" Tobias asked.

"Mister, there's a war on if you don't know it. This whole state is under marshal law. If you refuse, I got the right to shoot you right here on the spot, and I will too. So you ain't got no choice. And I'm not going to stand here and argue. Them Federal troops could have already landed by now. Are you ready to go?"

"You done said I got no choice. Do I need to take along my shotgun? And I ain't got a horse."

"You don't need to take nothing but yourself. If it gets down to where you have to shoot, we'll give you a gun. And I've got log wagons just up north of here. You can ride from there."

Tobias turned to Emma. "Maybe I'll be back real soon. A battle sure couldn't take as much time as a cattle drive." Then he said to Zech, "You clean them squirrels there for your mamma. And take the whip and kill something ever day for the two of you to eat."

"They's rabbits on that patch of winter rye where I take Tuck and Buck ever morning, Pappa. I'll kill one ever time I go there."

Tobias embraced Emma briefly. Then once again he followed a mounted rider across the clearing and into the woods.

Tobias passed down the line and was handed a tin cup of thin beef stew and a piece of black bread. Then he sat on a log and started eating.

A man beside him said, "A soldier told me that them Federal troops has raided Baldwin and Gainesville and took everything they could get their hands on. Cows, horses, mules, corn. Whatever. They're even taking ever black they can find. And they're on their way here now. It could happen tomorrow."

"I wish it would and be done with," Tobias responded, chewing the tough bread. "I been here over two weeks and I'm ready to go back home and see to my wife and boy."

"I know what you mean. I don't ever want to cut down another tree. We must of chopped two thousand logs by now."

"I guess. And maybe more. They ought to have built a barricade from here to Tallahassee. If we're done with it I wish they'd let us go."

The logging camp was three miles south of the battle site, in a thick forest of hickory, pine, and oak. Logs were carried from here to the forts on huge oxen-drawn wagons.

Tobias finished the stew and said, "Did the soldier you talked to say how many troops the Federals have?"

"Maybe five and a half thousand."

"It's about even then. I guess the Rebs has a good chance to win. But I wish they'd get on with it. I need to go back to the scrub."

It was just past noon the next day when the men finished loading a wagon and started north across an area of open meadow. Tobias stopped the oxen and said, "Look yonder, over to the west. What are them soldiers doing?"

A line of horses were pulling cannons at a fast trot and were followed by cavalry and foot soldiers.

"Don't know. But it looks like ever man at the forts is hightailing it down here. Maybe they decided to not fight."

"Don't seem likely," Tobias said. Then he looked to the east and exclaimed, "Yonder! Over yonder! There's the reason!"

Three long columns of Federal troops were marching toward them, and the columns were flanked on both sides by cavalry.

Tobias then said, "Good Heavens! They're going to have the battle down here and not up there where they built all them barricades! And we're going to be caught right in the middle of it!"

"I guess they couldn't direct the Federals where to fight," the man next to Tobias said. "But I tell you one thing for sure. We better be gone from here when they start firing them cannons at each other."

"The woods!" Tobias said urgently. "Run back to the woods! It's our only chance!"

One of the men cut the oxen loose from the wagon and they all ran back toward the line of trees. They were halfway there when Confederate cannons belched fire and smoke. This was returned instantly from the east. Shells dropped and exploded fifty yards north of the fleeing men.

When Tobias reached the woods he ran right over a stump and fell hard to the ground. Then he crawled into a clump of bushes and watched as the tempo of cannon fire increased. The cannons continued to thunder for more than an hour before men in both armies rushed forward toward each other.

At one point the advancing soldiers overran each other and formed one big mass of slashing swords and firing guns. It was impossible to tell one army from the other except for the color of uniforms. As he watched the battle intensify, Tobias wondered what would have happened if they were all dressed in overalls as he was.

The plain was now engulfed with a low-hanging cloud of smoke, making it difficult to see what was happening. Once a troop of Confederate cavalry rushed through the woods and jumped their horses right over the brush where Tobias was hiding. He was not sure if they saw him or not, or of what they would do if they did. He knew there was no way for them to know that their own log cutters were hiding in these woods.

The battle raged back and forth for four hours, and then the Federal troops turned and retreated rapidly back to the east. Confederates swooped after them, rushing over a plain now littered with bodies—lifeless men in both blue and gray.

Tobias did not come out of the woods even after the battle had passed. He spent the night beneath the brush, and at first dawn he walked to the edge of the woods and looked out, seeing that the dead had not yet been removed. Then a troop of soldiers came from the north, picking up bodies and putting them into wagons. When one wagon came close Tobias ran to it and said, "Is it all done now? I'm one of the log cutters, and if it's over I need to go home."

"We whupped them," one soldier said. "Them Feds is back in Jacksonville by now. But it was a bloody one for both sides. We got to get these men up before the buzzards come after them."

"I guess it's done then," Tobias said.

"This battle is done, but it ain't over by a long shot," the soldier said. "There's more Feds where them come from, and we'll see them again. But I don't think nobody cares what you do now, fella."

Tobias turned and went back into the woods. He could see no sign of any of the other loggers, so he headed south alone. He had walked just over a mile when he cut around a canebrake and found the horse. It was tied to a bush, and the rider was lying on the ground, wearing a blood-soaked uniform.

He was a boy of no more than eighteen. Lead balls had caught him in the neck and chest, and Tobias wondered how he could have ridden this far from the battle before falling.

Tobias removed a pistol and scabbard from the soldier's side, and then he unfastened the ammunition belt and put it in one saddlebag. There was also a rifle strapped to the saddle. He said, "I might as well take all of this, fella, but I want you to understand I ain't stealing from the dead. It ain't no use to you anymore, and it will be a godsend for me out in the scrub. I won't bury you, 'cause they'll find you sooner or later and send you back home. And I know you'd rather be with your folks than here in these woods."

He then searched the other saddlebag and found a knife and several tins of beef. He opened one can and ate ravenously, washing it down with water from the soldier's canteen. Then he mounted the horse and rode south.

When Tobias rode into the clearing he could not believe what he was seeing. Then the realization of it caused his hands to tremble. The house was no longer there, nor the barn, nor the smokehouse. Where they once stood, there were now piles of ashes. Only the woodshed remained.

He moved the horse forward slowly, dreading what he might find in the ashes. Then he heard movement behind the shed. Slowly and cautiously, Emma emerged from a bush, and then Zech peeked from behind the shed.

"Tobias!" Emma shouted, rushing to him. "We didn't know it was you. We only heard a horse coming. We thought one of them had come back."

Tobias jumped from the horse. "What has happened here,

Emma? What is all this?"

"They came a week ago, fifteen of them. When they left the next morning they set fire to all but the shed."

Zech said excitedly, "They killed Tuck, Pappa! They cooked him and et him right here in the yard! And they took Buck with them when they left!"

Tobias was furious.

"They weren't Federals," Emma said quickly. "They were Confederate deserters, Tobias. Some of them still had on pieces of their uniforms. They must have known about the battle and all the men being gone up there, 'cause they weren't in no hurry at all."

"Our own people did this to us?" Tobias questioned, finding it hard to believe. "Rebs?"

"Yes, Tobias. They were the meanest-looking men I've ever seen."

"Did they do harm to you?" Tobias then asked.

"They did us no harm, but I begged them not to burn the house, and they did it anyway."

"Blast them! They didn't have to do this. They could have just took what they wanted and left. Did you save anything?"

"Not much," Emma replied. "They left soon as they set the fires, and me and Zech ran in and got what we could. But the house went up too fast. We got an axe, a saw, the frying pan and a few blankets. But we didn't get any clothes. It just went up too fast."

"They took the shotgun, Pappa," Zech said, "but I still got the whip. Where'd you get the horse?"

"Off a dead soldier. A Federal."

Tobias walked over and looked at the scorched ground where the house had been. He kicked the ashes and said, "Ain't no man ever gonna do this to me again! Not ever! I'll kill the first one who tries! And I'll kill a thousand more if I have to! So help me, I will!"

"We could live in the shed while you build another house," Emma said, frightened by the bitterness in his voice. "It's better

43

than what we had when we first came here."

"No! We'll go south. This time we'll go to a place where nobody can find us till the war is over. That's what I should have done in the first place."

"They didn't burn the wagon, Pappa," Zech said. "It's behind the shed."

"I don't know if this cavalry horse can pull it or not," Tobias said. "He's trained to run, not pull. But we'll try. There's tinned beef and hardtack in the saddlebag. Soon as we eat a bite we'll leave. This time we'll go to a place where they can't find us, just like the Indians done."

At first Tobias headed directly south, leading the horse and wagon through thick woods, sometimes having to backtrack when he came to swampy bottoms and then follow higher ridges of dry ground.

On the second day he came into the lower scrub, an area he had never before explored. Here there were rolling sand hills thickly covered with tiny, runty scrub oak and impenetrable clumps of Spanish bayonet. The dead trunks of pines pointed upward forlornly, some peppered with woodpecker holes, the limbless trees giving evidence of some great fire that had once rushed over the land, destroying all in its path.

Every small oak had bear marks on its trunk, deep slashes made by claws, and buzzards circled overhead constantly. Occasionally Tobias came too close to the bayonet plants and jumped back in pain as they cut into his flesh.

Emma held the reins as Tobias took the axe and tried to cut a path for them to pass. Even in the cold he was sweating, and damp splotches covered his overalls. Again and again the wagon wheels sank down into the sand and stuck, and when this happened, they all pushed as the horse strained and neighed loudly, bucking and straining again, trying vainly to move the wagon forward.

"It ain't no use," Tobias finally said, putting the axe back into the wagon. "This is the most hellish place I've ever seen. There ain't no way we can get through it with the wagon. We'll have to turn and go back, then take the trail down to the St. Johns and follow the river south. There ought to be open land along the river."

Tobias unhitched the panting horse and tied it to a bush, then the three of them pulled the wagon from the sand and turned it.

Kissimmee River
1866

The runty black cow snorted and tossed its head from side to side, as if daring the horse and rider to come after it. Tobias eyed it cautiously, trying to maneuver the horse to one side. Then the cow snorted again, wheeled, and darted off into a thick strand of trees, its wide horns making clanking sounds as they struck vines.

Tobias kicked the horse into full pursuit. He dodged low-hanging limbs and then felt his body crash into the side of a tree, causing him to depart the saddle, flip over backward, and hit the ground with a thud.

"Dang you!" he shouted as the horse disappeared into the brush. Zech was off to one side, watching. He ran to his father and said, "He done it again, didn't he, Pappa?"

"Cussed army horse don't know how to do nothing but run in a straight line!" Tobias said, getting up and brushing dirt from his overalls. "He ain't worth spit in a swamp. We'll never catch them cows till we get a horse that knows how to run around trees instead of into them. Even a mule would know better than that."

"I'll go fetch him back," Zech said. "You wait here, Pappa. He's just right down yonder."

Tobias hobbled over to a tree and sat down, and in a few minutes Zech returned with the horse. He said, "We going to try some more, Pappa? They's two more cows in the brush. I seen them."

"We best go on back now. I've got chores to do at the house."

"Can I ride the horse now?"

"You can have that blasted critter. Just be sure he don't walk head-on into a tree and knock your brains out. I feel like my tail is broke."

Zech scrambled onto the saddle and they went along a path that wound beneath huge oaks. Soon they came to a small plot of ground that was fenced with split cypress rails. Inside the pen there was one cow with the letters MCI burned into its side.

Tobias looked at the cow and said, "It ain't much, but it's a start. We ought to have a dozen by now. We'll try again tomorrow."

"Maybe we ought to build us a trap," Zech said, bouncing up and down in the saddle as if the horse were in full gallop. "We could catch 'em like you trap coons."

"That'd be some trap. A wild cow ain't a coon, and you know that. What we need is a horse with sense and some dogs."

The small cabin was in a clearing on the east bank of the Kissimmee River. It was built of cypress logs fastened together with pegs, and the roof was palmetto fronds. It contained two rooms, one a kitchen and eating area and the other a sleeping room. Tobias and Emma occupied the small private room and Zech slept on a pallet in the kitchen.

It took Tobias six months to find the place. They followed the west bank of the St. Johns, stopping for days at a time to let the tired horse rest and gather strength, taking what food they could from the woods and the water. Nights were spent beneath the thin protection of bushy cabbage palm tops or the outspread limbs of water oaks.

When they reached the source of the St. Johns in a lake that seemed to mesh into an impenetrable swamp, they camped there for a month, fishing with crude hooks Tobias made from thorn bushes and killing coons and rabbits with the whip. Then they turned inland and wandered again, finally coming to a dense hammock along the bank of the Kissimmee.

Tobias knew at once that this isolated place was what he was looking for. There were no other homesteads nearby, and the nearest trading post was at Fort Capron, fifty miles to the east.

Since arriving at the hammock, Tobias had been to the trading post only once, and it was then he learned the war was over, that the south had lost. He had gone there to buy salt, and he also paid a blacksmith two dollars of the fourteen dollars he earned on the cattle drive to make a branding iron. His pen stood empty for almost a year after that. There was nothing to brand, and for practice he burned the letters MCI into every log on the side of the house. And then one day he caught the lone cow. After herding it into the pen, he held it on the ground while Zech pressed the hot iron to its side. Tobias then stood for an hour just looking at the burned MCI that proclaimed the cow to be his own.

While scouting the surrounding countryside, he came upon an abandoned village where Seminoles once lived. The chickees were rotten and had fallen into decayed heaps, but there were also the remains of a garden that still contained corn, squash, beans and pumpkins, and a small plot of sugar cane. From this he started his own garden, and he hoped it would thrive in the black river bottom soil.

His next project was to build a small barn for the horse and add several rails to the cow pen fence. These woods too were filled with predators. Each night he tied the horse to a post just outside the cabin door. It was no good for chasing cows in a swamp, but it was his only means of pulling the wagon to the trading post or elsewhere.

Spring had just passed into early summer, and the woods were alive with the sounds of chattering birds and rambling animals. Squirrels barked and great blue herons squawked loudly as they glided along the nearby river. A red fox flicked its bushy tail and ran across the path as Tobias and Zech entered the clearing. Zech stayed on the horse, racing it back and forth between the cabin and the edge of the woods.

Emma was at a table in the kitchen area, chopping coon meat into small pieces and putting them into the frying pan. When Tobias entered she put down the knife and said, "Do you know when you might make another trip to the trading post?"

"I guess I ought to go pretty soon. I've got a whole passel of coon skins. Maybe they've got in some flour. A batch of biscuits would sure go good. Seems I ain't et one for ten years."

She hesitated for a moment, and then she said, "Do you have enough in trade for a Dutch oven? It's hard to make good stew or bake anything in this frying pan. I could fix better meals with an oven, and I sure miss the one we lost in the fire."

Her question brought immediate guilt to Tobias. He should have thought of this himself without being asked. Emma never complained about anything and never asked for things he knew she missed. It had been ten years since she had a new dress, and her shoes were the ones she wore when they left Georgia. And now she asked only for a cooking tool.

"I'm sure I have enough for that. I should have got one on the last trip. There's a lot of things I should have done for you that I ain't, Emma. And I know it. Someday I'll make it up to you."

"There's nothing I need that can't wait."

"I've about got the poles cut to add to the cow pen fence and the garden. I'll finish it this afternoon, and at sunup tomorrow I'll go to the trading post. There'll be enough skins for the oven."

He went back outside and down to the garden, studying the plants that had broken through the rich soil, hoping that wild hogs would not raid him constantly as they had in the scrub. He also thought of the hardships his family had endured during those years in the scrub and on the trip here. Zech was eight years old now and had never tasted an apple or eaten a piece of sugar candy. There had been no jackknife to play with and no kite to fly and no whistle to blow. He felt a sudden urgency to do something for both Emma and Zech, to somehow better their lives. If he did not hurry, the void would become too big for him to ever fill.

Just then Zech came riding by at full gallop, his slim body seemingly glued to the saddle. He reined up, made the horse rear on its hind legs, and shouted, "I bet you I could ride him in the swamp, Pappa! I bet you I could!" Then he raced away to the far side of the clearing.

Tobias watched after him, noticing that boy and horse seemed to be one and the same. He thought of that night in the scrub when a man-child picked up a shotgun weighing as much as he and killed a bear without fear or hesitation. He said, "I'll just bet you could, Zech. I bet you really could."

✠

Ten miles down the river Tobias left the woods and turned east. Here he entered a prairie dotted with palmetto and broken occasionally by cypress stands and clumps of cabbage palms.

There was an early morning haze over the land, adding to the majesty of its vastness. Flights of egrets and herons glided gracefully over the brown grass and then landed in cypress stands, turning the trees into solid masses of white and gray.

Mile after mile the wagon creaked forward, and it seemed to Tobias that the prairie was endless. Here there was no circular border of thick forests like on the Alachua savanna, but like the savanna, he could see herds of deer moving across the land, and also wild cattle. Once he came within a hundred yards of a small herd, and when he stopped to look, the cows jerked their heads up quickly, standing alert as they stared at him for a moment, then wheeled and bounded away. For a half mile they thundered over the ground; then they stopped and ignored him, and continued to graze.

At noon he stopped at a cypress stand and ate the fried coon Emma had prepared for him, washing it down with water from the canteen that had come with the horse. To stretch his legs he walked over to the stand. The little island of pond cypress was so thick he found it difficult to enter. As he made his way toward the center, he thought that in this one stand alone there were enough cypress poles to fence the entire prairie.

He was startled when he heard the sound just ahead of him, a combination grunting-growl. He stepped cautiously around a tree and came face to face with a wild boar. Man and animal looked at each other for a moment, both equally surprised by the other's sudden presence, then Tobias slowly backed away, leaving the boar sole claim to its prairie home. He hoped it would stay there and not come his way.

It was late afternoon when Tobias reached the trading post. The cypress shack was on the west side of an inlet to the north of Fort Pierce. He hitched the horse and stood for several minutes gazing out across the water, thinking that someday he would bring Emma and Zech here to walk the beach and gather shells, or just sit on the sand and watch the gulls and pelicans at play.

The proprietor of the trading post, Elias Thompson, was a short fat man in his fifties, with a bald head and tomato-red face. When Tobias entered he said, "Howdy. I seen you coming a good while ago. That wagon's a load for one hoss to pull. What you need is a buckboard. It ain't as heavy, and it rides better on the prairie. Oxen is what you ought to have to pull that farm wagon."

"I had oxen once," Tobias said. "But all I got now is the horse. It'll have to do."

"What can I do for you?" Thompson then asked.

"I've got coon skins to trade. A lot of them."

"You got any cash money? I mean silver or gold coins, not Confederate paper. That stuff ain't worth shucks but some folks still tries to pass it off on me."

"I got a little. And it's coins."

"Well, them coon skins ain't worth much. And besides that, I got hardly no supplies at all. Things is scarce everwhere now. Fellow come through here the other day told me it's so bad up in Georgia and Alabama that folks is eating pine cones and sassafras roots. Folks is in real bad shape on account of the war done tore up everthing. Only goods I can get comes on a schooner out of Baltimore, and it sure ain't much. What is it you got in mind?"

"Mainly I want a Dutch oven, and a little wheat flour if you got it. And I could use some salt."

"I got no flour at all, and I ain't seen a Dutch oven in five years. It all went into cannon balls. But I got some salt."

"I wouldn't give my cash money for salt," Tobias said. "Will you take the skins in trade?"

"Yeah, I'll take 'em. Next time the schooner comes I'll send 'em north. Folks up there has still got the money to buy stuff like that. The schooner captain told me what they really want now is polecat hides. Bring as much as two dollars each. Now ain't that something? Polecat hides. I reckon the women up there fancy a coat with white stripes. Next time you come in, bring me some if you can figure out a way to relieve a skunk of his hide without getting the worst end of it."

"I'll think on it," Tobias said. "But I don't relish the idea of trapping skunks. I got sprayed once and had to stay out in the barn for a week."

"Where you live?" Thompson asked.

"On the east side of the Kissimmee, a full day's travel from here."

"I hear tell them little steamboats is going to start running the river again, down to Lake Okeechobee. I bet you could sell them boatmen some alligator hides. 'Gator hides bring from a buck fifty to three dollars now, depending on the size. And the tail meat is as good as beef. You could probably sell fresh deer meat too. Nowadays it's easy to sell anything a man can eat if you can find somebody with cash."

"I've never seen a boat on the river since I've lived there. But if they come again I'll know it. My place is right off the bank."

Tobias went outside, brought in the skins and put them on the counter. Thompson examined them briefly and said, "Them's real good hides. I can let you have ten pounds of salt in trade."

"Done," Tobias said, disappointed about the other things but glad to at least get salt out of the long trip.

When Thompson came back with the salt he said, "You got a gun?"

"I've got a rifle and a pistol, both of them military."

"You want some shells? That's one thing they got plenty of up north, leftover ammunition. I bought three whole cases off the schooner. I can let you have a couple of boxes for a dollar cash."

"Are they forty-fours?"

"That's right."

"I'll take them," Tobias then said, surprised by the offer. "But I want four boxes. Here's two dollars cash."

Tobias put the shells and the salt into a cloth sack. "Next time the supply boat comes, ask about a Dutch oven. I want one real bad, and I'll pay cash if I have to."

"I'll do that."

Thompson followed Tobias to the wagon and said, "You going to travel out there at night?"

"Nope. I'll go a ways before it gets too dark and make camp. Then I'll move on at sunup."

"You best be real careful," Thompson warned, a seriousness in his voice. "Since the war there's been a lot of drifters in these parts. There's a lot of men scouting around now, looking for something to eat. And maybe for somebody to kill too. One day last month about fifteen come by here in one pack, riding horses, and they was the meanest-looking bunch I ever seen. Looked as if they'd as soon kill a man as look at him. They plumb scared me to death, and my boots shook till they finally rode off. You best watch out for yourself. A man ought not be out on the prairie alone."

"I'll keep a sharp eye," Tobias said. "And I rightly thank you for the warning."

As the wagon creaked away, Thompson shouted, "What you need is a buckboard! You decide to trade off that wagon let me know and I'll see can I find one!"

Tobias waved back to him.

The last rays of sundown were vanishing rapidly when Tobias stopped at a small hammock and unhitched the horse. Then he gathered palm fronds, placed them on the wagon floor, and covered them with a blanket. Because of snakes, he would sleep in the wagon rather than on the ground.

He started a fire and then sat by it, eating the last small scrap of coon meat. Shadows from the fire flickered through tree limbs and vanished upward, like dancers performing a mystic ritual. From somewhere across the prairie came the lonesome cry of a whippoorwill.

Tobias had heard no sound of footsteps, but when he glanced to the far reaches of the fire's light, he saw two men and a woman standing there, looking at him. He jumped backward quickly and grabbed the rifle, remembering Thompson's warning.

One of the men said, "We did not mean to frighten you. We saw your fire and came to it. We mean no harm."

As they came closer Tobias recognized them as Indians. He stared at them intensely, trying to bring forth something long since forgotten. There was a familiarity about them, something in their faces that tugged at his memory.

Then it came to him. He said, "I know you. I don't remember the names, but you came to my place in the scrub when the men were chasing you for killing a calf."

"We remember you well," one of the men said. "You are Tobias MacIvey. We have never forgotten what you did for us, and all of our people know of this. But we never expected to find you here. Do you not still live where you did?"

"No. Some men burned the place while I was away and we left after that. We live now in a hammock on the east bank of the Kissimmee, about a day's journey from here."

"I know the place you speak of. My people once had a village not far from there. I know it well."

"I found your place and took seed from the garden," Tobias

said, putting down the rifle. "I'm sorry, but I have no food to offer you now."

"We have food. We will prepare it here if we can share your fire."

"You are welcome," Tobias said. "And you can stay the night if you wish. It would be better for all of us to be together. I've been told there are many strangers wandering the countryside."

One of the men went into the darkness and returned pulling a sled made of two poles covered with deer hide. Several bundles were on the sled. He said, "I do not blame you for not remembering our names. That was a long time ago, and it was also a very bad day when we met. I am Keith Tiger, and this is Bird Jumper. And she is my wife, Lillie."

"I won't forget again." Tobias promised.

The men sat with Tobias by the fire as the woman took a pot from the sled and filled it from a deerhide pouch. Then she poured water into the pot and set in on the fire.

"It is sofkee," Keith Tiger said, noticing Tobias' curiosity as he watched Lillie. "We make it by soaking crushed corn in wood ash lye. Then we boil it with water. It is a favorite of our people. When it is done you will eat with us."

Tobias appreciated the offer since the small portion of coon left him still hungry. He said, "When you left the scrub you said you were going to a land far in the south to join your people there. Why are you here now?"

"We are on our way to Fort Capron for bullets. The man who owns the trading post at Fort Dallas will not sell guns or bullets to an Indian, and we have heard that the man here will. We need them badly to kill game, and we are on the way to trade for them."

"I had coon skins," Tobias said, "and all I could get for them was salt. For everything else he wanted cash. What do you have to trade?"

"Flour."

"Flour?" Tobias questioned, his interest aroused immediately. "You've got flour?"

"Yes," Keith Tiger responded, amused by Tobias' reaction. "Koonti flour. It is as good as the white man's flour. We like it better. It is made from the root of the sago palm, and it is free for the taking."

"I've never heard of it, but I reckon I've eaten a ton of cattail flour."

"This is better. We will tell you how to gather it and how to prepare it. In hard times, koonti will nourish you and keep you alive. It saved my people from hunger many times during the wars."

"I'd be right pleased to know all about it," Tobias said. "And the man at the trading post did say he can sell anything a man can eat. You ought to make a good trade."

Keith Tiger motioned toward the sled; then the woman went to it and removed one of the bundles. As she handed it to Tobias, Tiger said, "Take some of the koonti with you. We have enough to share. Tell your woman to use it as she would the white man's flour."

"I really appreciate this," Tobias said, accepting the bundle. "I'll have my wife make biscuits as soon as I get back home. And I have something to share too, just in case things go wrong at the trading post." He removed two boxes of the shells from his saddlebag and handed them to Tiger. "I've got more, and I don't need to shoot as much game as you do to feed a whole village."

The Indian's eyes flashed pleasure and gratitude. "This is truly a great gift to my people," he said. "We will use them wisely, and we do thank you."

"I'm just glad I had them to share."

Tiger then said, "I see you have a horse now. I remember you did not have one in the scrub."

"I took him off a dead soldier during the war. He's fair at pulling the wagon, but he ain't no good at all in the woods and swamps. He's too big, and he runs in a straight line. Ever time I've chased a cow with him I've nigh on got my neck broke."

"You remember I told you once before that what you need is a marshtackie. A marshtackie can take you through the swamp and the thickest of woods as swiftly as a deer. It is the best cow horse there is."

"Well, I sure ain't had no luck with that fellow. So far I've got only one cow."

"Where do you keep your cow?" Tiger asked.

"In a pen close by the house in the hammock."

"That is not good. You could not do this at all with a herd, even a small one. In the summer you must let them wander the range freely, grazing wherever they find grass. You must follow the herd and not keep them penned. When my people had cattle they would let them range as far as a hundred miles and more in a summer. In the winter, turn them loose in the woods and swamps and they will survive. And in the spring, round them up and put your mark on the new ones. If you keep them penned they will die. The marsh grass in flood areas along the rivers has salt, and without this your cattle will become sick. The best salt grass is along the St. Johns."

"You mean if I want to own cattle I'll have to leave the house and follow them wherever they go?"

"This is true. There were times when my people had herds that stretched as far as the eye could see, and we followed them everywhere. Those who wandered with the herds were called Ishmaelites by the white soldiers. I do not know what the word means, but I think it is something bad. They did not say this of those who stayed in the villages and farmed, only those who wandered the land. But if you do not wish to follow the herd, it is best that you stay home and grow pumpkins."

"Ishmaelites," Tobias said, as if weighing the word. "Maybe I will do as you say. I wouldn't like to be just a pumpkin grower."

"If you catch a cow in the swamp, put your mark on it and let it go. Then catch another and mark it. You can return for them later. If you keep them in a pen all the time they will die."

By now the pot in the fire was bubbling, and the mixture had formed a thick gruel. Lillie removed it from the fire, then she handed a huge wooden spoon to Keith Tiger. He passed it to Tobias and said, "You must eat first. It is the custom of our people."

Tobias dipped the spoon into the pot, put it to his mouth and chewed. "It's good," he said, swallowing and then smiling. "It's really good. I hope we have corn this fall. I'll tell Emma about this."

He passed the spoon back to Keith Tiger, and after he dipped it into the pot, he passed it to Bird Jumper. They would all eat from the same spoon and pot. When Bird Jumper ate, he passed it back to Tobias. Lillie would wait until the men finished before eating.

Later that night, after two hours of talking, Tobias yawned and said, "I guess I better turn in now. It's been a long day, and I need to hit the trail by sunup tomorrow."

Keith Tiger said, "We must start early too. We have been traveling mostly at night. It is best that no one sees us. But I am glad we came to your fire. If we had not recognized you, we would have remained in the darkness." He then handed the sofkce spoon to Tobias. "Take this as a gift to your woman. Perhaps she can make use of it. We have many more of them at the village. And if you ever have need of my people, go to the far shore of the great lake Okeechobee. From there, walk south. You will not see us, but we will know you are there."

Tobias took the spoon and put it into his saddlebag. He said, "I thank you for this. It will make Emma proud, and I know she'll have use of it. I'm glad you stopped here for the night, and I wish you much luck with the trading."

"We'll have more food together before we depart at sunup," Tiger said.

Tobias then climbed into the wagon and lay down on the palmetto bed, thinking for a long time of the strange word Ishmaelite.

♉

The morning after Tobias arrived home from the trading post he left the house early and strode briskly through the woods toward the cow pen. Zech had to trot to keep up with him. He said excitedly, "Where we going in such a hurry, Pappa? What we going to do?"

Tobias felt good, his stomach full of koonti biscuits. His lanky legs covered three feet per step. When he reached the pen he gazed for a moment at the cow, then he opened the gate and propped a stick against it to keep it open.

"What you doing, Pappa?" Zech asked anxiously, completely puzzled by his father's actions. "You going to turn him loose after all that ruckus we had catching him?"

"If I don't he'll die."

"How come? He looks fine to me."

"Look there at the ground," Tobias said, pointing. "Not a blade of grass left, and we sure don't have any hay or corn to feed him. He's got our mark. I'll turn him loose now so's he can eat, then we'll catch him again later. Go back to the house and fetch the horse and the branding iron. We'll catch another one this morning and mark him right there in the woods."

Zech turned and ran toward the clearing, still not understanding what had come over his father.

The cow too seemed puzzled. It stood still, eyeing the man and the open gate. Then it shook its horns and backed into the far side of the pen.

Tobias went inside and circled the cow. When it still did not move he said loudly, "Shu! Shu cow! Git!"

The cow backed further against the fence and snorted.

60

Tobias said, "Dang critter! As much as you fought getting in here, now you won't go out!"

Then he started jumping up and down, flailing his arms wildly, shouting, "Git! Git! I said git!"

The cow watched Tobias for a moment more, then it rushed forward, bounded out the gate and into the woods, bellowing loudly.

Just then Zech came back, riding the horse at full gallop. He reined up, got off and said, "I got the iron, Pappa. But if you're going to turn them loose, how come we got to catch another one?"

"Just do it, Zech," Tobias said. "Let's go down by the hickory flat and see what's there."

When they reached the grove of hickory trees Tobias mounted the horse. They remained very still, listening. After a few minutes Zech whispered, "I hear one, Pappa. He's over to the right in the brush."

"I'll go after him," Tobias said. "If I can get up to him I'll jump off and grab him by the horns. Then you run in and help me."

Tobias moved the horse toward the sound, and when he came around the side of a clump of huckleberry bushes, a runty black bull was standing there. It immediately turned and ran.

When Tobias kicked it in the flanks, the horse bounded forward quickly. For fifty yards horse and rider rushed after the bull, then the bull made a sudden turn to the left. The horse crashed headlong into a thick growth of muscadine vines and became entangled. It kicked and bucked, trying to break free, then it threw Tobias right over its head and into the vines, entangling him even worse.

Zech ran up and said, "Gimme your hand, Pappa! I'll pull you out!"

The horse continued to buck as Zech pulled and strained, and finally Tobias popped free. They broke the vines from around the horse's legs and backed it out of the entanglement. Tobias then shouted, "Idiot! Fool! You could have turned with the bull!"

Zech said, "It ain't all his fault, Pappa. I was watching. You

61

didn't try to turn him quick enough. You got to give him better directions so he'll know what to do."

"Maybe so, but this ain't going to work. I tell you what, Zech. You get on the horse, and I'll climb up in a tree. Try to turn the bull under the tree and I'll drop down on top of him and catch him. It just might work."

Zech got on the horse and rode off into the brush as Tobias climbed the nearest tree. As soon as he found the bull, Zech circled slowly to the right and came up behind it. Then he charged, herding the bull back the way it had come.

Tobias sat on the limb, watching. The bull was coming straight to him, with Zech in hot pursuit. Just as the bull reached the tree, Tobias turned loose, dropped down and landed solidly on the bull's back. He grabbed the horns with both hands and locked his long legs round its stomach.

The bull continued running full speed for twenty yards, then bull and rider crashed to the ground. The breath was knocked from him, but Tobias managed to shout, "Get the fire going, Zech! Hurry! Get the iron hot! I don't think I can hold him for long!"

Before Zech could even start gathering sticks for a fire, the bull jumped up, bucked around and around, and started running again. Tobias tightened his legs and hung on. The bull changed directions twice, and then it ran under a low-hanging limb that caught Tobias in the chest. He let go the horns and grabbed the limb, and for a moment both bull and rider left the ground and hung suspended in midair; then Tobias' legs turned loose and he flipped backward, hitting the ground upside down as the bull dropped down and bounded away.

Zech shouted, "You done good, Pappa! You was really riding him till he run under that limb!"

Tobias got up and examined himself to see if anything was broken. He said, "I wasn't trying to ride him! I was trying to throw him! What we need is a rope. When I get one on the ground you can tie his legs, then he can't get up afore we put the mark on. Next time we'll bring rope."

Zech was awed by his father's performance. He said again, "You done real good, Pappa. You had that bull going some before he knocked you off. Hadn't been for that limb you could have rode him slam back to the house. We going to try it again?"

"Maybe tomorrow. I'm a mite sore just now. But there's got to be a way if we can figure it out."

It was early morning a month later when Zech ran into the clearing, shouting, "Come quick, Pappa! Hurry! Down to the cow pen!"

Tobias rushed outside and followed the fleeing boy, having to run full stride to catch up with him. When they reached the pen Zech shouted, "Look there, Pappa! Look!"

Inside the pen there was a small black stallion, its sleek body glistening with muscles. On its back was mounted a McClellan saddle. Tied to the outside of the fence there were two dogs, both tall, gray and shaggy, looking almost exactly like wolves.

Zech jumped up and down with excitement. "Where'd they come from, Pappa! Who brought them here?"

"Can't say," Tobias said, "but that horse didn't put himself in there. That's for sure. But I think I know. He's a marshtackie."

Zech ran into the pen and leaped onto the saddle. He whirled the horse around and around, shouting, "Look here, Pappa! He can turn quicker than a rabbit!" Then he kicked it in the side, bounded the fence in one leap and made a wide circle through the woods.

When he came back to the pen, Zech jumped off and said, "He flies like a bird, Pappa. We'll get cows now. Ain't no cow can out-run him, even in the swamp. He needs a name. What we going to call him?"

Tobias thought for a moment, and then he said, "Ishmael. We'll call him Ishmael. That's a good name for a horse."

"What about the dogs?" Zech then asked. "What we going to

name them? A dog's got to have a name when you call him."

"We'll name one after ole Tuck. And the other Nip. Nip and Tuck. How's that!"

"That's fine. That's real fine." Zech then went over and patted one of the dogs on the head, causing its tail to wag vigorously. He said, "You're Nip. And you're Tuck. I'll bet you can keep them wild hogs out of the garden."

"I expect they will," Tobias said. "They look like they could take on a bear. But I swear they could pass for wolves."

"They ain't, Pappa. They's good dogs. I can tell."

"We best go on back to the house now and tell your mamma about this. You scared the life out of her when you come running into the clearing, shouting like you was. She don't know what the ruckus was about. We best go tell her so she won't worry."

Zech untied the dogs, jumped back on the horse and bounded away. The dogs took after him, barking loudly. Tobias said, "If that sight don't put Emma up a tree, nothing will."

When Tobias reached the clearing Emma was outside, looking at the horse. The dogs were circling her, their tails wagging. She said, "What is all this, Tobias? Has someone lost their horse and dogs?"

"Well, it looks like Christmas done finally come for us. Let's go inside and talk about it."

Zech galloped away as they went into the cabin and sat at the table. Tobias said, "The Indians brung them. It couldn't be nobody else."

"Why? Why would they do this? They owe us nothing."

"They think they do. For what we did for them in the scrub. And it could be they just wanted to do it. Whatever the reason, it's a blessing. I could have never bought that horse and them dogs, not in a hundred years. There ain't that many coons in the swamp."

"Are they wild, the horse and the dogs?"

"Don't seem to be. They're probably trained real good. Keith Tiger told me his people had great herds of cattle before the soldiers took them away, and the horse they used was the marsh-tackie. They've probably been keeping some of them horses and dogs all this time, hoping that someday they would have cattle again and be able to use them. But that ain't likely to happen, at least not anytime soon. I guess they wanted somebody to put the horse and the dogs to use again."

"First the flour, and now this," Emma said. "I wish they would have come to the house. We could have given them something to eat and thanked them."

"I would have liked to see them too. Maybe they just didn't want to make a big deal out of it. It could be the Indian way."

"I still wish we could have thanked them. I know this means a lot to you and Zech."

"Emma," Tobias said, putting his hand on hers, "it means more than you know. At least we got a chance now. Before this we didn't have no chance at all. We were just fooling ourselves, me and Zech, and I knowed it. I just didn't have the heart to tell him. But now we got a chance."

The two dogs ran straight to the bull, as if they knew beforehand exactly where they would find it. Nip rushed in and grabbed it by the nose, and Tuck sank his teeth into its left rear leg.

Zech was riding just behind them, the small horse darting effortlessly around trees and jumping over vines. Tobias followed on the other horse.

When the bull tried to break free, Nip sank his teeth in deeper, causing a trickle of blood to stain the tip of his nose. Then the bull stood motionless, its eyes wild and staring downward at the dog.

Tobias jumped from his horse and grabbed the bull by its horns, putting all his strength into a twisting motion that finally sent the bull sprawling on its side. As Zech tied its legs together, the dogs turned loose and backed away.

Tobias started a fire, and when the flames were burning brightly he put the branding iron into the center. He said, "It seems to me we're still doing this wrong, running around all over the woods and making a fire ever time we put on a mark. We ought to build a pen down here and wait till we get five or six cows in a bunch, then brand them all at one time."

"It do make sense," Zech replied. "And I bet you that Nip and Tuck could bring in cows by themselves, without no help at all from us. I already seen them do it. They can make a cow go any way they want to. All we'd have to do is show them the pen and say git 'em."

"We'll start a pen tomorrow. Fact is, we'll build two, and put them about a mile apart. That ought to be even better."

"I can bring them in by myself too, Pappa. The other day Ishmael made a cow walk a straight line right through the brush. Seemed he knowed ever move that cow was going to make, and then he made it first. I think he's part cow himself. He sure knows what a cow is going to do."

When the iron glowed red, Tobias took it from the fire and pressed it to the bull's side. Smoke boiled upward from burning hair as the iron seared the letters MCI into the bull's hide. He kicked twice and tried to get up, then Tobias released the ropes. The bull struggled to its feet and ran off into the woods.

The dogs watched attentively, awaiting a signal for them to hunt again; then Tobias patted one on the head and said, "Go git 'em, dogs! Git 'em!" They immediately streaked away into the brush.

Zech said, "Them dogs is a sight, ain't they, Pappa?"

"They surely are. I don't know how we ever got along without them. They keep this up they's going to be MacIvey cows all over the place. You best put out that fire now. And do it real good. Seems like a fool idea to be running around building fires all over the swamp."

The sound of yelping came from a half mile away and Zech said, "They done struck another one already."

"Sure sounds like it. They don't even give us a chance to rest. Let's ride on over and see to it."

This time they did not race the horses, knowing that the dogs would hold the cow, even to sundown if necessary. When they reached the spot, the dogs were running around and around a thick clump of palmetto, barking and growling at the same time.

Tobias watched for a moment, and then he said, "That sure ain't no cow they've got in there this time. Don't go in yet. It could be a bear in them bushes."

The dogs continued circling and growling, and Tobias took the rifle from the saddle holster. He said, "Whatever it is, it sure don't want to come out. Must be something besides a bear else the horses would have done smelled him by now and put on a show. Ain't no horses nowheres going to stand still for a bear, not even Ishmael."

For five minutes the dogs continued circling the palmetto, then Tobias said "We're going to have to flush it out, whatever it is. Get a big stick and throw it in there. I'll keep the gun aimed."

Zech dismounted and picked up a hickory limb. Tobias said to him, "Don't go any closer. Throw it from as far back as you can."

Zech whirled around and around; then he released the limb. It arched upward and crashed down right into the center of the palmetto clump.

Nothing happened for a moment more, and then they heard a rustling sound, as if something were crawling. Then a black head peeked through a frond.

The black man crawled forward slowly, watching the dogs, his eyes pure terror. He glanced upward and saw the rifle pointing at him, and then he said, "Don't shoot me, mister. And call off them critters. I don't mean no harm." His voice trembled as he spoke.

Tobias and Zech were both so surprised they did nothing but stare. Finally Tobias said, "Get the dogs away from him, Zech. Make them hush up."

Zech called the dogs to him and held them as Tobias dismounted, the rifle still in his hand. He said, "Fella, what are you doing hiding in there? I could have shot in there blind and killed you."

"The dogs," the black man said, his voice still shaky. "They got to me before I could go up a tree, and there weren't nowhere else for me to go. I thought they was wolves."

"They do favor wolves a mite," Tobias said. "But they won't hurt you now. You can come out of there. We don't aim to do you any harm."

When the black man stood up he was even taller than Tobias, at least six and a half feet, and his forearm was as large as Tobias' thigh. He was dressed in a tattered blue shirt and had on a pair of pants that seemed to have been made from a feed sack. He appeared to be about the same age as Tobias, and he was the blackest black man Tobias had ever seen. When he spoke, his white teeth gleamed like elephant ivory.

He said, "You ain't got a little scrap of food, has you? I ain't et since day befo' yesterday."

"Don't have nothing here," Tobias said, "but there's vittles back at the house. We'll be glad to feed you. Where'd you come from, anyway?"

"Just to the south of Tallahassee."

"Tallahassee?" Tobias repeated. "You mean you walked slam down here from Tallahassee?"

"Sho' did. I been driftin' now for nigh on a year. I been shot at and stomped and chased by dogs, but this the first time I been treed by wolves."

"They ain't wolves," Zech said, listening curiously. "They's dogs."

"Well, you could 'a fooled me. I would have swore fo' God they was wolves."

Tobias said, "I'm Tobias MacIvey, and this is my boy, Zech. Who be you?"

"Skillit."

"Your name's Skillit?"

"That's all I ever been knowed as. Skillit."

"Well, Skillit, I sure would like to hear what you've got to say fur yourself. But I know you're about to starve, so let's go to the house and see to your belly first. We'll talk later."

"That would sho' be fine. But just don't let them wolves get to me."

"They ain't wolves," Zech said again. "They's dogs. Their names are Nip and Tuck. And they can catch any cow you ever seen."

"I just bet they can," Skillit said.

Tobias watched the black man as he wolfed down the bowl of stewed squash and then chomped a fried coon leg, bone and all. Emma watched too, thinking that he was about the hungriest man she had ever seen. She said, "Would you like more squash? That's the last piece of coon meat till I cook some more."

"I sho' would, missus. I'd be right proud to et another bowl. You be's a fine cook, a fine one."

Tobias said, "Soon as I get a smokehouse built I aim to shoot a cow. Fresh meat wouldn't keep no time at all in this heat. We'll have beef soon as I'm done with the smokehouse."

"I ain't never et a smoked cow," Skillit said, stuffing his mouth with squash. "Only hog. And not much of that. Sow belly mostly."

"It's right good," Tobias said. "I smoked one once before when we lived up in the scrub."

Zech said, "You ride a horse? I bet you ain't never seen a horse like Ishmael. He's a marshtackie."

"I've rid plenty of them," Skillit said. "And mules too. When I was a boy I used to ride a goat. Turn your back on him, he'd knock you over a fence."

Zech was fascinated by the black man. He said, "You been a slave?"

"Zech!" Emma snapped. "Why you ask him a question like that?"

"It's all right, missus. I been that too. I was born on a plantation in Georgia. My daddy and my granddaddy was slaves. When I was four years old I was sold to a man at Tallahassee and went to the farm there. I guess I'd still be a slave had'n been for the war."

"What happened to you after the war?" Tobias asked.

"When the war ended they said all us was free, and we could do whatever we wanted. Some folks went up North, and some

70

stayed where they was. I claimed me a little piece of land and built me a cabin on it, and then I started to farm. Had a fine garden. Wad'n long after that that some men come to the house one night. Said they didn't want no black man buildin' a house or runnin' a farm. They was all dressed in white sheets and had hoods over their faces. I told them I was supposed to be free and I didn't see how a garden could hurt nobody. They rawhided me good, whupped me like I ain't never been whupped befo'. Then they tromped down my garden with their horses and set fire to the cabin. Ever since then I been driftin' south, sleepin' wherever I could, and stealin' chickens when I could find one. I guess someday I got to find me a place and stop."

"They whup you with a whip?" Zech asked.

"They sho' did."

"We got a whip that kills rabbits and squirrels and coons and rattlers too. You want to see it?"

"Zech!" Emma said again. "He don't want to see no whip. Hush up now, and let Skillit talk. We want to hear."

"That's about the end of it," Skillit said. "I guess I should 'a turned north 'stead of south. They don't seem to be nothin' down here but woods and swamps. You the first white folks ever give me a meal."

"Where will you go from here?" Tobias asked.

"Don't know. Don't even know where I'm at now."

"So far as I know there ain't nothing in the far south but swamp and Indians," Tobias said. "I've never met a white man who's been there. It was Indians from down there who gave us the marsh-tackie and dogs. They was Seminoles."

"How come they do that?" Skillit asked.

"We done them a favor once. I got a idea, Skillit. Why don't you stay on here for a while? You would be a big help to me and Zech. We couldn't pay you nothing, 'cause we ain't got nothing. But we could build you a little cabin to stay in. The garden ought to come in soon, and if you help me with the smokehouse, we'll kill us a cow."

"You mean you'd let me stay here?" Skillit asked, not sure he was hearing what Tobias said.

"What do you say, Emma?" Tobias asked.

"It's fine with me. He would be a big help to you and Zech. And it's just as easy to cook for four as three. It won't be no bother at all."

"Will you stay?" Tobias asked.

"I sho' will!" Skillit said, grinning and flashing the ivory teeth. "I's awful tired of driftin'. I'm beholdin' to you, Mistuh Tobias! And to you, Missus Emma! I never knowed them wolves was doin' me such a favor by putting me in them bushes."

"They ain't wolves," Zech said. "They's dogs." Then he turned to Tobias and said, "Can Skillit ride your horse, Pappa? I found an eagle nest down by the river, and I want to show it to him. It's got babies in it. Can he, Pappa?"

"He can ride whenever he wants."

Zech jumped up and said, "Come on Skillit! But you better watch that big ole horse. He ain't no marshtackie. He runs straight, and if you don't watch him he'll knock you off on a tree."

When he reached the door, Skillit turned and said, "Soon's we're back we'll start on that smokehouse, Mistuh Tobias. It won't take us no time at all to build one. No time at all."

Zech grabbed his arm and pulled him out the door, saying, "Come on, Skillit! Come on!"

Tobias and Emma were both smiling.

CHAPTER ELEVEN

A thin spiral of smoke drifted upward as Tobias put on more wood and placed the branding iron on the fire. Zech and Skillit stood just outside the gate, waiting for the iron to get hot.

Inside the pen, six cows milled about, poking their huge horns at the rails, trying to find a weak spot in the fence. Nip and Tuck were lying under a huckleberry bush, panting from the heat.

Tobias said, "It's ready now. Zech, you do the tying when Skillit gets one on the ground."

"Don't need no rope," Skillit said. "That just take up more time. You just stand back out of the way, Mistuh Zech. Let me handle it."

Skillit was shirtless, and his black skin glistened with sweat. Summer was boring in now with its full fury, and it seemed that even the water of the river was warm.

When Tobias came over to the pen, Skillit went inside and grabbed a cow by the horns. In one quick motion he had it on the ground and was on top of it. Muscles became taut in his arms and back as the bull struggled uselessly. Tobias pushed the branding iron to flesh, then Skillit released it and grabbed another one. In an instant the cow was on the ground and the iron made its mark again.

Tobias said, "Lordy, Skillit, with you here we can brand as many cows in a half hour as it used to take me and Zech a week. You're the strongest man I ever seen."

"It ain't nothin' workin' these little ole cows. I could down a mule if'n I had to."

As soon as the branding was finished, the cows were turned loose. Tobias said, "That's about enough for today. It's too hot to

73

do this. Let's go on back and finish your cabin."

Skillit picked up his shirt and said, "Mistuh Tobias, what you gone ever do with all these cows? You can't et all of them, not even with someone around with a belly like mine."

Tobias scratched his head. "You know, I ain't never thought of that. Me and Zech stayed so busy trying to catch one and put on a mark, I never put no mind to what I'd do if we did catch it. I been told that come spring we ought to round them up and let them graze as a herd on the prairie. They sure don't seem to gain no weight in these woods. After that I guess we ought to sell them sommers. They ain't worth a red cent to us roaming the woods. But I don't rightly know where to take them for the selling."

"Place where I stayed had a lot of cattle. During the war they all went to the soldiers, but they sho' ain't no Confederate army around no more to buy 'em."

"Next time I go to the trading post I'll ask Elias Thompson. He ought to know. But they sure don't put nothing in your pocket like this. We need to get us some cash money."

"What's that?" Skillit asked, grinning. "In all my life I ain't never had even a single coin of my own. I guess you done noticed these cracker sack britches ain't got no pockets."

"You will," Tobias said. "We'll just keep on marking like we got good sense. It ain't costing us nothing to brand them."

They were about halfway to the clearing when a shrill tooting sound came from the direction of the river. Zech stopped his horse and said, "What's that, Pappa? I ain't never heard no bull holler like that."

"I'd say it's a steam whistle," Tobias said. "I ain't heard a sound like that since we left Georgia."

"I've heard it before," Skillit said. "Trains up to Tallahassee made that sound when they wanted to run cows off the tracks."

"Well, there ain't no train out there coming through the woods," Tobias said, "so it must be on the river. Elias Thompson told me he heard the boats was going to run the river again down to Okeechobee. That must be one of them. He said they might want to buy stuff or trade. Let's go and see."

The whistle blew again just as they reached the river, then the boat came into view. It was a stern-wheeler, forty feet long, with black smoke boiling from its one stack. The deck was crowded with crates, and a sign across the wheelhouse said MARY BELLE.

Tobias jumped up and down, waving his arms and shouting as the boat came abreast of them. Then the stern-wheel was reversed, sending bubbling brown water rushing beneath the boat and into the bank. The boat stopped slowly, backed up, and turned into the bank.

A man came out to the rail and shouted, "What is it? You want passage down to Okeechobee?"

"No," Tobias answered. "You want to buy something, or trade?"

"What you got?"

"What you want?"

"Crazy fellow!" the man shouted. "You stop us for a fool question like that? You got something to sell, say it!"

Tobias said, "We got beef."

"What kind?"

"Cows."

The man shook his head, exasperated. "All beef is cows! Are you talking about them wild swamp critters?"

"We catch 'em in the swamp."

"No! I don't want none of the scrawny yellowhammers! They don't even make good soup. You got deer?"

"We could."

"Pay you three cents a pound, dressed. But it's got to be fresh killed. If it ain't, you can just feed it to the buzzards. We'll be back by here three days from now."

"How about 'gator hides?" Tobias asked.

"Two bucks each if they're big enough."

"Coons?"

"Twenty five cents a hide."

"That the best you can do?"

Just then the whistle shrieked loudly, causing both horses to buck. The man shouted, "We ain't got all day, you idiot! You got something to sell, be back here in three days!" Then the boat pulled away from the bank and continued downstream.

"Seemed to be a mite riled up, didn't he?" Tobias said.

"I guess," Skillit said, trying to calm the horse.

"They must be a hundred 'gators in that big pond down by the hickory flat," Tobias said. "We get 'em all, that's more money than I ever seen."

"Could be," Skillit said. "But a 'gator don't part with his hide easy. Don't count yo' money yet."

Zech said, "Pappa, why don't me and Skillit ride back to the woods and see if we can find deer signs? We'll be back to the clearing real soon."

"While you do that I'll go on to the house and tell Emma. That whistle probably scared her real good."

Tobias watched as Skillit mounted the horse. He said, "You know, Skillit, it's a good thing we got that big ole army horse. You get on one of them marshtackies your feet would drag the ground."

"That's the God's truth," Skillit said. "That little hoss ain't made fo' a big fellow like me. I'd as soon ride that goat I had when I was a boy."

"We find a deer trail you want us to put Nip and Tuck on it?" Zech asked.

"Nope. You heard the man say it has to be fresh killed. I ain't wasting a bullet on buzzard bait. We'll go after a 'gator first."

They set out for the pond early the next morning, Tobias and Zech on the horses and Skillit following, carrying an axe, a six-foot cypress pole, and a length of rope. Just past the hickory flat they tied the horses to a bush and walked the remaining distance.

Nip and Tuck had been left behind at the house for fear they would strike the scent of a cow and go after it alone.

The bank of the pond was covered thickly with button bush and pickerel weed, but on the south side a mud flat formed an open area that ran forty feet out into the water. A fallen cypress limb to the left of the flat was covered solidly with turtles, and at the sound of approaching footsteps, they rolled over sideways and splashed into the water.

Six alligators were lying on the flat, motionless, their jaws cocked open. They paid no heed as the two men and a boy came to within thirty feet of them and stopped. If they were even aware of the intruders, they did not show it.

Skillit said, "How we going to go about this, Mistuh Tobias? I ain't never even tried to kill a 'gator."

"Me, neither. But it appears they're sleeping. That ought to make it easy."

For a few moments they just looked, and then Tobias said, "We'll try the one nearest to us. Ease in there, Skillit, and bash him on the head with that pole. Then me and Zech will come in and help pull him out."

"Are you sho' about this?" Skillit asked. "What if he don't bash? He got a mighty hard-lookin' head to me."

"That pole could knock down a bull. Just give him a good one."

Skillit eased forward, and when he stepped out onto the flat, his feet sank down into the mud. He took two more steps forward, each time making a sucking sound with his shoes; then suddenly the alligators started hissing.

Skillit looked back and said, "What I do now? Them things is givin' me a warnin', like a rattlesnake."

"They ain't even looking at you," Tobias said. "That hissing don't mean nothing. They can't bite you with their heads turned away from you."

As Skillit took another step forward, the hissing grew louder. The alligators were sideways to him, still motionless. He pulled one foot from the muck and leaped forward as best he could,

77

lifting the pole above his head. Before he could start the down-swing, the nearest alligator whirled around quickly and charged, its massive jaws snapping wildly. The pole came down and hit the alligator on top of its head, then it bounced away, ricocheting off the fallen cypress tree and landing in the water ten feet beyond.

Skillit fell backward into the mud and rolled over. He struggled free just as the alligator's jaws snapped to within a foot of his face. Then he scrambled up the bank and ran back to Tobias and Zech.

"I told you!" he exclaimed excitedly. "I done told you them things don't part with their hides easy! What we gone do now?"

Three of the alligators pushed off into the water and swam away. One of the remaining ones was still hissing, and the other two became silent again.

"I guess I'll just have to shoot one," Tobias said. "He can't bounce off a bullet like he did that pole." He took the rifle from its holster and came closer to the flat. "I best hit him halfway up from his tail, around where the heart ought to be. If I hit him in the snout it probably wouldn't do nothing but make him mad."

Tobias aimed carefully and fired. The alligator jumped two feet sideways and lay still as the other two scrambled into the water.

"Let's just stay back a minute and see if he moves," Tobias said.

They continued to watch, and then Tobias said, "He's dead for sure. Let's go in and get him, Skillit. Zech, you stay up here out of the way."

As they started across the flat Tobias said, "I'll get the tail and you get his head. The way he's lying, we'll have to pull him out sideways."

Skillit had just reached the head when Tobias grabbed the tail and jerked it. The huge tail lashed out like a whip, striking Tobias in the side. He landed six feet out in the water and went under. The 'gator then whirled around, jaws snapping, and caught the bottom of Skillit's pants in its teeth. Skillit kicked frantically, trying to break free, shouting, "Oh Lordy! Oh Lordy!"

Tobias came up spitting water, and then he managed to shout, "Get the gun, Zech! Shoot him! In the head, Zech! Shoot!"

Zech scrambled for the rifle as Skillit's pants were jerked off, making flapping sounds as the 'gator swished its head from side to side, popping the cloth in the air.

Zech aimed quickly and fired, and was knocked flat on his back. The alligator pumped blood from a hole directly between the eyes. He bucked up and down for a moment and then became still.

Tobias and Skillit scrambled up the bank simultaneously. Skillit said, "That darn 'gator done tore up my britches, Mistuh Tobias! What I gone do? That the only pair I got!"

"Emma can patch 'em," Tobias said, still spitting water. "Don't worry about it. You all right, Zech?"

"I'm O.K., Pappa. It just knocked the breath out of me."

"You ready to try again?" Tobias said to Skillit. "We done come too far to quit now. Let's get him out and see can we skin out the hide. And we can get your pants out of his mouth."

"I guess," Skillit said without enthusiasm. "But I tell you the truth, Mistuh Tobias, this ain't worth no two dollars. I'd as soon skin out eight coons or shoot a buck. I don't want no more trouble with them 'gators."

"Might be best we stick with coons," Tobias said. "I'm a bit shook up myself. Tomorrow morning we'll let them 'gators be and try to kill us a deer and a few coons."

Spring
1867

The holding pen was built just past the edge of the woods at the point where forest ends and prairie begins. Inside there were one hundred forty-eight cows, all with the MCI brand.

Zech put his hand on the gate latch and shouted, "You ready, Pappa?"

"Let 'em go!"

Zech threw open the gate and one cow ambled out slowly, then a few others followed and milled about. Others stayed inside, swishing their tails and bobbing their horns.

Tobias shouted, "Don't get in front of them, nobody! And don't push! Just let 'em eat and we'll follow!"

Tobias and Zech then mounted their horses, standing ready to rush after strays. Skillit was on the wagon seat with Emma beside him, and Nip and Tuck were off to the right, looking bewildered, waiting for something to happen.

The horse pulling the wagon was tall and black, with rib and hip bones showing beneath its hide. Tobias had been at the Fort Capron trading post when a man from St. Louis came through with a string of thirty ex-army horses. He purchased one for twenty dollars, knowing the old nag wasn't worth it but hoping he could fatten it on prairie grass and bring back some of its strength. He had to have something to pull the wagon on their first summer grazing drive and this was the best he could do.

They had worked steadily for months selling hides and deer meat to the riverboat, and after purchasing the horse, Tobias had enough left for a three-gallon cast iron cooking pot, two cowhide whips, salt and flour, and a used tarpaulin for the wagon. There still was no Dutch oven.

Zech had visions of following a thundering herd across the prairie, cracking his whip constantly, riding wildly as he forced escaping cows back into the herd; but by now a noon sun was directly overhead and the cows were still within a hundred yards of the pen, grazing contentedly. The wagon stood ready, but the wheels had not turned even one spoke.

Tobias rode up to Skillit and said, "Kinda slow, ain't it?"

"Sho' is. But this pore old hoss is glad of it. I'm gone turn him loose now and let him eat. If them cows decides to move, I'll hitch him up again."

Tobias said, "It's best we keep heading south. Over to the east, along the coast, there's too much palmetto and rattlers. Them snakes was thick as skeeters last time I was over there."

Emma adjusted her bonnet and said, "There ought to be some shade out here sommers. The sun is really coming down on me just sitting here like this. There's not even a breeze like back in the hammock."

"You get too tired go in the wagon and rest. The tarp will keep the sun off."

"I tried that, and it's hotter than an oven in there. I wish the cows would do something so we could move about some."

The afternoon drifted by slowly, and by sundown they had moved less than two miles. Skillit pulled the wagon to the edge of a cypress stand, unhitched the horse and started a fire. Then he cut thin poles, gathered palm fronds and built a lean-to where he and Zech would sleep. Tobias and Emma would share the wagon.

Emma made a stew of smoked beef and onions, and she baked

sweet potatoes in the edge of the coals. There was still no coffee, but she boiled hot tea from sassafras roots and sweetened it with cane syrup.

They ate from tin plates and then sat by the fire, deciding who would stand first watch. Someone would circle the herd all night, changing guard every four hours.

It was decided that Zech would go first when there was less chance of danger. Skillit said to him, "Mistuh Zech, when you come in tonight, be real careful befo' you lie down to sleep. And in the mornin', look real good befo' you make a sudden move. I knowed a man who slept one night on the prairie, and the next mornin' he grabbed a boot and slapped it on without lookin' first. They was a rattler in the bottom of it. His leg swelled up big as a tree trunk, and he like to have died. You be real careful. Them snakes sho' love to crawl in and sleep with people."

"Lordy, Skillit," Emma exclaimed, her eyes widening, "can they climb wagon wheels too?"

"I've seen 'em go up a tree easy as nothin'. You best look in yo shoes too."

Emma shuddered. "I'll sleep with them on!"

Tobias said, "Skillit, you're going to spook Emma before we even get started. Let's worry about keeping the cows in a bunch and forget the snakes. If one comes in the wagon I'll know what to do."

"Yes sir, Mistuh Tobias," Skillit said, grinning, "just like you knows how to hit a 'gator on the head with a cypress pole."

Tobias laughed, and then he said, "Before anybody goes on watch we ought to work out a signal. If there's trouble, and you need help, crack your whip three times real fast. Three cracks and we'll come to you quick as we can. And if the cows break and run for any reason, get out of the way. I've seen what they can do when they stampede. You understand me, Zech?"

"Yes, Pappa. I'll get out of the way. But if they run off in the dark, how we going to ever find them?"

"We will. They can't hide on the prairie. Just don't do something foolish. It ain't worth it."

Nothing happened during Zech's watch, and at ten o'clock he rode in and was relieved by Skillit. An hour later the cry of a wolf came from about a mile away. It was answered immediately by Nip and Tuck, and before the sound could spook the cows, the dogs raced around them, nipping legs, forcing them to remain in a circle. Then they stopped and sat alert, waiting anxiously for the cry to come again so they could go after it; but it was heard no more.

A full moon bathed the prairie when Tobias rode out to the herd. Cabbage palms stood like silent sentinels in the distance, and cypress stands were dark silhouettes on a sea of yellow. The quiet land seemed awesome, too vast for any man to ever conquer. Animals could survive its hazards, but Tobias wondered if he could.

He also wondered if he was being foolish, taking the advice of an Indian he really hardly knew, leaving the relative safety of his hidden hammock and following cattle into the unknown. But the cows did not grow in the swamp, and even the boatmen didn't want them. Out here there was grass to fatten them and ready them for market, and they would be worth something someday. He did not want to go on forever skinning coons and killing deer and growing just enough vegetables to survive. And this was apparently the only way out of the trap.

But what worried him most was Emma. He did not know what hardships lay ahead for her, things he and Zech and Skillit could overcome easily but would be an ordeal for her. Drifting a prairie was not exactly a woman's way of life. But she had to come along, for leaving her alone in the hammock was unthinkable. There was safety in numbers, safety from predators and from the bands of men Thompson said were roaming the countryside. He hoped that this wandering life would be uneventful, but one thing he knew: she would not complain, and no matter what came their way, she would have the strength to face it.

They followed the herd southward for a month, sometimes moving several miles in a day, other times not moving at all. The cows grew larger each day, and even their hides took on a sleek luster. Tobias swore he could actually see them put on weight with each mouthful of grass they swallowed. Even the old nag horse seemed to thrive on the rich prairie and grow stronger.

Several times they passed within sight of wild herds, some of them five times larger than the one they tended. But they did not go after them. Tobias thought it would be too much for the three of them to handle. It would take more men and more horses to capture and brand cows in such large numbers, and his mind was already searching for a way to hire drovers to join his little band.

One night when they were eating supper Zech said, "Pappa, who owns all this land out here?"

Tobias wondered why a boy Zech's age would even ask such a question. He said, "The Lord."

"You reckon He would give us some of it?"

"You've got it now. You can roam it wherever you please. The Lord put it here for everybody."

"But what if somebody else comes here besides us with a herd? How could we keep the cows apart?"

"It's big enough for everyone. There ain't enough cows and people in the whole world to fill it up."

Zech then said, "Skillit told me that the place where he was a slave was owned by a man. He owned all the land and nobody else couldn't come on it. If we owned the land we could put a fence around it, like the pen we built, and then we wouldn't have to follow the cows. We could just turn 'em loose 'cause they couldn't get out."

"That's foolish boy talk," Tobias said. "Nobody will ever fence this land. There's too much of it. This right here ain't a drop in the bucket. There ain't no man ever even seen all of it. The Lord put it here for everyone to use."

Emma was listening. She said, "Somebody might own it some-day, Tobias. All the land in Georgia is owned. You know that."

"A man would have to be a fool to buy something he can use for nothing," Tobias replied. "This ain't Georgia. There they farm the land, here they don't. This land ain't worth nothing except to graze cows. The whole place is wilderness. Georgia ain't."

Tobias then changed the subject. "Speaking of cows, it's about time I found out what to do with the ones we got. I figure we're probably out to the west of Fort Pierce by now. In the morning I'm going to ride over to the east and find it. Somebody there will know about the market."

"Will you be gone long?" Emma asked.

"Not more than a day and a night. It couldn't be far to the coast. But I got to find out where we can sell the cows."

"If you find lard, buy some. We don't have any more, and I can't make biscuits without it."

There were orange groves on the outskirts, and a dirt road ran past them and into the village of Fort Pierce. There was no activity on the sultry streets as Tobias walked the horse slowly, going past a dock where a coastal schooner was being loaded, then coming to a barnlike building with a sign: GENERAL MERCHANDISE. After tying his horse to a rail, he went inside.

The store was deserted except for a man sitting beside the counter, swatting flies with a matted palm fan. He said to Tobias, "Flies gets bad this time of year. Skeeters too. Sometimes I wish they'd go after each other."

"You got lard?" Tobias asked.

"How much you want?"

"A bucket."

The man went behind the counter and brought out a one-gallon can.

"Twenty-five cents. Be anything else?"

"You got a Dutch oven?"

"Nope. But I got some frying pans."

"I got a frying pan." Tobias sniffed the air. "Is that coffee I smell?"

"Sure is. Just ground a fresh batch. It came in on the schooner yesterday."

"How much is it?"

"Dollar for a five-pound bag."

"I'll take it. And a coffee pot too if you got one."

The man went to a shelf and returned with a tin coffee pot. "Dollar-fifty for both."

As Tobias was counting out the money, he said, "What they do with them oranges I seen coming here?"

"Ship 'em up north on the schooner. And some goes up the inland waterway to Jacksonville on them little boats."

"How much they sell for?"

"Bringing five cents a hundred-pound weight right now. Man can make a good living with oranges. In a good season you can clear up to three dollars a tree. And they're going to be worth more than that. It's a smart move to plant a grove."

"I just might do that."

The man put all of Tobias' purchases into a brown paper sack. "Anything else now?"

"Just some information. You know anything about selling cattle?"

"Right smart. A man in my business has to keep up with things. What you want to know?"

"Where to sell them."

"You got a herd?"

"Yes. Out on the prairie west of here."

"Well, there ain't no market for cows in Fort Pierce except a few at a time to the butcher shop. If you sell them out there on the prairie you'll get about four dollars a head tops. Best place to sell now is over on the west coast. The Cuba trade is getting real good again. You take them over there to a shipping point you'll get at least twelve dollars a head, maybe more."

"Where over there?"

"Best place is Punta Rassa. And they're shipping out of Tampa too."

"Where's Punta Rassa?"

"Down south of Fort Myers."

"Where's Fort Myers?"

The man gave Tobias a penetrating look. "I tell you what you ought to do, fella. You got a herd, point it straight west. When you come to a big body of water, that will be the Gulf of Mexico. You can turn right or left. If you turn right, sooner or later you'll come to Tampa, unless you go past it and end up in Pensacola. If you turn left, you'll come to Fort Myers or Punta Rassa. If you miss both of them, you're headed for Key West. But it's a long swim down there."

Tobias picked up the sack and said, "I thank you for the information." Then he walked out.

During the ride back to join the herd his mind was calculating figures. Four dollars a head for one hundred forty-eight cows was more money than he had ever seen or hoped to see. With that he could buy Emma a wood stove instead of a Dutch oven. And many other things too. But twelve dollars a head boggled his imagination and was beyond comprehension. And all that additional money just to drive the cattle over to a place called Punta Rassa, a thing he and Zech and Skillit could do easily. He could see visions of someday soon hiring drovers and moving herds ten times as large as his present one, masses of cows all cutting a trail to Punta Rassa.

When he found the herd it was late afternoon and they had already made camp for the night. Emma was by a fire cooking supper, and Zech and Skillit were out with the cows.

Tobias tied the horse to a wagon wheel as Emma said, "Did you get the information you wanted?"

"Sure did. And the lard too." He took the can from the sack and handed it to her.

"That's good. I'll make biscuits for supper. I know Zech and Skillit are hungry."

"There's more too," Tobias said teasingly. "Turn your head and close your eyes."

When he put the sack beneath her nose she sniffed and then cried, "Coffee! You got coffee!"

"And a pot to make it in."

"I'll go now and fill it with water," she said eagerly. "Then you can sit and watch as it boils. I bet the smell will bring Skillit in. Zech won't know what it is."

As soon as the pot was bubbling Tobias poured a tin cup of the steaming liquid and sipped slowly. "Coffee and biscuits at the same time," he moaned. "It's been a long time, Emma."

Zech and Skillit rode in and tied their horses, and Skillit said immediately, "Do I smell what I think I smell?"

"What you think you smell?" Tobias asked.

"Coffee?"

"Sure is. And it's ready now. Pour out a cup."

Skillit picked up the pot and said, "A voice been tellin' me all day something good was goin' to happen to ole Skillit. And now it's come to pass. Praise the Lord!"

Emma turned from the cooking pot and said, "What did you find out about the cattle, Tobias? With all the excitement about the coffee I forgot to ask."

"How would you like to see a place called Punta Rassa?"

"Where's that?" Zech asked.

"Over on the west coast, clear across the state. They're buying cows there now for Cuba, at twelve dollars a head. As soon as our cows hit about five hundred pounds each we're heading west. I figure it ought not to be more than three weeks, maybe less."

"Punta Rassa," Emma repeated. "That's a pretty name. Does it mean anything?"

"It means twelve dollars a cow, and we got a hundred and forty-eight of them. I can't even figure that high."

"I'll go out there and make them ole cows eat faster," Zech said. "I want to go now. How far is it, Pappa?"

"Don't know. But it's over there. All we got to do is head west."

CHAPTER THIRTEEN

✝

It was mid-afternoon in the middle of the next week when the sky in the east turned solid black. Clouds boiled like smoke and inched upward, blocking out more and more blue; and an increasing wind rattled the fronds of cabbage palms and shook the palmetto clumps.

Streaks of lightning flashed downward and then turned horizontal, forming fingers that ran crazily for a moment and disappeared into the earth. The boom of thunder broke the stillness of the prairie and caused great flights of egrets to rise upward and move away to the west.

Tobias rode up to the wagon and said to Skillit, "Must be a storm coming from out over the ocean. Looks to be a good one. This thunder keeps up, the cows is liable to run in four directions all at the same time."

"You want me to unhitch from the wagon and ride herd with you and Zech?"

"You best do that till we see what this storm is going to do. We might need your help. Are you all right, Emma?"

"I'm fine. I'll stay with the wagon till it blows past. Then we can make camp and have supper."

Soon the sky overhead was black too, and the winds increased to a steady howl, bending the prairie grass flat against the ground and filling the air with dead fronds from palm trees. Skillit rode up to Tobias and said, "Just look at that, Mistuh Tobias. I ain't never seen anything like it, and I sho' don't like the looks of it."

Droves of small animals—foxes, rabbits, raccoons—were running together, enemies no longer, moving rapidly westward; and deer bounded across the land, leaping bushes as they rushed past the smaller animals and disappeared.

They rode around and around the herd, trying to hold in the frightened cattle, and even the horses became skittish and whinnied nervously. Nip and Tuck worked full speed as they went for cow after cow that broke free and tried to run away.

The first pelts of wind-driven rain stung like bees as they slashed into Tobias' face. All light was vanishing rapidly, giving the prairie the yellowish look of late sundown.

Tobias turned one cow with his whip as Skillit galloped up to him and said, "What we goin' to do, Mistuh Tobias? We can't hold the cows no longer. There just ain't no way we can do it."

"We got to try," Tobias said. "They'll be ready to start to Punta Rassa by next week. If they run now as scared as they are, they'll be scattered all over come morning. Tell Zech to go and see to Emma. Me and you and the dogs will try."

As Skillit rode off, the rain came in a blinding sheet, obscuring cows, hammocks and sky. Tobias rode back in the direction of the wagon, groping slowly, feeling the wind knock the horse sideways and cause it to stumble.

When he finally found the wagon, both Skillit and Zech were there. The dogs were tied to a wheel and were huddled beneath the wagon floor, whimpering. The tarpaulin top popped constantly, sounding louder than cracking whips.

Skillit came close to Tobias and said, "This marsh is the lowest land we been on since we started the drive. There ain't no place for the water to run off. If it keeps on rainin' like this the whole place goin' turn to a lake."

"I know," Tobias agreed. "But we can't turn back now. It's too late. It's ten miles back to higher ground, and we'd never make it."

Skillit pointed south and said, "Yesterday afternoon when I scouted ahead I seen a Indian mound, right over yonder. We go there, we be out of the water. It's only a mile. We can look for the cows tomorrow."

"Hitch Ishmael to the wagon too and we'll make a run for it. You take my horse and lead the way. I'll throw the dogs in there with Emma and Zech."

Both horses strained to their limit as the wagon inched slowly across the soggy ground. Wind gusts hitting the tarp almost turned the wagon over before they took it off; then all protection for Emma and Zech was gone.

The mound loomed above them just before they became engulfed in total darkness. A few minutes more and it would have blended black into black and become impossible to find. They tried to drive the wagon up the slope but the horses slipped and fell backward. Finally they unhitched them and led them upward to the flat top.

The mound was fifty feet across and covered with dwarf cypress. They tied the horses and dogs and then huddled together, linking their arms and bracing themselves against the runty trees. By now the rain was not rain but solid water, tons of wind-driven water that felt like a river rushing over them. It poured into their eyes and noses, almost suffocating them, causing them to gasp for breath and hold their hands against their faces in hope of relief.

The storm raged unabated for eight hours; three hours before dawn it returned from solid water to a torrential downpour. When a faint light finally broke the darkness, the rain still came down with such force as to limit vision to less than fifty yards.

Tobias felt around him and touched flesh; then he said, "Emma. Are you all right, Emma? Zech? Skillit? Is everybody here?" He opened his eyes but his sight was blurred by the night of pounding water.

Emma said feebly, "I'm not sure. I've never been so soaked. I feel like my skin is washed off."

"I'm fine, Pappa," Zech said. "But I need to check on Ishmael. I hope he ain't floated off."

Skillit stirred and said, "I knows now how it feels to be a ole catfish. That storm must a went right up the coast. If we'd been in the center of it, it would of blowed us off here like leaves."

"It was bad enough," Tobias said, pushing himself to his feet. He walked to the edge of the mound and looked downward, seeing solid water. Only the tip of the wagon seat was visible.

In another hour the rain slackened to a drizzle, and they all looked out over a vast lake stretching as far as they could see. The water had come eight feet up the side of the mound.

Emma said, "The wagon, Tobias. Everything in it is gone. It's all ruined. The salt and the flour and the coffee and the lard. Everything."

"The cows too," Tobias said. "Ain't no way they could have got out of that alive. They done all ended up as buzzard meat."

"Maybe the Lord didn't mean for us to own them," Emma said, brushing her eyes. "Maybe He means for them to be wild and free, like the deer and the birds."

"This ain't the Lord's doing," Tobias said. "It was only a storm. We'll start again, but I will not spend another year popping cows out of swamps one at a time. This time we'll find a better way to do it."

"The horses is O.K., Pappa," Zech said. "And the dogs too. But they seem to be powerful hungry."

"We're all going to be hungry before we get out of this. Our bellies has rumbled before and we got through it, and we'll do it again. Soon as the water goes down we'll start out of here. It's going to take more than a storm to keep me from Punta Rassa. And that's the God's truth, so help me. We're going to see Punta Rassa."

Tobias then turned to Skillit and said, "Are you still with us, Skillit? You want to try again, or have you had enough by now?"

"I ain't goin' nowhere but with you, Mistuh Tobias. This is the onliest family I ever had, and ain't no storm goin' take it away from me. I'm ready whenever you are."

CHAPTER FOURTEEN

Spring
1868

Tobias stood by the corral gate, listening to the popping of whips far in the distance. Then came a faint sound like the drone of bees, and he felt a trembling in the ground. He watch intensely as the tiny black specks grew larger and formed a small herd of cows thundering straight toward him. When he could see their horns point upward he opened the gate and moved off hurriedly to the side of the corral.

Zech turned at the last possible moment and just missed crashing headlong into the rails; then Ishmael started bucking and kicking, as if to show the cows who had won the race. Nip and Tuck ran around in circles, and then they plopped to the ground, panting.

Tobias came back and closed the gate. Zech and Skillit calmed their horses and dismounted. Skillit said, "Mistuh Zech, you don't quit runnin' that little hoss flat-out like that, you gone go right over a cow's back one of these days."

"He wasn't wide open," Zech said. "I let him go, he'd be a mile out in front of the cows. He just likes to run in real close and bite their hind legs, like Nip and Tuck."

Tobias was busy counting. He said, "This sure beats one-on-one in the swamp. Must be over thirty in that bunch. It pains me just to think about how we used to spend a whole day trying to catch one cow, and then most likely he'd get away. We got all we can handle now. Soon's this bunch is marked we'll round up the whole herd and pen them for a final count. Then we'll get started."

"How long you figure it take us to drive all them cows to Punta Rassa?" Skillit asked.

"Don't rightly know, but we'll do it like we done with the herd we lost, go real slow and let 'em graze on the way. Time we get there, they ought to be fattened up and in good shape."

"Well, I sho' hope we make it there this time. I get a little something to spend, I needs a new pair of britches real bad. These I got about to fall apart. They done got patches on patches, and they ain't nothing more Missus Emma can do for them. And they's something else I need to see about too."

"What's that?" Tobias asked, mildly curious.

"Best not say," Skillit replied, grinning. "They might not have none, so it best I wait and see."

"What I want is a pair of boots," Tobias said. "We sell the cows, everbody gets boots. And a Dutch oven for Emma. Or maybe one of them spank-new wood cook stoves. She ain't never had one of them. What you want, Zech?"

Zech thought for a moment, and then he said, "A sack of apples for me and Ishmael. You reckon they got apples over there, Pappa?"

"I reckon. But is that all you want?"

"Well, maybe a brush too. Then I could brush Ishmael down and make him look real shiny. He's never had a chance to look his best, and I know it would feel good to him."

"We'll do it!" Tobias said, slapping Zech on the shoulder. "We'll get it all. Britches, boots, oven, apples, and brushes. And maybe whatever else it is that Skillit's got in mind. But right now we best stop spending money we ain't got and get on with the branding.

And we got a few calves with this bunch. We need to get them back to the right mammy so's they can suck."

"Let's get them cows marked and them calves mammied-up!" Skillit shouted enthusiastically. "These old britches might not hold up till we gets to Punta Rassa. Then I'd be in a worse fix than what the ole 'gator done to me. I'd have to stay hid in the woods and miss all the fun. And I sho' wouldn't like that."

When they reached the homestead later that afternoon, Zech and Skillit took a bundle of raccoon hides down to the river to hail one of the boats. Another stern-wheeler had been put into service, the *Osceola*, and they had sold the boatmen enough venison and hides to purchase supplies for the trip to Punta Rassa.

Emma was at the cooking pot when Tobias came inside and sat at the table. He said to her, "You figure we got enough of everything to make the trip? We done branded the last bunch, so we'll be ready to leave soon."

"We can make do. You'll have to shoot meat along the way. It's getting too hot to carry along much meat, even if it's smoked. How long have the supplies got to last?"

"A few weeks. That time I helped drive the cows for the Confederates we went a far piece in two weeks, and this ought not be much further."

Emma put down the spoon and sat at the table. "That's what worries me, Tobias. When you went on that drive you were with men who had been there before. They knew where they were going and how long it would take. Now you don't. And there were a lot more men. Zech's not a man, Tobias. I know he tries to act like one instead of a boy. But he is a boy. It's really just you and Skillit."

Tobias remained silent for a moment, and then he said, "You're right, Emma, and I know it. It worries me too. We got over seven hundred cows, and that's more than we herded for the army with seven men. Lord, what would the three of us do if we run into something like that pack of wolves? But I don't know what else to do. We just got to sell the cows. It's our only chance."

"Why don't you find some help? There must be a lot of men somewhere who need work. Didn't Mister Thompson tell you there's men everywhere who are hungry and looking for anything to do? You could try to get help up at Kissimmee. That's the closest place."

"He did say that. But I ain't got no money to pay drovers, and nobody works for free."

"Pay them at the end of the drive. That would make them want to get the herd there as much as you. If we lose the herd with just the three of you, we end up with nothing again. Seems to me that paying a few wages is better than risking nothing at all."

Tobias smiled. "You know, Emma, you got a heap more sense than me. This family would fall apart without you. It just might work. I can promise to pay them when I sell the cattle, and feed them along the way. If a man's hungry enough he'll go for it. It's worth a try."

Emma was pleased that he agreed. "I just fear for the three of you trying it alone. Zech would kill himself for you if need be, but he's still just a boy."

"I'll go to Kissimmee at daybreak tomorrow. I ain't never been there but I can find it. All I got to do is follow the river. And soon as I come back with some help we'll be on our way." He took her hands in his and said, "You're the only MacIvey with brains, Emma. Except Zech. Just you and Zech. Me, I'm a dumb ole coot and I know it. I'm as dumb as that army horse, running in a straight line full speed ahead without looking where I'm going. It could get me busted wide open, and all of you too."

"That ain't so, Tobias," she said gently. "Hadn't been for you we'd still be up in Georgia, probably starved by now. Wouldn't many men strike out like you did. And like you always say, we're going to make it. Somehow. Now you just go on and look for them drovers."

*T*obias followed the river hammocks until he came to Lake Kissimmee. Here he skirted the east shore and then headed through a marsh area, soon coming to two more lakes. Late in the afternoon he met a family traveling south by ox cart, and they told him it was just a few more miles into the village. He decided to make camp for the night and continue at daybreak.

The next morning he ate a sparse breakfast of smoked beef and a biscuit, saving most of his food for the drovers on the return trip. Then after a short ride he approached Kissimmee along a dirt road deeply embedded by cows' hooves.

The main street extended for two blocks and was lined with unpainted clapboard buildings containing two general stores, a small café, a blacksmith shop, and three saloons. Wooden benches bordered the sidewalk in front of each store, and vacant lots separating the buildings were overgrown with weeds.

Tobias first rode all the way through town and into the residential section containing a half dozen frame houses with small front porches and drawn window shades. A dog ran from one yard and barked as he passed, and in another, chickens pecked at the bare ground. This was the most houses he had seen in years, and he observed carefully the details of each, comparing them with his own homemade cabin.

When he came back into the business section, loud curses were coming from one of the saloons. He watched curiously as a lone rider rode up to a window cut into the side of the building, was handed a filled glass in exchange for a coin, drank it in one gulp and sauntered off, never dismounting his horse.

Just then a man crashed through the swinging doors and landed flat on his back in the street. He got up painfully, brushed dirt from his pants, then walked down to one of the stores and sat on a bench.

Tobias rode by slowly, studying the man out of the corner of his eye. He was around thirty, six feet tall and thin as a cypress pole, with a bushy black beard. On top of his head was a huge black felt hat covered with dust. He stared dejectedly at the ground and paid no heed as the horse passed.

At the next store Tobias dismounted, tied his horse to a rail and walked back to the man. He hesitated for a moment, not knowing how to make the approach, and then he said bluntly, "You looking for work?"

The man glanced up, "Doing what?"

"Brush popping."

"What's that?"

"Working cows. Herding."

"What do it pay?"

"Fifty cents a day plus keep. But I can't pay till I sell the cows. You got a horse?"

"Piece of one. I rode him in the army."

"Which army?"

"Reb. Do I smell like a Federal?"

"Nope. More like a skunk. When's the last time you went down to a creek and washed?"

"Don't rightly remember. Must 'a been sometime back in sixty-five."

Tobias shifted his feet and said, "You want the job or not? I got a herd to move to Punta Rassa and I ain't got time to stand here jawing with you."

"One thing for sure. I ain't had a dollar on me in over three years. And I've et so many possums I feel like I could hang by my tail from a tree limb. When do I start?"

"I'm riding out of here just as soon as I can. I'm Tobias MacIvey. What's your name?"

"Frog"

"Frog? Frog what?"

"Just Frog. That's all the name I need. I got a buddy down the street. Can he go too?"

"Yes. I need two drovers. What's his name?"

"Bonzo."

"Lordy me," Tobias said, shaking his head. "Frog and Bonzo. This going to be some cattle crew. Go and tell him we'll leave from right here in a half hour. And both of you better be on time."

"Could I have fifty cents in advance?" Frog asked. "What for?"

"I done been throwed out of ever saloon betwix here and Tallahassee, and I'd like to just one time have a drink and pay cash for it. That way I wouldn't end up flat on my back in the street."

"No!" Tobias replied harshly. "I ain't paying my hard-earned money to put whiskey in your gut! Now you go on and fetch your buddy back here!"

"It was just a thought," Frog said, turning and walking away.

Tobias went into the store and said to the clerk, "You got cheese?"

"How much you want?"

"Two one-pound blocks. And wrap them separate."

The clerk cut two chunks from a hoop, wrapped them and handed them to Tobias. "Now what else?"

"Can you make a sign?"

"What kind of a sign?"

"A small one. About three feet long."

"Sure. We got stencils."

"How long will it take and how much will it cost?"

"Seventy-five cents, counting the board. It won't take but a couple of minutes, but you'll have to be careful with it till the paint dries. What you want it to say?"

"MacIvey Cattle Company."

"How you spell that name?"

"M-a-c-I-v-e-y."

The clerk said, "Why don't you just write it all down for me on this piece of paper and I'll copy it."

"If I could write it all down, I'd make the sign myself," Tobias said impatiently. "I can count cows and money but I ain't no good at writing. And besides, that's what I'm paying you for."

"Very well. It won't take but a minute."

As the clerk went to the back of the store Tobias said, "Punch two holes in the top of the board so's I can tie it to the side of a wagon."

While waiting he walked around the store, looking at the sparsely stocked shelves, thinking that goods here were not much more plentiful than at Fort Capron. But the emphasis here seemed to be on things needed by cattlemen.

On one counter he found a basket of pink ribbons, and when the clerk came back, he said, "How much are these?"

"Five cents each. Purty, ain't they? We got them in about a month ago but don't have much call for ribbons. Mostly men in these parts."

"I'll take one. You got a Dutch oven?"

"That I don't have."

"How much I owe?"

"All together it comes to a dollar twenty-fine."

Tobias paid the bill and picked up the sign carefully so as not to smear it. He said, "Much obliged," and started out.

The clerk called after him, "Don't touch the paint for an hour. It ought to be dry by then."

Frog and Bonzo were standing in the street, holding their horses, when Tobias came from the store. He did a double take when he saw Bonzo, then he said, "You two look like twin brothers. You must be cut from the same mold."

"We ain't," Frog said. "It just appears that way. I ain't no kin to this varmint."

Tobias scratched his head. "I thought I looked like a cattail stalk, but you two are worse than me. You look like you need worming. When's the last time you et?"

"Can't say for sure," Frog said, "but right now I could eat a cut off a saddle."

"Here, take this," Tobias said, handing each of them a package. "I bought it for you." He watched as they opened the cheese and ate eagerly, then he said, "My wife's a good cook. Her name's Emma. She can make a polecat taste like ham. She'll put some

meat on them bones. I got smoked beef and biscuits in the saddlebag. We'll have that for supper."

"How long it going to take to get where we're going?" Bonzo
asked, stuffing his mouth.

"We'll be there in the morning. Best we take it easy on the way.
Them horses you got looks like they'd faint dead away if you put
them in a trot. Bones stick out worse than on you. What they need
is some good prairie grass. Let's mount up and go soon as I finish
tying this sign to my saddle. You can eat on the way."

Tobias secured the board; then they mounted and rode down
the dirt street. He wondered what Emma, Zech, and Skillit would
do when they saw Frog and Bonzo come riding out of the woods.
He felt sure that Nip and Tuck would put them up a tree.

Frog said, "Mister MacIvey, don't you worry none about these
horses. They old and skinny but they tough. And me and Bonzo
might look like rotten bean poles, but we're like these old nags.
We knows how to hang in there. And we thank you for the cheese.
You the first one who just up and give us something besides a hard
time."

"Just hope you enjoyed it," Tobias said. "It might stop up your
innards but it'll fill your belly for a while. We got some riding to
do afore dark and the next meal."

As Tobias and the two men rode into the clearing, Emma and
Zech came from the house. Tobias stopped his horse and said
uncertainly, "Emma, this is Frog and Bonzo, my new drovers."

"Howdy, ma'am," they said in unison, removing their hats.

"This is my son, Zech."

"Howdy, Zech. Pleased to meet you."

They all dismounted as Emma and Zech continued to stare at
the gaunt strangers. Tobias watched their reaction closely. Zech
said, "What kind of horses is them?"

"Just horses," Frog responded.

"They's worse than the one Pappa bought at Fort Capron. Looks like they needs some grass."

Emma said, "Are you men hungry? I fixed a big pot of stew in case Tobias brought somebody back with him."

"They's always hungry." Tobias said. "Last night they ate everything but my saddlebag. From now on you best make stew in a wash tub instead of the cooking pot. Where's Skillit?"

"In his cabin," Zech said. "He's putting in some shelves. I'll go and get him."

Before Zech could move, Skillit came from the cabin. Frog took one look and exclaimed, "Where'd you get him? That's the biggest man I ever seen."

"His name's Skillit," Tobias said. "He's my right-hand man. You and Bonzo can bunk in with him tonight."

"Pleased to meet you, Skillit," Frog said pleasantly, remembering what Emma said about stew. "I'm Frog, and this here is Bonzo."

Just then Nip and Tuck came running from the woods, yapping loudly. They bounded across the clearing and came straight for the two men.

Frog and Bonzo reached Skillit's cabin just ahead of the dogs and scrambled to the roof. The dogs then ran around and around the cabin and tried to climb the wall.

"I knew it!" Tobias shouted. "I just knew they'd do it! Call 'em off, Zech!"

Zech whistled, and the dogs came to him. Frog and Bonzo peeked over the edge of the roof, and Frog said, "Where'd you get them wolves?"

"They ain't wolves," Zech said. "They's dogs. Their names are Nip and Tuck. They ain't going to hurt you. They just didn't know who you are."

"You better make an introduction afore I come down off of here," Frog said. "They done scared the livin' daylights outen me."

Skillit was watching it all, grinning.

"They won't do it again," Tobias said. "Soon as they know

103

you're part of the crew they'll like you."

Frog and Bonzo climbed down from the roof reluctantly. Then they all went into the house and took tin plates from a shelf.

*J*ust before they went to bed that night, Tobias and Emma sat at the table alone, talking. Emma said, "Where'd you find those two, Tobias?"

"On the street in Kissimmee. But don't let their looks fool you. They're tough. I've done seen it. They'll be a big help to us."

"I'm not worried about that. It's the supplies. I've never seen men eat like them. They keep it up we'll have to kill and cook every cow we got before we reach Punta Rassa."

Tobias smiled. "It's just that they're empty right now and have been that way for a long time. They're bound to fill up soon."

"I hope so. I don't know how I could keep a cook fire going all day every day during the drive."

Tobias then took the ribbon from his pocket and held it behind him. "I bought a little something for you in Kissimmee. It ain't much, but I thought you'd like it."

When he handed it to her she said, "It's real purty, Tobias. Real purty. And I thank you. But I won't wear it myself. I'll put it away. Pink is for a baby girl. I'll save it."

Tobias felt his face flush. He reached out and touched her, and then he said, "You'll use it someday, Emma. Now that I got some help, things are going to change for us."

☦

The line of cattle stretched out over a quarter mile, moving slowly, the men and dogs on the sides, the wagon in the rear. Frog told Tobias he had never been to Punta Rassa but knew of men who had, and that they should go south to Fort Basinger where there was a ferry to take the wagon across the Kissimmee River. From that point on it was unknown territory.

When they reached the fort, Tobias was charged two dollars to load the wagon on a small wooden barge that was pulled across the river by ropes. The cattle, horses and men swam, and it reminded Tobias of the time he stood on the bank of the St. Marys and watched the cows cross the water in a long black line of bobbing horns. Only this time none were lost, and there was no crowd of hungry spectators watching, hoping for a drowned cow to wash ashore.

They were two days past the river when a rider came across the plain and to the wagon. Tobias saw him speak briefly to Emma, then he rode back to meet him. The man said, "Name's Sam Lowry. Are you MacIvey?" He had seen the MacIvey Cattle Company sign on the side of the wagon.

"Tobias MacIvey."

"Where you headed?"

"Punta Rassa."

The man shifted in his saddle. "You want to buy some cows?"

"What you mean?" Tobias responded, not expecting such a question.

"I got a little spread couple of miles north of here. I seen you coming. I farm mostly, but I got sixty-five cows. Ain't no way I can get them to market by myself, so I'll sell them to you for three dollars each. You can put 'em in with your herd."

Tobias calculated in his mind what they were said to be worth in Punta Rassa. If the market was as Thompson indicated, there would be a profit of nine dollars per cow. He said, "I don't have that much money on me. Tell you what I'll do, though. I'll take them and pay you on the way back."

"Well, I don't know about that. I wanted cash. How do I know you'll come back by here and pay me?"

"You've got the word of Tobias MacIvey," Tobias said firmly. "I've never broken my word to no man, and I'm not going to do it for sixty-five cows. When we come back I'll pay you."

"For sure they ain't doing me any good just chewing grass. You've got the look of an honest man, and your missus has too. I'll take a chance with you and do it. You want to sign some kind of a paper?"

"Don't need no paper 'less you want it. You got my word. And next time we come through with a herd I'll pay you cash for whatever you got. I'll make a stop ever time at your place."

"Sounds good enough. But we ought to at least shake on it."

Tobias clasped the man's hand. "It's did."

Frog and Bonzo rode to the homestead with Lowry and drove his cows back to the herd. This pushed the number past eight hundred.

That night after supper, Tobias was sitting in the wagon with Emma, waiting his turn for second watch. She said, "Next time we make a drive, we better bring a whole barrel of flour, or maybe a wagon load. Frog and Bonzo ate twelve biscuits each. They eat more than Skillit, and look how big he is."

"Don't seem right for a man to eat that much and stay thin as a snake. But look at me. I ain't much better. Maybe some men don't get fat no matter what they eat."

"Zech's going to be the same way. He keeps getting taller all the time, but he don't have no meat on his bones. Seems I'm the only one who puts on flesh."

"You're just right," Tobias smiled, patting her shoulder. "Don't no man want to sleep with a snake. I'll take you over any skinny woman I ever seen."

"Oh, Tobias, be serious!" she said, smiling too.

Tobias then said, "You know, Emma, I been thinking about the cows we got from Lowry. They must be men scattered all over the place with small herds and no way to get them to market. We get enough cash money, I could ride ahead of the drive and buy cows for three dollars each. What we got here now ain't nothing to what we could have. We could end a drive with thousands of cows and not even have to go to the trouble of catching them."

"That's true," Emma agreed. "But when you just give your word for payment, like you did today, what will you do if we lose this herd like we did once before. How will you pay anyone?"

"That ain't likely. We're bound to get through with some of them. We got the men to do it. But if we make Punta Rassa with only sixty-five cows they belong to Lowry. I gave my word."

"Yes, you did. And I know by now how a MacIvey thinks." She took his hand and held it. "If I were Lowry, I would trust you.

Tobias smiled again. "It's worth thinking on, buying cows along the way."

For three days they moved over a marsh flat just to the south of a dense swamp. The grass here was rich and bountiful, and Tobias thought it would be a good place to bring cows for summer grazing.

It was just before midnight on the third day when Tobias was awakened by the sound of a whip cracking three times, a signal of danger. He dressed hurriedly, jumped from the wagon and saddled his horse.

Skillit and Zech heard it too and were already mounted. Frog and Bonzo were with the herd.

The cracking came again, and Skillit said, "Whatever it is, they must figure they need help bad. They keep poppin' them whips, they'll spook the cows for sure."

There was a full moon flooding the marsh, and the herd was easily visible a quarter mile away. As they rode forward, they could hear bellowing and the dull thump of hooves striking the ground.

Zech said, "You want me to go back and untie the dogs, Pappa?"

"Not yet. Let's see what the trouble is first."

They rode to the right of the herd and found Frog. He said, "I'm sure glad you got here this quick. We couldn't hold the cows in much longer without help."

"What's happening?" Tobias asked, puzzled. "I don't see anything to stir them up."

"You will. Look over yonder to the edge of the swamp."

Tobias shifted in his saddle and looked to the north; then he said, "Oh Lord! Wolves! A whole passel of 'em, just like I seen on the Confederate cattle drive."

Dark forms darted everywhere in the moonlight, running forward, turning back to the woods, coming forward again, each time getting closer to the herd.

"I don't know how to handle something like this," Frog said. "You'll have to tell me what you want me to do."

"Even if they don't attack, they'll stampede the herd," Tobias said. "We got to keep 'em back. Frog, you and Bonzo keep circling the herd. Zech, you and Skillit go back to the wagon and turn the dogs loose. Then bring all the firewood we got back here. Me and Skillit will use torches, and Zech, you go to the herd and help out there. If the cows break, get out of the way and let 'em go. We'll round them up in the morning. Just don't get in the way. And hurry now!"

Tobias' horse danced nervously as he waited for Zech and Skillit to return. When one wolf rushed forward, he unfurled his whip and charged it, slashing at the darting form again and again, feeling cowhide touch flesh as the wolf howled in pain and turned back. The horse bucked and kicked, terrorized by the wolf-smell, almost throwing him from the saddle.

Nip and Tuck streaked through the yellow grass, barking and snarling, two gray forms moving so fast that Tobias lost track of them. They rushed right through the wolves; then they came back and positioned themselves halfway between the woods and the herd, apparently fearless of what stalked in front of them.

Skillit rode up with a burlap sack full of pine knots. He said, "I didn't mean to be so long, but I built a fire by the wagon. Missus Emma is all fretted up and I didn't want to leave her in the dark."

"That's good," Tobias said, dismounting. "You done right. Tie the horses to a bush while I light the torches. We best stay on foot with the fire. We can move around better this way."

Tobias and Skillit then ran constantly, moving with the wolves, thrusting fire forward when a dark form came close, smelling singed hair and running again. The sound of whips blended with bellowing as the cows charged in one direction and were turned back, then stomped their hooves and charged again, crashing into each other.

One wolf broke into the outside circle of the herd and a shrill, almost human scream overwhelmed all other sound as a calf hit the ground and struggled frantically to get away. Nip and Tuck were on the wolf's back instantly, snarling, teeth snapping, hair flying, biting chunks from the wolf and jumping back, then rushing in again to send the wolf sprawling across the ground.

Some of the cows broke away from the battle site and ran, and no amount of men or whips could stop them. Tobias glanced at them briefly as they thundered away and disappeared in the direction of the swamp.

A death cry came from the wolf as the dogs ripped its throat open. It stumbled back toward the woods, leaving a trail of hot blood, falling and then scrambling forward, howling again as its life rapidly poured out onto the ground. The mournful sound seemed to frighten the other wolves. For a few minutes they moved back and forth among themselves, bewildered and

109

undecided; then they ran swiftly to the edge of the woods and disappeared.

Tobias and Skillit put out their torches, mounted and rode to the herd. Frog came to them and said, "About thirty broke out, Mister MacIvey. We couldn't stop them. It was when that wolf got in there."

"I know. I seen it. We're just lucky it wasn't more than that. We'll find them in the morning. All of us need to stay out here the rest of the night in case the wolves come back. Where's Zech?"

"Over to the right," Frog said. "He had that little hoss going like a jackrabbit. And I sure wouldn't want him to turn that whip on me the way he was using it on them wolves."

"Go and tell him to stay with his mamma till the rest of us come in. She's probably up in the top of a tree by now. Tell him to hurry on in to the wagon."

Once more during the night, the cattle tried to break but were turned back, and when daylight came, they started grazing as peacefully as if nothing had happened.

Tobias noticed one calf with a cut across its side but it was not a serious injury. He figured it was the one the wolf knocked down. Skillit came up to him and said, "How many of us you want to keep staying here?"

"Tell everybody to go back to the wagon. The cows are calm now, and we all need some food and rest."

Emma had biscuits and beef waiting when they rode in. She also dipped into their meager supply of coffee, and the aroma made the men jump from their horses and grab tin cups from the wagon.

Frog took a deep drink and said, "Zech, I ain't going to say nothing more but good about them dogs of yours. When that wolf got in there, if it hadn't been for the dogs them cows would 'a been scattered over Georgia by now. They really done a job on that wolf."

Both Nip and Tuck's faces were covered with caked blood. Zech patted one of them and said, "They's good dogs, and they ain't scared of nothing."

Emma passed around a plate of hot biscuits. "I thought everybody was getting killed," she said. "I've never heard so many different sounds at one time."

"It was a ruckus all right," Tobias said. "I just hope it don't happen again. Maybe we've seen the last of them."

Zech said, "Pappa, if the wolves come back, why don't we just shoot them?"

"That'd scare the cows as bad as the wolves." He yawned, and then he said, "Frog, you and Bonzo stay here and get some sleep. You're probably shucked out since you haven't been to bed all night. Me and Zech and Skillit will look for the cows that ran off."

"We'll stay, but I'll keep one eye open. If anything happens we'll go out to the herd real fast."

As soon as the coffee was gone, Tobias, Zech and Skillit mounted up and rode to the north side of the herd. Tobias said, "The last time I seen them they were heading straight for the swamp, about a quarter mile west of the wolves. Let's go down that way and see if we can pick up their tracks."

The ground close to the line of cypress trees was soft, and they easily found the trail of hoof prints. When they entered the woods, they could see ferns that had been stomped flat by the cows. Tobias said, "I hope they didn't go far. If they did, we'll never get them out of there."

Bald cypress trees towered over a hundred feet into the sky and were surrounded by thick clumps of knees, and the ground was covered solidly with lush ferns and beds of velvet moss. There was an eerie quietness about the place, no barking of squirrels and no flapping of wings.

The ground took a sudden downward slant that led into a cup-shaped slough, and here the hoof marks went down a foot into black muck. Tobias stopped his horse and said, "Lord have mercy! Just look at that!"

Forty yards ahead of them, cow horns were sticking out of the ground, nothing but horns, and not even the bare tip of a head could be seen.

"They done buried themselves alive in that sinkhole," Skillit said, his eyes wide. "Even the buzzards can't get at 'em. They ain't nothing left but worm bait."

Zech started backing Ishmael. "I don't want to look, Pappa. Let's leave. I don't want to see it."

"I don't either. That ain't a fit way for even an animal to die. I don't want to see this place again."

For another week they stayed on open prairie, skirting just to the south of the line of trees that marked swampland. Then one day the trees appeared on the horizon ahead of them as well as to the north; and as they moved forward, a wall of tall cypress blocked their view to the south.

For two more days they moved westward, letting the cows graze and set their own pace, and each day the corridor between the north and south trees became narrower, and the wall ahead of them loomed closer.

Tobias rode from the wagon and over to Skillit on the herd's right flank. "I don't like the looks of this," he said. "Seems like we're heading into some kind of dead-end canyon, right into a swamp. I hope there's a way through it. If there ain't, we've got three or four days of backtracking to do."

"Don't look good. And we sho' ought not push 'em into a swamp after what we seen back at the other one."

By late afternoon, the wall in front of them was only a half mile away, and the north and south corridor had narrowed to less than a mile. Heat coming from the ground was stifling, and the air was so thin the horses puffed as they walked.

Tobias told the men to stop the herd and circle them until they were settled, then come back to the wagon for supper. He hoped there were no bears or wolves here, for if the herd spooked for any reason, there was nowhere for them to run and seek safety.

Emma cooked the last of the smoked beef and also baked sweet potatoes. As the men ate silently, she said to Tobias, "Tomorrow you've got to either shoot a deer or kill one of the cows. There's no meat left, and the flour is almost gone too. We'll have to make koonti to get us through."

"I'll see to it as soon as I can," Tobias said. "What worries me more than vittles is this fix we're in. In the morning I'll scout ahead and see if there's a way out of here without turning back."

"This place spooks me," Frog said. "I got a feeling somebody is watching us. I don't know how to explain it, but something ain't right. Times like this it pays to be a dumbo like Bonzo."

Bonzo either didn't hear the remark or ignored it. He stuffed a burned potato peeling into his mouth and chomped, paying no heed to the conversation.

"I got the same feeling," Skillit said. "Black man say someone walkin' on yo' grave. It strong enough to make my flesh crawl."

"You men!" Emma exclaimed, dipping herself a plate of stew. "You're seeing ghosts everywhere. All you're doing is remembering the wolves, and we may never see those wolves again. And when it comes down to the truth, all you really worry about is your stomachs, whether or not some woman can fill them up."

"There's fact in that," Frog said. "The only thing that counts in life is a woman's cooking pot. Is yours empty now, Miz Emma?"

"Almost," Emma said, taking his plate. "There's a little left. But you just proved what I said."

Zech was listening, but he seldom broke into a conversation when adults were talking; but now he spoke up. "Ishmael feels it too, Pappa. I can put my hand on his neck and feel him tremble. He knowed the wolves were coming before we seen them, before the cows got riled up. He sees things nobody else can see, and he has a way of letting me know. He ain't happy here, Pappa. He says we ought not be here. He's a Indian pony, and he has a way of knowing things we don't know."

Everyone became silent for a moment, wondering if this were truth or fantasy coming from a small boy who talked as if he really believed it; then Tobias said, "Ishmael is a horse, Zech, and that's all. He's just a horse like all the others. It's time we stopped this gibberish and go on watch. Me and you will go first. That way, if Ishmael has something special to say, maybe I can hear it too."

"You don't have to believe it," Zech said. "I was just trying to tell you Ishmael ain't happy here. I can tell when he is and when he ain't."

Tobias got up from the fire. "Let's go, before you get me too spooked to ride watch. Tomorrow morning we'll leave this place one way or another."

There was no moon during the first of the watch, and it was impossible to distinguish cows from trees. Tobias and Zech rode only by sound, hearing the swish of a tail or the thump of a hoof, circling what they hoped was the herd. The fire back at the wagon was their only beacon, and without it, they would have had no sense of direction at all.

Tobias sat still in the saddle for a moment, staring blindly into the darkness, thinking what a catastrophe it would be if danger struck the herd in such a sea of ink. If the cows ran, there would be no way of knowing which direction they took; and with swamp on three sides of them, they would have to hunt for the cows one at a time, just as he and Zech had once hunted them in the swamp beyond the hammock.

He moved the horse forward again, feeling his way, not wanting to bump into a cow and frighten it; then he stopped and listened, hearing a faint tinkling sound, like bells. The sound went away, and then it came again, this time closer. The next time he heard it, it seemed to be moving back into the swamp.

Zech rode up to him, moving swiftly, the small horse surefooted in the darkness. "Did you hear something, Pappa?" he asked, holding the reins tight to stop the horse's dancing.

"I thought I did. But it could have been the wind in the trees.

Did you?"

"It sounded like bells. I heard it two or three times, and then it went away."

"That's what I heard too, something tinkling. It's for sure nobody's belled a milk cow and turned it loose out here. It must have been something in the trees. Whatever it was, I haven't heard it again."

Just before the watch ended, the moon came from behind a cloud bank, casting a yellow glow over the herd and the trees. Although he had felt no movement, Tobias discovered that the cows were a quarter mile closer to the edge of the swamp. He wanted to move them back again but did not do so for fear of spooking them.

When he got back to the wagon after being relieved, Emma stirred and said, "Well, did you see any buggers out there tonight?" She said it in jest, not really expecting an answer.

"No, Emma, I heard bells. Zech heard it too, and I told him it was just the wind in the trees. But it wasn't. It was bells."

"Bells?"

"It was a tinkling sound at first. It came close to the herd once, and then it went away. Neither one of us didn't hear it no more."

"Why would anyone be out here in the wilderness with bells?"

"I don't know. But come sunup I aim to find out."

Tobias left before breakfast the next morning. Zech wanted to come with him, but he said no, he would do this alone. If there was a way through the swamp he would find it and come back as soon as possible.

He approached the line of cypress trees reluctantly, walking the horse slowly, looking back at the grazing herd and at the wagon beyond. It seemed to him that all this land they had moved over for three days was a funnel, directing them to this one impassable

115

spot. His instinct was to turn back now, to backtrack the herd and leave this place as hurriedly as possible, but he walked the horse straight into the woods.

The land looked the same as where the cows buried themselves: towering bald cypress, thick clumps of lush ferns, fallen rotten limbs covered with moss, palmetto clumps and cocoplum bushes. There were also pools of stagnant water covered with slime, cut in places by moccasin trails.

Tobias followed a small ridge of higher ground, moving gingerly, remembering what happened to the cows that ran into the sinkhole muck. He already knew there was no way to move cattle through here but he did not turn back. He was a mile into the swamp when he heard it, the bells, the one thing he had come looking for—not a passage for the herd but the strange sound that had come out of the night.

It was off to the right, no more than a hundred yards distant, tinkling, moving and then stopping, then moving again. He sat in the saddle in a daze, not thinking of the herd or of Emma or Zech or anything but the bells, somehow knowing that if he sat still it would come to him.

The horse whinnied and backed away a few steps as the sound grew louder; then it came past the last clump of palmetto and stood before him.

The man was beyond age, so old that his skin was cracked like alligator hide. He was almost seven feet tall, and his hair was tied on top of his head with bands of reeds, making him seem even taller. He wore only a girdle of silver-colored balls and small brass bells, and around his neck there were six strings of shells. His wrists were covered with bracelets of fish teeth, and his entire body was stained red.

Tobias stared, unbelieving at first and then believing, but feeling no fear. He knew this was not an apparition or a hallucination but a man, a flesh and blood man beneath all those strange trappings. There was a calmness about him that dissipated fear, making Tobias calm too, an overwhelming calmness that flooded his body and caused him to slump forward in the saddle.

For several moments no word was spoken, and then the old man said, "I am a Timucuan, the last of my people. I am the keeper of the graves. Soon I will join the others. We came here a long time ago to hide from the Spanish soldiers. I am the only one left, and I have lived beyond my time."

Tobias said, "We didn't know. We are lost and trying to find a passage for the herd."

"Do not bring your cows in here," the old man cautioned. "In here there is only death. If you come in here you will never return. Go back the way you came. This swamp is a burial ground for all who enter. My people have known this to be true."

"Is there no other way? We're trying to reach the sea to the west. If we turn back it means three or four days of traveling."

"It is best that you travel those days. Only death awaits you if you enter. Do not go into the south swamp either. Go all the way back and around the swamp. It is the only way."

Without speaking further, the old man turned and walked away. Tobias wondered if he had really seen this or not, but as he listened to the bells fading into the distance, he knew.

Zech rode to him swiftly as soon as he emerged from the woods. He asked anxiously, "Did you find it, Pappa?"

"Find what?" Tobias responded absently.

"A way to get through."

"There is no way to get through. We'll have to turn the herd and go back. It's the only way."

"The bells, Pappa? Did you find the bells?"

"It was the wind. Only the wind. Ride on ahead and tell the men to move the cows out of here right away. Hurry now!"

Tobias sat still for several minutes, thinking of the old man who had been in there alone for such a long time; then he put his horse into a trot and headed for the herd.

*F*or two days they turned back eastward, following the south line of trees, seeing the funnel gradually widen until the swamp on the north lay on the far horizon.

Tobias was strangely silent, even at night around the supper fire. They killed one cow and dressed it, and the fresh beef satisfied all but Tobias, who seemed to be preoccupied with something besides food. He could not dismiss the strange Indian from his mind, and he wanted to get away as quickly as possible and never return.

At dawn on the third morning he rode into the edge of the swamp alone. The trees were not so thick here, and for a half mile the ground was solid. From this point forward there was water, and the trees became even thinner. He stared at what seemed to be an opening on the far side; then he turned and went back to the wagon.

Everyone was at the breakfast fire except Bonzo, who was with the herd. Tobias took a strip of fried beef, ate a few bites and threw the rest to Nip. He said, "I think the swamp is narrow here. There's water, but it don't look too bad. If we can push through here it will save us a couple more days of backtracking. Then we'll be away from this place."

"There's really no hurry, is there?" Emma asked. "The cows seem to be doing fine on the grass."

"I want to try it anyway. We'll cut out six cows. Me and Zech and Skillit will take them in there. If we make it with no trouble, Zech can wait on the other side while we come back and push the rest of the herd through."

"You want the dogs to come with us?" Zech asked.

"Maybe they ought to. They could be a big help in there, and the water don't look too deep for them."

"Are you sure about this?" Skillit asked doubtfully, hoping Tobias would change his mind. "Don't seem to me it make no difference we get to Punta Rassa one day or another, just so we get there."

"It's worth a try. If we can't make it, we'll turn around, come back and head east again."

"You the boss," Skillit said resignedly, getting up and mounting his horse.

They cut six cows from the herd and entered the woods, and when they reached the point where water met solid ground, the cows hesitated and tried to turn back. Nip and Tuck bit at their rear legs, forcing them forward, and soon they were wading through a foot of water.

"So far it's not too deep for the wagon," Tobias said. "If it don't get no worse than this we can make it easy."

Ishmael started to buck, and the splashing water caused herons to flap out of a cypress tree and squawk loudly. Tobias said, "Calm him down, Zech, afore he scares the cows and makes them run."

Zech steadied the horse, and they moved forward again, churning up black mud as they rippled the calm surface. Skillit said, "I don't like this, Mistuh Tobias. Something don't seem right about this place."

"We'll go a bit further. If it gets deeper, we'll turn back."

The dogs were now having to jump to stay above the water level, and they were useless in herding the cows. Suddenly the lead cow plunged downward, went under and came up bellowing; then it seemed that dynamite was being set off beneath the surface. Violence came from everywhere, all at once without warning, tails slashing and jaws popping. One cow was snatched under instantly; then it came up fighting to break free, its head firmly locked in an alligator's mouth. It bellowed and went under again as blood bubbled to the surface and spread out in a widening circle.

"'Gators!" Tobias shouted, clinging to the saddle as his horse reared up. "Turn back! Turn back!"

Nip was already swimming toward high ground, but Tuck went straight ahead, heading for the panic-stricken cows. Zech kicked Ishmael in the flanks and plunged after the dog, the water now almost over the saddle.

Tobias watched, frozen with fear; then he managed to shout frantically, "No, Zech! No!"

The small horse swam right into the death orgy, staining its hide with blood; then Zech grabbed the dog and pulled it onto the saddle and turned back. Water exploded all around him as Ishmael churned desperately, gradually moving away.

Skillit had already snatched Nip up and was galloping through the water. Tobias continued to watch, unable to move, as the black surface turned solid red; and it was only after Zech rushed by him that he wheeled his horse and followed.

When they reached the edge of the woods, they stopped and put the dogs down. Tobias said weakly, "You could 'a got killed back there, Zech. You shouldn't ought to have done it. A dog ain't worth the chance you took."

"I wasn't going to let no 'gator eat Tuck, Pappa. I knew Ishmael could do it. I could feel it."

"Lord, what I could have caused," Tobias sighed, putting his hand on Zech's shoulder.

"It wasn't your fault," Skillit said quickly, concerned by the stricken look on Tobias' face. "Wasn't no way to know that place is a 'gator den."

"I knew. I knew before we went in there. He warned me, and I didn't pay heed. He told me there is only death in there, and I went anyway."

"You ain't making sense, Mistuh Tobias," Skillit said. "Who warned you?"

"Back there. In the swamp. He said not to enter, to go around."

"You want to go to the wagon and take a rest? Maybe we ought to stop here for a day or two."

"No! Get the herd started. We'll go east as far as we have to and go around the rest of this swamp. I should 'a listened."

"We'll move on then," Skillit said, still looking at Tobias strangely. "But don't blame yo'self for anything. At least we know not to come this way again. It was worth something. Best we lose a few cows than a whole herd."

"Next time we'll know," Tobias agreed. Then he watched the two dogs as they streaked through the grass toward the herd, Zech and Ishmael close behind them.

When they rounded the tip of the swamp and turned westward again, they came into open prairie land. The herd moved lazily, grazing in one spot until it was cleaned, then drifting on.

Tobias gradually dismissed the Timucuan from his mind, and all of the men seemed to regain confidence after the experience of being boxed into the dead-end swamp. Tobias also made mental notes of the route they should take the next time.

One morning they approached a lake with a dense hardwood hammock on the east side. Tobias was riding right flank, and he saw the rider come from the woods and head in his direction. He left the herd and met him halfway.

This man said directly, "I got a few cows to sell. Are you interested?" He was an older man, around sixty, with solid white hair and a beard to match.

Tobias responded, "Well, yes and no. I don't have money to pay cash. I picked up sixty-five head from a man named Lowry back at the Kissimmee for three dollars a head and promised to pay him on my way back. I could do the same for you. How many you got?"

"A hundred and ten. And I ain't got no help to move them. What's your name?"

"Tobias MacIvey."

"Windell Lykes."

"Pleased to meet you."

Both men looked at each other as if sizing each other up, and then Lykes said, "How do I know you'll come back and pay me?"

"Same way as Lowry. You got my word, and I've never broken it to no man. So far we've lost near on forty cows and Lowry will get paid for every one of his. What we lose is mine. And like I told Lowry, next trip through I'll take whatever you got and pay cash."

The man scratched his head for a moment, pondering a decision. "You coming straight back here after the drive?"

"Straight back. I live over on the east bank of the Kissimmee."

"Well, O.K., it's a deal. Where you taking the herd? Tampa?"

"Nope. Punta Rassa. I've been told the price is better there."

"You're too far north for Punta Rassa. You need to cut south."

"You been there?"

"Several times, but not driving a herd. Is this your first trip there?"

"For a fact, and we done got lost on several occasions. Maybe you could give us directions."

"Well, best thing you can do is go due south till you hit the Caloosahatchie. It's the first river you'll come to. It goes into Punta Rassa, but you'll have to cross the river to get there. It's on the south bank, right at the Gulf. There's a ferry about four miles north of there that can take your wagon across, but you'll have to swim the cows."

"Is there 'gators in the river?"

"Mister, there ain't no water in Florida without 'gators, less you got a tub of it in your house. And one's liable to get in there too if you leave the door open. But I ain't heard of nobody losing cows to 'gators on the Caloosahatchie. It's pretty deep water, and 'gators lay up mostly in shallows."

"Just thought I'd ask."

Tobias unfurled his whip and cracked it two times; then he saw Skillit and Zech ride away from the wagon and come toward him. He said, "They'll go with you and bring in your cows."

"Don't you want to count them first and sign a paper?"

"If you say you've got a hundred and ten, that's good enough for me. You get paid for a hundred and ten. And I don't need a paper if you don't."

"Fair enough. I hope we get to do business again."

Tobias turned his horse; then he looked back and said, "Thanks rightly for the directions. I was beginning to believe there ain't no such place as Punta Rassa. I'll see you again soon, and we'll take good care of your cows."

Four days later they reached the Caloosahatchie and then followed its bank until they found the ferry. It was late afternoon when the last cow staggered from the river, but they made the crossing without incident.

Tobias could not believe they were within four miles of their destination. Although this close, Punta Rassa still seemed to him to be as distant as China, and just as unreachable.

He also had a strong feeling that something bad would happen yet, a storm, a flood, wolves, alligators, something. Or Thompson's information about the Cuban market would be in error, and there would be no buyers on hand who wanted the cattle. The long path to this point had been too filled with disappointment, disaster and grief for him to feel premature joy.

They moved the herd a mile down the river and then circled them for the night. Tobias would ride on alone the next morning and seek a buyer, then return and share the news with everyone, good or bad.

At supper that night everyone seemed strangely quiet, as if they too did not yet believe. Tobias had surmised that Frog and Bonzo would try to get advance pay and ride off to the village, leaving the rest of them alone to protect the herd; but they made no mention of this. Even Zech showed no boyish enthusiasm of reaching trail's end, and he spent an hour after dark quietly rubbing Ishmael's neck and talking to him.

Tobias noticed all of this, thinking that perhaps they were all tired beyond realization and it was just now hitting them, like hunters who pursue the prey through the woods relentlessly for

an entire day, and after the kill is finally made, fall down exhausted. Whatever the reason, it was the quietest night the camp spent.

They still posted the same guard as they had in the wilderness,
and an hour before midnight Tobias was still awake, awaiting his
turn. He sat on the wagon seat as Emma aroused from a fitful
sleep and came to him. She sensed at supper he was restless, anx-
ious for the night to pass and the dawn to come, that he would not
lie down and rest either before his watch or when it ended.

She sat beside him silently, watching a full moon come over
cypress trees lining the banks of the river. Spanish moss swayed
from limbs like blobs of cotton and absorbed the moonbeams,
changing the dull gray beards to glowing yellow. The cattle were
visible in the distance, quiet now, standing deathly still, resembling
not flesh and blood creatures hounded by predators but miniature
statues on a kitchen shelf. The herd was all together now for the
last time, a mass rather than individual fragments, and she
thought of all those days and weeks and months Tobias and Zech
and Skillit struggled to assemble what stood on this small plot of
ground and would soon be no more. They had survived only to
come to an end, and the cycle would begin anew when they
returned to the homestead.

She finally said, "Don't be too disappointed if this doesn't turn
out right, Tobias. It's not the end of everything."

For a moment he made no answer, and then he said, "I was
going to say the same thing to you, and ask you not to be disappointed. You beat me to it."

"I would be disappointed only for you and Zech. You've
worked too hard to fail now. I know what it means to you."

"I'm not sure I know myself what it means," he said, putting his
hand on hers. "All those times me and Zech chased some scrawny
cow through the woods and didn't catch it, it wasn't the money. I
want the money now for you and Zech. For me, I guess I just been
trying to prove something to myself. All my life when I tried to do
something worth anything I never made it, not here or back in
Georgia. It was the same with my daddy, and he finally gave up

and quit trying. When he did, it killed my mamma, just as sure as those 'gators killed the cows back in the swamp. And it was just as awful to see. Then it got Daddy too. We almost made it in the scrub, me and you and Zech; then somebody comes along and burns it all for no reason. Ever time I try, it seems somebody burns it or floods it or kills it. Maybe this time the Lord won't throw a roadblock in front of me. But if He does, I'll just stumble over it and try again. I'm not ready to give up yet, and I ain't going to quit no matter what happens tomorrow morning."

She leaned over and put her head on his shoulder. "I've known that all along, Tobias. And whatever happens, we'll work it out together. That's the way I want it to be."

"Emma . . ." he said hesitantly, unsure of his words; then he started again, "Emma, . . . I'm not always a gentle man, and I know it. I guess it's because of the things I seen growing up. I want to be, but I don't know how. You could have done better than me, a fine woman like you, and I always knowed that too. I ain't much to look at, but someday I'm going to make you proud, and Zech too. I'm not going to quit trying till I do."

She reached up and kissed him. "You're the most gentle man I've ever known. I'm proud now, and Zech is too."

Tobias passed several large holding pens and then turned down a rutted road leading to the waterfront. There were two stores, one containing a café and a post office, the other general merchandise. Between them was a saloon, and behind this a livery stable, feed store, and blacksmith shop were housed together in a barnlike structure. Across from one store a two-story clapboard house offered rooms for rent. The whole area reeked of cow manure, and Tobias wondered how the people who lived and worked here could stand the constant odor.

At the end of the street a dock ran one hundred feet out into the bay, and adjacent to the dock there was a cattle chute. A small shack on pilings was at the left of the dock, and at the end, a sidewheel steamer belched smoke from its two stacks. Two more steamers lay at anchor further out in the bay.

The village had a desolate look, almost forbidding, peppered with fierce-looking Spanish bayonet and clumps of salt-burned palmetto. Sea grapes covered large sand dunes to the right and left of the dock. Tobias had pictured it differently, the name Punta Rassa conjuring visions of something exotic, things he had never seen before. But except for the cattle dock and the more numerous buildings, it was no different from Kissimmee. He was more than mildly disappointed.

Several men were sitting on the porch of one store, and Tobias rode up to them and dismounted. Two one-gallon jugs of Cuban rum were on the floor in front of them. He said, "I'm looking for a cattle buyer. You know where I can find one?"

"Down yonder," one of the men said, pointing. "The shack on the dock. You want to see Cap'n Hendry."

Tobias tied the horse to a hitching post and walked to the dock. He knocked on the closed door and a voice came to him, "It ain't locked. Come on in."

There were three men inside, two sitting on tall stools at shelves containing ledgers, the other in a rocking chair with his feet propped on a desk. The man in the rocker was dressed in black leather boots, brown canvas pants and a blue chambray shirt. He wore a large straw hat with turkey feathers on one side.

Tobias said, "Name's Tobias MacIvey. I was told I could find a cattle buyer here."

"You come to the right place," the man said, getting up from the rocker. He was a tall, slim man of about fifty. "I'm Sam Hendry. Where's your herd?"

"Three miles up the river."

"How many you got?"

"Can't say for sure. We lost some on the drive, and ate a couple. I figure it to be around eight hundred and fifty, maybe a few more than that."

"They in good shape?"

"Real good. We moved slow coming here and let 'em eat all they wanted. They ought to go over five hundred pounds each."

"That's the kind we need," Hendry said, showing interest. "Some men run them yellowhammers down here like they was rabbits instead of cows, and time they get here they're not much more than skin and bones. Then we have to fatten them ourselves. If yours are in good shape like you say, we'll pay sixteen dollars a head. If not, twelve is tops."

Tobias felt a faintness flush through him, causing his throat to turn dry. Even after hearing it, he still could not believe that the cows were actually worth cash money. To him they were still just stubborn critters they had popped out of swamps and chased across prairies. He finally managed to croak, "Sounds fair to me. When you want to see them?"

"Drive the herd on down here and put them in one of the holding pens. We'll take a look and make a head count. We pay in

Spanish gold doubloons worth fifteen dollars each, five hundred and twenty-five dollars to a sack. You better go to the store and buy a trunk to carry it in, unless you've got a big wooden box with you."

"Yes sir, Mister Hendry, I'll do that. And I'll go back right now and move the herd."

"Captain Hendry," the man corrected. "If I'm not here when you get done with it, I'll be in my office in back of the general store."

Tobias had an overwhelming urge to run, but he walked casually up the street to his horse. He moved slowly until out of sight of the men. Then he let out a whoop that could be heard back at the dock and put the old horse in a gallop.

When he reached the wagon he was breathless. He jumped from the panting horse and said in gasps, "We done it! We done it! Sixteen dollars a head! Spanish gold!"

"Calm yourself down a bit," Emma replied, "and then tell us what happened."

"Captain Hendry. He's the buyer. He said if they're in good shape, he'll pay sixteen dollars each. If not, twelve is tops. You know how much money that is, Emma?"

"Not really. I'm not sure I can count that high."

"It's a bunch. I'm going to buy a steamer trunk down at the store just to haul it back to the hammock. But right now we got to move the herd. He said bring them to a holding pen so he can look and make a head count. Ride on out there, Skillit, and tell everybody to start moving the cows. I'll come on later with Emma. I'm going to tie the dogs in some bushes and leave 'em a pan of water. They follow us into town, somebody is liable to take them for wolves and shoot them."

Skillit leaped on his horse and said, "We'll have them cows down there in no time at all, Mistuh Tobias."

"No!" Tobias exclaimed. "Walk 'em slow. Real slow. They need to keep ever pound they got. Just take it easy."

*T*obias sat in a chair in front of the desk, watching Hendry make figures with a pencil. He scratched for a moment more; then he looked up and said, "Well, MacIvey, you've got eight hundred and sixty-five head, all in good shape, so the price is sixteen. That comes to thirteen thousand, eight hundred and forty dollars. You want to count all of the money?"

"No sir, Captain Hendry, that ain't necessary," Tobias replied, overwhelmed by the figures. "I trust you to do the right thing. But if you got one of them gold coins on you right now, I'd sure like to keep it separate. It's the first I ever earned."

Hendry took a doubloon from his pocket and handed it to Tobias. "You want the rest of the money now?"

"I'll buy a trunk first and then come back with the wagon. But I'd like to have eight more coins now. We all need boots, and I want to treat everbody to a meal in the café. My boy's never been in a café."

"You've got them."

While Hendry counted out the coins Tobias said, "Captain Hendry, I ain't never had this much money in all my life, and never thought I would. Will somebody here try to take it from me?"

"I figured that would cross your mind, especially since this is your first time in with a herd. Won't nobody here pay any more attention to that gold than they would biscuits. I've seen men come in with six thousand head, then dump all those sacks of doubloons on the store porch and go in the saloon, just leaving it set there. If somebody took it, they couldn't put it on a horse. If they used a wagon, you could catch them in less than a mile. You've got nothing to worry about here in Punta Rassa. Of course I wouldn't go back out in the wilderness and flaunt it around. Somebody out there would take the challenge for sure."

Tobias then accepted the coins. "I thank you for the advice.

We'll be back in about an hour for the rest of the money."

He went outside and up the street to where the horses and the wagon were tied in front of the café. Zech was prancing Ishmael, and the others were sitting on the edge of the porch. Tobias said, "It'll be a while before we pick up the money. Let's go in the café and get something to eat."

It was an hour before noon and there were no other customers in the building. They all took chairs at a table covered with a red checkered oil cloth. The waiter, a short, fat man wearing a dirty apron, came to them and said, "What'll it be, folks?"

Tobias said, "What you got?"

"Well, today we're serving country-fried steak, pork chops, fried snapper, and fried chicken. Take your choice."

"What else goes with it?"

"Rice and gravy, black-eyed peas, turnips, cornbread, and biscuits."

"Sounds good," Tobias said. "We'll take six fried chicken dinners, but cook us a whole chicken each. And all the rest of that stuff plus a gallon of hot coffee. You got eggs too?"

"Yeah, we got eggs," the waiter said, eyeing Tobias curiously.

"Fry us three dozen on a side platter. Zech's never eaten a egg, or chicken either. What kind of pie you got?"

"Apple."

"We'll take six."

The waiter looked at the scratch pad. "Now let me get this straight. Six fried chicken dinners, a whole chicken each. Three dozen eggs, six apple pies and a gallon of coffee. You sure that's all you want?"

"That ought to do for a start. If it don't, we'll let you know."

The waiter then pointed to Skillit. "When the food's done, he'll have to eat out back. We don't serve blacks in the dining room."

"What'd you say?" Tobias asked quickly.

"There's a table on the stoop outside the kitchen. He can eat there. We don't serve blacks in here."

"Excuse me a minute," Tobias said, getting up. "I left something in my saddlebag. I'll be right back."

Emma said, "Tobias, don't you . . ."

"I said I'd be right back!" he snapped.

Frog also got up. "I need to check my saddlebag too. I'll go with Mister MacIvey."

They both returned carrying military pistols. Tobias sat down and placed his pistol on the table. Skillit said to him, "Mistuh Tobias, this ain't worth trouble. I'd as soon go out to the stoop. It don't make no difference to me. The chicken will taste just as good out there as in here."

"Sit still," Tobias said. "Ain't no member of the MacIvey clan going to eat on a back porch, not here or anywhere. If one of us gets kicked out, we all go. And that's a fact."

The waiter came back from the kitchen and announced, "Mister Lassiter is the cook and the owner. He says he ain't going to . . ."

Tobias and Frog cocked the pistols, and then Tobias said, "You go and tell mister whoever-he-is that he's about to serve his first black in here. If he don't, we'll all leave. And if we do, you're going to have some real bad trouble with the roof next time it rains."

"Very well," he said distastefully, eyeing the pistols. In a moment he returned. "Mister Lassiter says he can bend the rule this time, but he don't understand why anyone would make such a fuss over a black man. He says don't shoot no holes in the roof, and he hopes you enjoy the chicken."

"We will," Tobias said, "if it ever gets here."

Frog uncocked the pistol. "He just learned that some things you do for the first time ain't nearly so bad as you thought it'd be. Ain't that right, Mister MacIvey?"

Tobias smiled. "If you say so, Frog. And I tell you what I'm gonna do. After I pay you and Bonzo the wages I promised, I'm gonna give each one of you a hundred dollar bonus. How would that suit you?"

"Just fine," Frog answered, surprised and pleased. "That much money will probably burn a hole in my pockets, but it's real fine. We thank you, don't we, Bonzo." He kicked Bonzo under the table.

"That's real fine," Bonzo echoed quickly. "We didn't expect that much. We're obliged to you."

"You said that real good, Bonzo," Frog said. "I'm right proud of you."

Just then the waiter started bringing steaming platters and bowls to the table. Zech helped himself to a chicken breast and two fried eggs. He gulped them down and said, "That's real good, Pappa, a heap better than coon. How come we don't get us some chickens? I'd take care of them."

"We will someday. But it might be hard to keep them in the hammock. Foxes and panthers eat chickens, and wolves do too. It's like inviting them to supper. And coons steal eggs. We'd have to watch over them real careful."

"Nip and Tuck would help me do that. It's real good, Pappa. The best I've ever et."

"Wait till you get to the apple pie," Emma said, smiling. "You'll like that too. I know how to make pies but it's hard to do in a frying pan. If we ever get another Dutch oven or a cook stove I'll bake you a pie every day. And cookies too."

Frog and Bonzo heard none of it. Their plates were piled with bones, and the side dishes were empty. Tobias said, "I'll order more rice and peas and turnips and another pone of cornbread. Maybe we'll need more chicken too afore we're done."

Skillit smacked his lips. "Mistuh Tobias, this worth all them floods and wolves and 'gators too. You keep the vittles comin', we might be here for a week."

"We can't stay that long," Tobias said, "'cause I got to go to the store and buy a trunk. I told Captain Hendry we'd be back for the money in a hour or so. But we might eat ever chicken in Punta Rassa before we head back to the hammock." He then took the gold doubloon from his pocket and handed it to Zech. "This's the first coin Captain Hendry gave me. I want you to have it, Zech, and keep it. If you don't ever spend it, you'll never be flat-out broke like I always been."

Zech turned the coin over in his hand, looking at the engravings. "It's real purty, Pappa. But if you don't mind, I'd rather spend it and buy some apples for Ishmael. I promised him."

"I'll buy the apples. You keep the coin. I don't want you to spend it, now or ever."

Zech put the doubloon in his pocket. "I'll keep it, Pappa. I promise. When we get back to the hammock I'll put it away. Can I have some more chicken now, and some more biscuits and gravy too?"

"Eat all you want," Emma said, piling his plate. "Maybe it will put meat on those bones. You're beginning to look just like your daddy."

"Speaking of bones," Tobias said, "save all them chicken bones for Nip and Tuck. And I'll have the waiter sack up a whole fried chicken for each of them. They've earned it too, much as anyone. We'll feed 'em good this afternoon."

The waiter came from the kitchen with another platter. "Mister Lassiter sent you some snapper. He cooks real good fish, and he thought you might like some. Way you folks eats, he wants all of you to come back ever time you brings in a herd." He put the platter down, motioned at Skillit and said sheepishly, "Mister Lassiter says him too."

"We'll just do that," Tobias said. "You got a good café. Tell Mister Lassiter this is right neighborly of him, right neighborly."

*T*he four men placed the steamer trunk in the wagon. Tobias opened one sack and counted out coins to Frog and Bonzo. Skillit watched and said nothing as no money was offered to him.

Frog put the doubloons in his pocket and shook his pants leg to make them jingle. "Just wanted to make sure I ain't dreaming," he said. "Me and Bonzo's got a little chore to do, Mister MacIvey. Where you want us to meet after you get done in the store?"

"Right here, I guess. Then we'll go back out of town and make camp. We all got some talking to do."

Emma, Zech and Skillit followed Tobias into the building. A clerk came to them immediately and said, "Yes, sir, what can I do for you today?"

Tobias said, "Well, we want a bunch of things. Boots for everyone, and dresses for my wife, Emma. That'll do for a start."

"I'm sorry, sir. We don't carry ladies' apparel. There's just no call for it here. For that you'll have to go up to Fort Myers. But we do have boots."

"Aw shucks!" Tobias said, disappointed. "You ought to get in some stuff for women. If you ain't got dresses, I guess you best see to Skillit first. He needs the most."

"Which one is Skillit?"

"Him," Tobias said, pointing. "This here's my boy, Zech."

The clerk studied Skillit carefully, and then he said, "He's really a whopper. What you got in mind?"

"Everything. Boots, socks, britches, shirt, underwear, the whole works. And a felt hat too."

Skillit beamed. "You mean I get all that, Mistuh Tobias? I was only expectin' britches."

"That and anything else you want."

The clerk said, "As I said, he's awful big. I hope we have his size in everything. I'll do my best. Why don't you folks just look around while I take care of him."

Skillit followed the clerk as Tobias said to Emma, "I'm sorry. Real sorry. I wanted to get you some dresses."

"Doesn't matter," Emma said, trying to ease his disappointment. "Maybe they've got a pair of boy's boots that will fit me. That would do me fine on trail drives. And I don't need new dresses in the hammock."

"Maybe they've got something else you want. Look around and see."

The three of them wandered around the aisles until Skillit and the clerk returned from the back of the store. Skillit was dressed in brown leather boots, blue denim pants, blue chambray shirt, and a wide-brimmed black hat. The pants came four inches up the boots.

Emma said, "My, my, Skillit, you sure look nice."

Skillit grinned broadly. "Don't hardly know myself in all this. It's the first sto-bought stuff I ever owned. And it don't matter none about the britches being short. I can tuck 'em in the boots and never know the difference." Then he looked to Tobias. "Can I have this too? It's only ten cents." In his hand he held a red bandanna.

"Sure you can. Put it on and let's see how it looks."

Skillit put the bandanna around his neck and tied it in front. "Always did want one of these things," he said. "Foreman on the plantation at Tallahassee wore one."

"It looks real nice with the blue," Emma said.

"Now let's get the other boots," Tobias said. "Skillit's done put us all to shame."

Skillit grinned again; then he went over to a mirror hanging on one wall.

"Don't forget the apples, Pappa," Zech said anxiously.

"Don't you worry about that. I won't forget. We'll get a whole sackful before we leave. And you need britches too, and a hat if he's got one your size."

"I'd like a hat too," Emma said. "It might not look right on a woman but it would sure keep the sun off me out on the prairie."

After everyone had been outfitted Tobias motioned for the clerk to follow him to the back of the store. He whispered, "You by any chance got a cook stove?"

"Just so happens I have," the clerk answered, whispering also but not knowing why. "Follow me."

They went into a storeroom. The clerk said, "We've had this thing for over a year and nobody's bought it. It's a mite fancy for folks here. Came down by ship from New Orleans. You want it, you can have it for cost plus the shipping charge."

Sitting in one corner was a dust-covered cast-iron stove. The left bottom section was an oven and the right side was the firebox. The flat surface on top contained four round cooking plates. Two warmer ovens formed a top over the entire stove, and the door of each oven was decorated with golden angels playing harps. All four legs were shaped like clusters of grapes and were also painted gold. A unicorn was engraved across the main oven door and was charging a cringing devil on the firebox door. Both were gold painted and outlined in blue.

Tobias gulped, not believing he had finally found such an item. He said, "It's the purtiest thing I ever seen. How much is it?"

"I can let you have it for thirty-six dollars plus the twelve-dollar shipping cost."

"Sold!" Tobias said quickly. "I'll pay you for it now, but I don't want to pick it up till in the morning. Can you have somebody clean the dust off it?"

"Surely," the clerk said, breathing a sign of relief. "You've made a wise decision, Mister MacIvey. This should make your missus real proud. It's a mighty fine stove."

"When you total up the bill, don't say nothing about it in front of Emma. I want it to be a surprise. And when we get back up there, sack up a dozen apples for Zech."

"Be glad to. And they're on the house. You've been a good customer and we hope you'll come back every time you're in Punta Rassa."

"Thanks. I appreciate it. That's right nice of you."

Emma selected two baking pans and a long kitchen knife, and when everything was paid for they all went back out to the wagon. Everyone, including Emma and Zech, wore a new wide-brimmed black felt hat.

Zech took an apple from the sack and put it in front of Ishmael's nose. The horse sniffed, and then he grabbed the apple with his teeth and chomped vigorously. After swallowing, he jerked his head up and down, whinnying loudly.

Zech said, "Good, ain't it." Then he put another apple into Ishmael's mouth.

The horse ate six. Zech put the rest in the wagon and leaped onto the saddle. He streaked down to the dock at full gallop, turned abruptly, then raced back to the store and made the horse rear up, kicking its front legs high into the air, as if fighting.

Captain Hendry was standing on the store porch, watching. He came to Tobias and said, "That your boy?"

"Sure is. His name's Zechariah, but we call him Zech."

"How old is he?"

"Going on eleven."

Hendry leaned against the wagon. "He rides that horse like a tick on a hound's back. He must have been born in a saddle."

"He does right well," Tobias said, pleased by the compliment.

"Where'd you get that little horse? He's right swift."

"Indians gave him to us. His name's Ishmael."

"Ishmael? That's a queer name for a horse. You want to race him?"

"Do what?" Tobias said, surprised.

"Race him. That's my one weakness, a good horse race. I've got a Tennessee bay I'd like to put against him. Just to make it interesting, I'll bet the deed to a hundred and fifty acres just up the river. You can put up seven of those doubloons I paid you. That's good odds, about the same as seven cows against a hundred and fifty acres of land. What say? Is it a bet?"

Tobias was still too surprised by the challenge to answer. He scratched his head, trying to think clearly, and then he finally said, "Well, I don't know, Captain Hendry. I've never done nothing like that. Let's see what your horse looks like."

Hendry turned to a man sitting on the porch and said, "Go to the stable and tell Willie to saddle Thunder and bring him out here."

"Yes sir, Cap'n Hendry. Right away."

Tobias said, "While he's getting the horse I'll speak to my family. I still ain't sure this is the right thing to do."

"Don't do it if you don't want to," Hendry replied. "I never push a man into anything. It's up to you."

Tobias went back to the wagon and said hesitantly, "I don't exactly know how to explain this, but Captain Hendry wants to race a horse against Ishmael. The bet is seven doubloons against a hundred and fifty acres of land just up the river. I said I'd talk it over before I give an answer."

"Let's do it, Pappa!" Zech said eagerly. "Can't no horse outrun Ishmael."

"Maybe yes, and maybe no," Tobias said. "You ain't never been in a horse race. It's a heap different from running down cows."

"What kind of horse he got?" Skillit asked.

"A Tennessee bay, name of Thunder. He's having it brought out here now."

"How long is the race?" Skillit then asked.

"He ain't made no mention of that yet."

Just then a man came around the side of the store, leading a red stallion twice the size of Ishmael. Skillit said, "Lawd-a-mercy, Mistuh Tobias, look at that! You could set a cow on top of him."

Tobias stared, and then he said, "Ain't no way! We can't race Ishmael against a elephant like that. He wouldn't have a chance."

"Yes he would, Pappa!" Zech insisted. "Size don't mean nothing. Ishmael ain't afraid of him. I can feel it."

Skillit said in a low voice, not wanting anyone standing nearby to hear, "Mistuh Tobias, I seen men up in Tallahassee race horses just like that one. They go like the wind for a mile, then they tucker out. Zech can ride Ishmael flat out for five miles on the prairie. I seen it. When he turn three miles, Ishmael just gettin' warmed up. Tell Cap'n Hendry it's a three-mile race or nothin'. Zech make that big hoss look like a fool."

"You really think so?"

"I done seen what that little hoss can do. He got more heart than any critter I ever knowed."

Emma was listening but remained silent. Tobias turned to her and said, "What you think, Emma? It's gambling, and maybe it's wrong. But it's no more than seven cows against the land, and the 'gators ate more of them than that on the way here. And I know Zech would enjoy the race."

"We been gambling just to get here," Emma replied. "Go on and do it if you want to. I don't think the Lord will frown on us for a horse race. Not if we look on it as fun for Zech and don't make a habit of it."

"Thanks, Mamma!" Zech smiled. "I knew you'd let me do it!"

"All right, all right!" Tobias exclaimed, wanting Zech to calm himself. "We'll do it, but just this once. And don't fret none if you take a whuppin' from that bay."

Hendry called over to him, "What about it, MacIvey? Is it a race or not?"

Tobias went over to the porch and said, "How far you want to race, Captain Hendry?"

"Well, it's usually a mile, but I don't care. Whatever you say is fine with me."

"Three miles," Tobias said.

"Three miles it is," Hendry agreed. "It's about a mile and a half to the last holding pen outside town. The race will be to there and back."

One of the nearest spectators shouted, "Hoss race! Hoss race!" As soon as he said it, men poured from the saloon and seemingly out of trees, forming a chattering crowd in front of the store.

One man waved his arms and shouted, "I'll take Thunder and give odds three to one! Who wants to bet on the little hoss?" There were no takers. "All right then, five to one!"

Frog and Bonzo came from the saloon and toward the store. Frog said to a man at the edge of the crowd, "What's happening? How come all the commotion?"

"Ole Cap'n Hendry's done got hisself another sucker. It's a race between his bay and that marshtackie. Odds is five to one."

"You mean Ishmael?" Frog questioned.

"Don't know nothing about no Ishmael. It's the black hoss that boy is riding. You reckon them folks is really dumb enough to race that little runt against Thunder?"

"Maybe so. How long is the race?"

"Three miles."

"Did you say three miles?" Frog asked, his mind clicking.

"Three miles is what I said. Ole Thunder'll be back here before that runt gets started."

"Who's taking bets?"

"Man right over there. With the red shirt and straw hat."

Frog waved his hand and shouted, "I got two hundred dollars on the black! Five to one and you got a bet!" He said to Bonzo, "Gimme that bonus money quick. We done got us a sucker bet. Ishmael'll put dust in that big hoss's mouth afore they turn the two-mile mark."

Several men snickered as Frog put the doubloons into a wooden betting box.

The man who brought the bay from the stable sprang onto the saddle; then he and Zech lined the horses up in the middle of the street. Hendry shouted, "When I fire my pistol, let 'em go!"

Ishmael danced nervously as they waited, and when the boom came, the bay lunged forward and pulled away rapidly. Before they reached the end of the street he was forty yards ahead.

Zech watched the big horse move away. He patted Ishmael's neck and said, "Not now, Ishmael. Let him go. Just trail him, like we do a cow. You can bite his legs later."

When they reached the holding pen marking the halfway point, the bay turned in a tight circle, never breaking stride. Zech wheeled Ishmael quickly, cutting the distance between them to thirty yards. Then the bay increased the gap back to forty.

Zech waited for several moments more, and then he said, "Now, Ishmael! Bite him now!"

Ishmael sprang forward as if until this point he had not been running at all. He stretched his neck out like a heron in flight, and his hooves barely touched the ground as he streaked across the rutted sand. In five seconds he was abreast of the bay and moving ahead; and when they reached the finish line, he was fifty yards in front of Thunder.

All but the man who had taken the bets cheered wildly, and even he showed respect for the little horse and its boy rider.

Hendry came to Tobias immediately and handed him a paper. "It's all yours," he said. "I'll have one of my men ride out in the morning and show you the land lines."

Tobias accepted the deed reluctantly. "I hate to take your land over a horse race, Captain Hendry. It don't seem right."

"Nonsense!" Hendry replied. "You won fair and square, and it's yours now. And besides that, it's nothing to me. I won that deed myself in a poker game."

"Well, I don't exactly know what we'll do with land in Punta Rassa. I guess I'll give it to Zech. He's the one who won it, not me."

Zech stopped Ishmael just short of the dock, then trotted him back to the wagon. "I told you he could do it, Pappa!" he said excitedly. "He ain't even got his wind up. Ishmael could run from here to the hammock and back if he wanted to."

"Not that far, Zech, but he sure did a job on that three-mile stretch."

Hendry ran his hand across Ishmael's neck; then he said to Zech, "That's some horse, son. He's not even sweating. You want to sell him? I'll give you three hundred dollars for him."

"No sir!" Zech said quickly. "Ishmael is my friend. I'd never sell my friend for no kind of money."

"I figured you'd say that, and I don't blame you. I just thought I'd make an offer. He's the first horse to dust Thunder like that. Tell you what I want you to do. Go in the store and get a whole bushel of apples for you and him, and tell the clerk to put it on my bill. He'll do it, 'cause I own the store. You and that little horse earned it."

Zech jumped from the saddle and said, "Thanks, Captain Hendry! Thanks a lot! Ishmael never ate a apple before we come here, and me either. We both like it, and Ishmael thanks you too!"

"Some boy you got there," Hendry said, watching Zech run into the store. "He'll make a mark someday."

"Thank you kindly," Tobias and Emma both said at the same time. Then they laughed. "I've never seen such a good loser as you," Tobias then said.

Hendry laughed too. "Oh well, it's all in fun. Keeps the blood flowing, and there's not much else to do in Punta Rassa. It's been a real pleasure knowing you folks."

"Same here," Tobias said.

Frog came to the wagon carrying the box of money. He said, "Just got four years' pay for nothing. Me and Bonzo'll ride out and find you a little later this afternoon. We need to spend some of these coins and find out how it feels to pay cash for a change."

"We'll be along the river where we first camped," Tobias said. "We got to get on out there now and feed the dogs. You and Bonzo don't be too late. We still got some talking to do."

After they reached the campsite and built a fire, Emma started supper while Zech fed the dogs. Tobias was alone at the wagon with Skillit. He said to him, "I wanted to wait till we got back out here to tell you this. Those sacks of gold in the trunk are worth five hundred and twenty-five dollars each. One sack is yours."

"Say whut?" Skillit asked, his eyes suddenly bulging.

"One sack is yours. You've earned it."

"Aw Mistuh Tobias, you don't need to do that, " Skillit said, still shocked. "You and yo' folks needs that money more than I do. These clothes you bought me is enough. If I could have just two or three coins for my own I'd be satisfied. You done enough for me already."

"Nope. Without you, me and Zech could never have rounded

up all them cows. And from now on, ever time we sell a herd your share will be a dollar for each cow."

"Oh goodness, Mistuh Tobias, I don't know what to say. I ain't never had even a dollar of my own, much less five hundred. What I gone do with all that money?"

"Save it and let it build up. You'll find a use for it someday."

"Can I open a sack and just look?" Skillit asked. "Then I'll put it back in the trunk with the rest."

"Help yourself."

Skillit climbed into the wagon, opened the trunk and removed one of the canvas bags. He untied the top and ran his hands as far as he could push them into the coins. Then he scooped out a handful and let them drop back into the sack one by one, mesmerized by the clinking sound as metal bounced against metal. He said, "It sho' is purty. I never thought all them ole yellowhammers we chased and marked would turn into this."

"Me either," Tobias responded, amused by the look on Skillit's face. "And I'm not sure I believe it yet. But that ain't nails in them sacks. It's gold."

"Can I put two or three in my pocket, just to hear 'em jingle?"

"Take all you want. It's yours. Just cut a nick in the sack so you'll know which one it is."

Skillit took a knife from his pocket and cut the sack, then he put three coins in his pocket and put the sack back in the trunk. He climbed out of the wagon and said, "I never thought somethin' like this would ever happen to me. I's worked all my life like a mule and never got a penny fo' it, and I gave up hopin' a long time ago. When you found me hid in them bushes I hadn't had nothin' to et for a week but roots and berries. Now I got a belly full of fried chicken, a new pair of britches and boots, and a sack full of gold. Mistuh Tobias, you's the best white folks they's ever been!"

"You've earned ever bit of it," Tobias said. "But we got to go back and try it again. We don't want to quit on this."

Frog and Bonzo came riding into the camp, each with a gallon jug sloshing in the saddlebag. They dismounted, then Frog pulled out the jug and said, "Cuban rum. Either one of you want a snort?"

"I don't drink that rotgut," Tobias said. "I seen my daddy die of that stuff time he was thirty years old, and I aim to live longer than he did.

"What I want to talk to you about is what you aim to do now," Tobias continued. "If you want to stay on with us you're welcome to do so."

"Well, I don't know, Mister MacIvey," Frog said hesitantly. "Me and Bonzo is kind of drifters, and I have to stay with him. He ain't got much to say, and nothing much to think with, so I have to look out for him. But you and Missus Emma has been real good to us, and I'd like to know what you got in mind."

"If you want to join us permanent, I'll raise the pay to a dollar a day, and it'll be all the time, not just on a drive. And for ever cow you and Bonzo round up and put in the herd, you'll get a dollar a cow when we sell 'em. You'll do the branding and cutting, and we'll keep a tab."

"Let me see if I got this straight," Frog said, scratching his head. "If me and Bonzo was to round up a hundred wild cows and put 'em in the herd, we'd get a hundred-dollar bonus to split. And if we got a thousand, it would be a thousand-dollar bonus. Is that what you're sayin'?"

"That's right. A dollar a cow. Plus a regular salary and all you can eat."

"We just quit driftin' for a while," Frog said, grinning. "You got a deal, Mister MacIvey. We'll pop ever cow out of ever swamp and prairie in Florida. Next time we come to Punta Rassa we'll have a herd that stretches ten miles."

"It ain't that easy," Tobias cautioned. "Don't count your money before you get it. This time you just helped drive the cows, not round them up. We lost a whole herd one time to a storm. And we still got to run through wolves and 'gators. But we'll sure try."

Frog then said, "Where's Zech?"

"He was over there a few minutes ago cramming chicken down them dog's throats. You need to see him?"

"I got a ten-pound bag of sugar for Ishmael. That little hoss done made me more money than I ever seen in a lifetime. How come you all didn't bet on the race?"

"We did. Won a hundred and fifty acres. We might be camped right now on land Zech owns. One of Captain Hendry's men is going to show me the land lines in the morning."

"Well I'll be!" Frog exclaimed. "Wasn't no way that big hoss could outrun Ishmael for three miles, and I wondered why you didn't take advantage of it. I guess I done joined up with the right outfit for sure. I'll go and find Zech. I want to feed Ishmael myself."

"Apples and sugar," Tobias said. "Don't spoil that horse. He won a race, but he's still got to work for his keep."

Frog turned to leave. "Just one thing, Mister MacIvey. Me and Bonzo wants to ride up to Fort Myers and see what it's like. Would it be O.K. with you? We'll catch up with you in a few days."

"That's fine with me. We got to stop going back and pay Lykes and Lowry for their cows. And we're just going to mosey along anyway, shoot a deer or two and eat, and camp when we want to. We ain't in no hurry, and it'll probably be two weeks or more before we get back to the hammock. But if you miss us on the trail, are you sure you can find my place?"

"We'll find it. And we'll scout out a better trail than we had coming down here. I don't ever want to get boxed in again like we did in that 'gator swamp."

"I had the same thing in mind," Tobias said, "Are you and Bonzo staying for supper? Emma brought some chickens back from the store and she's making stew."

Frog sniffed the air and said eagerly. "We'll stay. We can head out for Fort Myers later."

Bonzo followed Frog, and Tobias said to Skillit, "Well, it seems we still got us a cattle company. I'm glad they're staying."

"Me too," Skillit said. "Them two looks like scarecrows, but they sho' got guts beneath all them bones. And if it hadn't been for you, Mistuh Tobias, I'd a joined them in a snort of that rum. It's like hoss racin', it ain't too bad if you don't do it too often."

"Don't let me stop you. It's ever man to his own liking. And by the way, what happened with the chore you wanted to do in Punta Rassa? You never told me what it was."

Skillit was surprised that Tobias remembered. "I asked around in town this mornin' and they ain't no colored folk in Punta Rassa. I'll take care of it some other time."

Tobias sensed that Skillit didn't want to discuss whatever it was he wanted to do. "Well, whenever. If it's something you need time off for, take all you want."

"It can wait, but not too much longer. I'll see to it later."

"Watch it now! Be careful! Don't scratch it!"

Tobias, Skillit, the clerk and one other man lifted the stove to the wagon floor and pushed it as far as possible from the edge.

Tobias said, "It'll have to ride there. Don't shove it against the trunk. It's a good thing we don't have any Georgia mountains to cross."

"Where you want me to put the stovepipe?" the clerk asked.

"Right behind the stove, where it can't roll out."

"We go across a wet marsh, we'll have to hitch another hoss to the wagon," Skillit said. "That thing's a heap heavier than it looks."

"We just might have to do that," Tobias said. "It do weigh a bit."

Tobias thanked the clerk and the man for their help before he climbed to the seat and started down the street. The extra weight caused the wagon wheels to cut a three-inch rut in the sand.

They moved slowly out of town and past the holding pens, then along the road bordering the river. Tobias cursed the pace, wanting to trot the horse, hurry to the camp and see Emma's reaction.

When they reached the camp Emma came to the wagon and stared open-mouthed. She finally said, "What on earth, Tobias? Where'd you get the stove?"

"At the store. I bought it yesterday as a surprise for you. You like it?"

"Lordy yes! It's the purtiest one I've ever seen." She climbed into the wagon and started opening doors and looking inside.

Zech rode up on Ishmael, gazed for a moment and then said, "What kind of a horse is that on the stove, Pappa? It's got a horn on its head."

"Don't know. But it's sure fancy, ain't it?"

Emma said, "I can hardly wait to try it out. Can I cook on it on the way back?"

"If me and Skillit and Zech can get it off the wagon. We don't want to set the wagon afire. We can sure do it when Frog and Bonzo joins us. I think I'll put in some of the pipe and see how it looks."

Tobias climbed into the wagon and put three lengths of stovepipe into the stove. Then he got out, backed away and studied carefully. "Looks fine. Just like the stack on them steamboats in Punta Rassa. I'll leave it there till we have to go under a tree."

"I ain't never seen a horse like that," Zech said again, still puzzled. "You want us to load the rest of the stuff now?"

"Yes," Tobias answered. "We need to go on and get across the river."

As soon as the wagon was loaded they moved up the road to the ferry. The ferry tender looked curiously at the "MacIvey Cattle Company" sign on the wagon, at the four new black felt hats, the wolf-dogs and miniature horse, the lanky, bearded man and the giant black man. He said, "That's a might fancy stove you folks got there. When I first seen you coming I thought it was a calliope."

Tobias drove the wagon onto the barge as Zech and

Skillit plunged their horses into the river and swam. When the ferry reached the other side the tender said, "Where you folks headed?"

"Over to the Kissimmee," Tobias replied. Then he whipped the horse and moved up the bank.

The ferry tender shouted, "Good luck, folks!" Then he continued staring until they turned past a clump of palmetto and passed from view. As he started back across the river he muttered, "Shoot! I thought for sure it was a circus coming."

✝

Spring
1875

Tobias roared. "They done it again!"

He kicked the stump of an orange tree and said, "Cussed cows! They're stupid critters!"

He was inside a three-acre plot surrounded by a split rail fence. A half dozen cows were standing in a group, swishing their tails and looking at him. Rows of small orange trees had been eaten to the ground and looked like dead sticks protruding from the sandy soil.

Tobias jerked one tree from the ground and threw it at the cows, causing them to wheel quickly and trot off to the far side of the fence. They turned, faced him again and shook their horns menacingly.

"Cuss you!" he shouted as he left the plot and walked hurriedly back into the hammock.

The house was three rooms larger now, one a kitchen built especially for the stove, another a bedroom for Zech, and a store-room containing two steamer trunks. The palmetto thatch was replaced with cypress shingles, and there was a porch across the front of the house. A cabin had been built for Frog and Bonzo, and Skillit had added an additional room to his cabin. There was also a barn down by the garden area.

Tobias stomped into the house and said, "The cows has et my orange trees again! That's the third time I've planted them, and them stupid critters has done it ever time!"

Emma continued chopping onions as she said, "Why don't you keep the cows away from them."

"Man who sells them to me says if I don't put cows in there to do the fertilizing, the trees won't grow. And that makes sense."

"Then buy taller trees."

"Taller trees," Tobias repeated. "How come I didn't think of that! If the trees is taller than the cows, then the cows can't eat them. That's what I'll do! Buy taller trees! I'll send Skillit for another wagonload."

Emma smiled as Tobias walked out briskly.

Tobias had made four more drives into Punta Rassa, each one larger than the one before. He now had regular buying points along the trail, and his last herd numbered over three thousand. Predators still stalked them, and many nights they kept fires burning to turn away wolves, but there had been no major disasters.

The old army horse died and was replaced by a tall black mare, and Tobias also purchased a buckboard and another horse to pull it. He bought two oxen which were used to pull the supply wagon during trail drives and when they followed grazing herds in summer months.

Other than this and the purchase of orange trees, the money from the sale of cows had been stockpiled, and now one steamer trunk was filled with sacks of gold doubloons and another started. Frog and Bonzo were the only ones interested in the coins as something to spend, and for two weeks after each drive they disappeared. To the others, the doubloons were just something to pile into a trunk and exchange for supplies when needed. The MacIvey clan's lifestyle changed none at all.

Zech had grown along with the homestead and was now as tall as his father and ten pounds heavier. But unlike Tobias, his hair turned a sandy brown. The most visible change in Tobias was the white specks that invaded his black beard.

*T*obias found Skillit down at the barn, mending a harness strap. He said straightaway, "I want you to take the wagon and get me some more orange trees. Same place as last, out west of Fort Pierce."

Skillit noticed the agitation in Tobias' voice and manner. He said, "Them cows done et yo' trees again, ain't they?"

Tobias ignored the question. "This time get taller trees. I don't want nothing less than six feet. Stand by each one of them, and if one's shorter than you, don't buy it. Get all you can cram on the wagon. Emma will give you the money."

"All right, Mistuh Tobias. I'll start right away. But would it be O.K. if I stay for a day or two? I got a chore to do while I'm down there."

"What kind of a chore?" Tobias asked, still agitated. "You been saying now for over five years you got a chore to do ever time you leave the hammock, and you ain't done it yet. If you got something you want to do, why don't you go on and do it 'stead of just talking about it?"

"It ain't never worked out yet," Skillit replied. "Maybe this time it will."

"Must be some chore," Tobias muttered. "Take what time you have to, but don't be gone too long. Soon as they get in with this last bunch of cows, we got to move the herd to grazing ground. Ain't enough grass left here for a billygoat to eat."

"Sho' ain't," Skillit agreed. "We don't get some rain soon, the whole place gone look like a frost hit it. I ain't never seen it be this dry for so long this time of year."

*Z*ech popped the whip just over the cow's head, turning it sharp right and into the pen. He leaped from the saddle and closed the gate, then he called for the dogs to leave the cows and come to him.

Frog wheeled his horse and said, "That's the last of this bunch. We can start back tomorrow."

The corral held sixty cows. They had spent idle winter months building small pens ten miles apart along the areas of the spring roundup, using them to brand and cut the cattle as they caught them and also contain them at night or while they hunted others.

Zech rode over to a nearby cypress stand and tied Ishmael; then he gave each dog a strip of dried beef. It was late afternoon, and long flights of herons and egrets drifted eastward. The sky in the west was cloudless and streaked with red and orange, marking the time when day creatures retreated and night dwellers emerged. Zech watched with amusement as a mother raccoon ambled by with her brood, chattering a loud protest of his presence.

Frog and Bonzo rode to the stand and dismounted. Frog stretched and groaned, and then he said, "Ain't nothing but a fool makes his living rubbing his butt against a saddle all day. Sometimes mine feels like it's busted. What you got left in the way of grub?"

Zech said, "Nothing but a couple of strips of dried beef and a few biscuits, and they're as hard as hickernuts."

"Don't even have that," Bonzo said. "Just one scrap of meat that looks like it ought to be buried."

"You want me to kill a rabbit?" Zech asked. "If you do, I best see to it now before it gets too dark."

"What I miss most out here is Miz Emma's vittles," Frog said.

"I ain't got nothing left. We ought to have brought more supplies or turned back two days ago. We could have come back and got them cows some other time."

"Pappa said we're not coming back after this," Zech said. "We're heading out for grazing. And besides that, none of these cows is marked yet. You and Bonzo'll get credit for all of them."

"Maybe so," Frog said, "but that don't help my belly none. I'd a soon have a big bowl of Miz Emma's hot stew just now as the sixty dollars over yonder in the pen." Frog scratched his head in thought, and then he said, "I got a good idea. We couldn't be over a hour's ride from Fort Drum, maybe less. We could go over there and get some fresh grub and be back here not long after dark."

"What about the cows?" Zech asked. "We can't go off and leave them unguarded."

"They ain't going nowhere inside that pen. And I ain't seen a wolf sign in three days. We could leave the dogs tied to the fence to watch after them."

"That'd be like using Nip and Tuck for fishbait," Zech said, shaking his head in disagreement. "Some bears or other varmints come in here, the dogs wouldn't have a chance tied to a rail. We'd have to take them with us."

"Ain't nothing going to happen to the cows," Frog insisted. "We can build a fire on both sides of the corral. That would keep off anything that comes around till we get back."

"You two go on and I'll stay," Zech said. "I'm not all that hungry anyway. I can make do on what I got."

"We ain't about to leave you out here by yourself. If something happened to you while we're gone, your Pappa would raise more hell than you ever seen. Either you go or nobody goes."

"You think I can't handle things by myself?" Zech asked angrily.

"It ain't that, and you know it. And there's no use in getting riled up. Your pappa wouldn't want nobody left alone at night on the prairie, not you or me or Bonzo. We going to go or not? If we ain't, then you might as well shoot that ole rabbit."

"Well, if your belly's in that bad a shape, I guess I'll go," Zech said reluctantly. "But I don't like it. I've seen what can happen to a cow at night, and you have too."

"Ain't nothing going to happen," Frog repeated.

As soon as the fires were glowing they rode eastward, cantering the horses as the dogs followed, moving at a steady pace across the palmetto prairie. The sunset reflected light ahead of them, a dim glow rapidly fading into the tops of cabbage palms; and cypress stands stood out like darkened castles looming upward from the flat land.

Just as the last sunbeam died they spotted a bonfire a mile to the north. Trading posts in the wilderness often put out such beacons at night, guiding unfamiliar travelers to a spot they could never find in darkness.

The horses panted slightly when the trio rode in and stopped in front of the store. Soft coal oil light spilled out from the two front windows and the open door, and several men sat on the building's porch, chewing and spitting silently.

Zech followed Frog and Bonzo inside, still doubtful about the journey and wishing he had remained behind. He wanted them to make their purchases quickly and head back to the corral.

Frog said to a man wearing a white apron, "You got cheese?"

"Enough to stop up a horse. How much you want?"

"Three pounds. And six cans of beans. You got bread and tinned sausage?"

"My wife bakes bread ever day, and we got sausages."

"Three each."

The man put the order into a brown sack and said, "Be anything else?"

"Them men out front just chewing their cuds like cows, or is that tobacco?" Frog asked.

"Tobacco."

"Then throw in a twist."

"That'll be two fifty," the man said, putting into the sack a link of twisted tobacco that looked like smoked sausage. He took the money and made change from a small wooden box. "You men just passing through?"

"Naw," Frog responded. "We got some cows penned out on the prairie west of here. We ran out of grub."

"If you ain't in a hurry, they's going to be a hoedown here soon as the folks come in out of the woods. You're welcome to stay."

Frog's face brightened. "You hear that, fellows? They're having a frolic here in a little while. You want to stay?"

"I do," Bonzo said quickly.

"What's a frolic?" Zech asked, annoyed that something might change their plans to leave immediately.

"Fiddles and dancin'," Frog responded. "Ain't you ever been to one?"

"If I had, I wouldn't ask what it is. We need to go now. We ain't got time for such stuff."

"Cows ain't everything, Zech. Just take it easy. We'll stay for a short spell and leave. You might enjoy it if you'd try."

They went outside, sat at the edge of the porch and started eating. People drifted in out of the darkness, on horses and in ox-drawn wagons, and soon a milling crowd filled the clearing.

Several men threw more logs on the fire, bringing the front of the store into focus; then three men with fiddles mounted the porch and played briskly. Another shouted cadence as men grabbed women, starting the first round of a square dance.

Zech watched sullenly as Frog and Bonzo joined the line of dancers, kicking their boots into the soft dirt, swaying, linking arms, then swinging down the line as they changed partners again and again.

He was unaware of the girl's presence until he looked up, and he wondered how long she had been standing there. She had flaming red hair that flowed past her shoulders, pale green eyes, and white skin not burned brown by prairie sun. A blue cotton dress came down to her shoes, and she wore a matching ribbon around her slim waist.

She said, "It's better on a wooden floor where you can hear the shoes tapping. The men are going to build a meeting hall soon so we can have the frolics inside. You look like you're not enjoying it. Don't you feel good?"

"Well, I . . . I . . ." Zech stammered, unable to form a coherent answer.

"I've never seen you here before. My daddy owns the store, and I usually know everybody who comes to the frolic. My name's Glenda Turner. What's yours?"

"Zech," he managed to say. "Zech MacIvey. We came in for food. We've got cows penned out on the prairie."

"You live nearby?"

"Up on the Kissimmee, about a day's ride from here. We're in the cattle business and we're finishing the spring roundup."

She waited for him to ask, and when he remained silent, she said, "You want to dance the next one with me?"

Zech felt like he had swallowed a pine burr that lodged in his throat. He forced out the words, "I don't know how. I've never been to a frolic before."

"That's too bad. Would you like some punch? I helped my mother make it and I know it's good. The bowl is on the table at the end of the porch."

"That would be fine."

Zech was still sitting, and when he got up to follow her, she came only to the top of his shoulder.

When they reached the table she filled a cup with red liquid and handed it to him. He downed it in one gulp and said, "That's real good. I've never tasted anything like it."

"It's sugar that makes it sweet. But it's better if you just sip."

His face turned crimson as he said, "I'm sorry I drank it so fast. Next time I won't."

"Here, let me get you another. How old are you?" she asked for the second time with no answer.

He shook his head, feeling as if he had jumped a ten-rail fence. "I'm sorry. I didn't hear you at first. I'm seventeen, going on eighteen."

"I'm fourteen, but my mother says I look older. Do you think I look older than fourteen?"

"I don't know. I've never been around girls. Only my mamma. But you look fine to me."

"Thank you. I've never been around boys very much either. There's not many young people in Fort Drum."

The music stopped between dances, and Zech noticed Frog and Bonzo out by a wagon with several sweating men, drinking from gallon jugs. He started to go to them and insist they leave, but said instead, "You want to see my dogs? They look like wolves. They're on the other side of the store."

"I'd like to. I've never seen a wolf, or a dog that looked like one."

They walked past the crowd of people and found the dogs sitting in the shadows, waiting patiently as Zech told them to do. He said, "This one is Nip, and that one Tuck. They're the best cow dogs that's ever been."

"Aren't you afraid of them?" she asked. "They're so big."

"They's good dogs. They won't hurt you. Touch one."

She put her hand on Nip's head, causing his tail to wag vigorously.

"See. I told you. He likes you. You want to see my horse too? His name is Ishmael, and he's a marshtackie. The Seminoles gave him to us."

They went to the rail where Ishmael was tied. Zech said, "He's little, but he runs like the wind. I won a race with him in Punta Rassa. Outran a big Tennessee bay twice his size." Then on an impulse he said, "You want to ride? We'll just go a short piece and come back."

"If you'll help me in the saddle. I can't get up there in this long dress."

When they came back to the store and the people and the screaming fiddle, he was jolted back to reality. He jumped from the horse, lifted her down and said, "I've got to find Frog and Bonzo and go now. There's bears and wolves out on the prairie, and the cows might be in danger. I didn't mean to take you so far."

"I enjoyed it," she said. "Will you be coming back soon?"

"I don't know. We're taking the cows grazing soon as we get back to the hammock, and after that we'll go to Punta Rassa to sell them. If I don't come back this summer I will in the fall."

"If you do, I'll teach you to dance. Will you promise me you'll try?"

"I promise. And I'll be back as soon as I can."

Frog and Bonzo were still at the wagon and Glenda watched as Zech turned quickly and walked straight to them. He said, "We best go. We've been here long enough. We've got to see to the cows."

They mounted and rode westward, putting the horses into a canter again, crossing a plain now flooded with soft moonlight. It seemed to Zech that the cabbage palms and palmetto had turned to lilacs. The scent clung to him and the saddle, coming from everywhere, making the ride last only moments before they approached the corral.

Even before they reached the pen, Zech sensed something was wrong. He put Ishmael into a fast gallop. He stopped just short of the rails and stared disbelieving into an empty corral.

Frog rode up beside him and said, "Now how did they do that? I checked that gate myself and it was shut tight. They must have pushed it open and took off."

"I told you we shouldn't have gone off and left them alone," Zech said, guilt in his voice, "I told you! We should have stayed here and watched after them."

"They're sommers close by," Frog said assuringly. "Cows don't run at night 'less they're afraid. If something had been after them they'd have busted down the fence, not just opened the gate and walked out. There's not a single rail even pushed sideways. We'll find 'em in the morning."

"I hope so," Zech said doubtfully. "I've never lost a bunch of cows like this, for no reason at all. We best start looking for them at first sunup. If we don't find them, I'll have a hard time explaining it to Pappa."

*F*rog looked down from his horse and said, "It's for sure nothing spooked them. The tracks is too close together for them to be running. They walked away from here calm as raccoons."

"We must not have locked the gate good," Zech said.

"Maybe so. But I could have sworn it was shut tight. I checked it right before we left."

"I'll put Nip and Tuck on the trail. They can sniff 'em out a lot quicker than we can follow the tracks."

Zech dismounted and whistled for the dogs. When they came to him he pushed their noses to the ground and said, "Go and find them! Go!"

They didn't bolt forward instantly and race away. Instead, they moved slowly and carefully at first, sniffing constantly, going off to the right and left to determine if any cow had wandered off alone.

The trail led south for four miles, then it turned west into an area of dense palmetto. Frog signaled for Zech and Bonzo to stop, and then he said, "You think this is really worth it, Zech? If them cows scatters out in this palmetto thicket, we'll have to pop them out one at a time. We can round up a new bunch quicker than this."

Zech knew what Frog said was true, but he was thinking of Tobias and the trust he placed in him to handle the roundup. He said, "Let's go just a bit further. The tracks is still all together. If we don't find them soon, we'll turn back and head for the hammock."

They followed the tracks for a half mile more, going deeper into thick scrub; then they came to a trail that ran straight into a narrow, dry slough bordered on both sides by Spanish bayonet and thick clumps of palmetto.

Zech was just about to call the dogs and turn back when it came, a shattering boom, ear splitting, coming from somewhere on the right just ahead of them. Tuck's head flew off and rolled forward, blood gushing from the stump and spilling out in a flood. Rifle bullets peppered the ground around Nip. He braked quickly, tumbling over and over; then he scrambled to his feet and retreated, running for the nearest cover. Then he fell again.

Ishmael jumped sideways instinctively, somehow knowing what he must do even before Zech realized what was happening. He staggered and then righted himself, almost throwing Zech from the saddle, then he bolted into a clump of palmetto.

Zech left the saddle and fell to the ground, stunned momentarily, before he heard someone close by shouting, "Bushwhackers! Bushwhackers! Stay hid! Stay hid!"

The popping sounds continued as Zech lay still. A limb above him shattered, sending a fine spray of palmetto fiber into his eyes. He brushed it away and pushed himself to a sitting position.

Then for the first time he realized what he had seen, Tuck's head departing its body, the instantly lifeless form tumbling over and over through its own blood; then Nip falling also, scrambling and falling again, not knowing if he had escaped death or not.

Fear gripped Zech, and then it turned to instant rage, uncontrollable rage. He snapped a frond from the palmetto and beat the ground with it, shouting, "No good thieves!"

The firing stopped as suddenly as it began. The voice of Frog came again, "Stay put! Don't come out yet!"

Zech ignored the warning. He jumped to his feet and staggered forward blindly, trying to see through tears that fogged his eyes. He walked into the open slough and to the body. He fell to his knees and touched the shaggy fur. Tuck's eyes were open, staring, seemingly puzzled as to what happened to him so swiftly. Zech reached out, grabbed the head and placed it back to the body.

Shouting came again, "Zech! Get outen there! They might not be gone yet!"

He went to the sound and located Frog's horse; then he ripped the pistol from the saddlebag and started running, screaming again, "No good thieves!"

Frog tackled him from behind and struggled to hold him, the two of them tumbling over and over like wildcats fighting. The pistol went off, spewing smoke into their eyes; then Frog shouted, "Don't be a fool, Zech! Anybody who'd do this for some scrawny yellowhammers would as soon shoot you as a buzzard! Let go the gun!"

Zech loosened his grip and lay still. He looked up, rubbing his eyes, seeing that it was Frog on top of him. He said, "What about Nip? Did they kill him too?"

"I don't now. Last time I seen him he was making for the bushes over to the left of us. Let's go and see."

The two of them got up, crossed the slough and entered the palmetto. They found Nip twenty feet inside the brush. He was lying on his side, whimpering, trying to lift his head but unable to do so. When he saw Zech he wagged his tail feebly.

Zech dropped down and touched him. "He's shot, but I can make him well. We'll take him back to the hammock."

"No, Zech. His guts is blowed apart. He's hurtin' real bad. You'll have to finish him."

Zech looked at the bloodied stomach, the gaping hole, realizing what must be done. "I can't do it, Frog. You'll have to." Then he walked away quickly. He cringed when the pistol fired, tears forming again in his eyes.

Bonzo was standing by his horse, his left arm hanging limp and blood-stained. When Zech saw this he went to him and said, "Are you hit bad, Bonzo?"

"Naw, ain't nothing but a flesh wound. The bullet went clear through. I'll be O.K. soon as I tie a cloth to it. The thief who cracked down on me ain't too good a shot."

Frog came from the palmetto and joined them. "Let's get out of here before them crazy fools decide to come back," he said.

"Not before I bury Nip and Tuck," Zech said. "I ain't going to leave them here for buzzard bait."

"Aw come on, Zech, how you going to bury them dogs without a shovel?"

"With my hands, if I have to. I'll not leave till it's done."

"I'll help then," Frog said, knowing he could not get Zech away otherwise. "I'll get some sticks to dig with."

They scraped a hole in the ground, using both hands and hickory, and put the dogs in a common grave. Zech covered them by himself, patting the dirt firmly, hoping some panther or wolf would not come along, find them and dig them up. He said, "I ain't never been able to read the Book. If I could, I'd say words, but I don't know how. I hope the Lord blesses them."

As they mounted the horses to leave, Zech said, "I ain't never going nowhere again without a gun. And if I ever find the thieves who done this, I'll blow their heads slam off, just like they done to Tuck."

"We don't even know who it was," Frog said. "And chances are we'll never know. There's varmints like them everwhere."

"I'll know. If I ever come on them, I'll know. Just like Ishmael knowed the wolves were coming. Someday I'll find them."

Zech looked back briefly at the grave; then he put Ishmael into a fast trot.

"Don't try to blame all this on yourself, Zech," Tobias said. "It ain't your fault. And it don't matter none at all about the cows. We got plenty more. I'm just glad all of you got out of it alive."

"But I know it's my fault, Pappa," Zech insisted. "I killed Nip and Tuck just as sure as if I pulled the trigger myself. If I hadn't gone to the store and stayed for the frolic, none of this would have happened. They'd be alive."

"Them men was backshooters, Zech!" Tobias said harshly. "Don't you understand that? Staying for the frolic might have saved your life."

"Maybe so. But I won't leave a herd unguarded again. And when we get to Punta Rassa you've got to get me a gun."

"I'll do that. You ought to carry one anyway. But don't go around shooting every man you think might have killed the dogs."

Frog said, "Mister MacIvey, what kind of a gun could blow a dog's head slam off, like it done Tuck's? I ain't never seen nothing like that before."

"In all my lifetime I've never seen but one that could do it. It was stole from me when we lived in the scrub. It's a ten-gauge breechloader with two forty-inch barrels. It was made by a gunsmith just for my daddy, and it's the only thing he left me besides grief. There may be others like it but I ain't seen one. It has my mark on the stock. Some of them varmints who bushwhacked you could be the same ones who burned my house."

"I'm glad they turned a rifle on Bonzo 'stead of that thing," Frog said. "If they had, he'd be scattered all over the prairie."

"I killed a bear with it once," Zech said, "and it like to have broke my shoulder. If I ever see that old gun again, I'll know it even without the mark."

Frog said, "I been trying to figure out what's missing around here. Where's Skillit?"

"I sent him after some orange trees five days ago and he ain't come back yet. I've done dug all the holes while he's been gone. Maybe he ended up in Georgia 'stead of Fort Pierce. I don't think nobody would bushwhack a wagon full of orange trees."

Bonzo sat on the stoop while Emma put a fresh dressing on the wound. When she finished she said, "You'll be as good as new in a couple of days. Go on now and join that man talk while I fix supper."

"Thanks, Miz Emma," Bonzo said. "I appreciate your doing this for me."

"You're welcome. And I'll see to your stomach next. It's probably in worse shape than your arm."

Tobias said, "Frog, you and Bonzo take the horses down to the barn. They probably need some rest after you run 'em like you did."

"I'll go and help," Zech said.

"No. You stay here. I want to talk to you."

Zech and Tobias sat on the edge of the stoop while the horses were led away. Tobias said, "Son, I know you're hurtin' now, hurtin' real bad. I've felt the pain myself, and I know how it is. But don't grieve too long for Nip and Tuck. Let it go soon. What you just seen and been through will come again and again. This whole wilderness is built on such as that, and it's going to get worse before it gets better, if it ever does. You've got to learn to take the bad as well as the good, no matter what comes along. Don't go on hurtin' too long."

"Pappa, I don't think I'll ever forget seeing what I seen. Not ever."

"Yes you will. There ain't no pain that don't fade away. We'll get other dogs, and you'll like them too, and a time will come when they take the place of Nip and Tuck. The new dogs will be the ones close to you, and the ones you remember, not the old ones. That's the way it is. Something you like and lose will be replaced, and it'll go on and on, over and over again."

"Would you forget Mamma if she left us?"

Tobias did not expect such a response. He said, "That's different. I'm not talking about people. I'm talking about critters. But there's men who can replace a woman, and a year later hardly remember her name or anything about her. Only the one with them at the time matters. But no, Zech, I would not forget your mamma. Or replace her either."

"That's what I thought you'd say. And I feel the same about Nip and Tuck. I don't think I'll ever want any more dogs."

Tobias put his arm on Zech's shoulder. "We don't talk much like this, and maybe we ought to do it more often. I guess we've both been too busy chasing cows. What I said I've said badly. I ain't good with words, and you know that. All I'm trying to tell you is to be strong. Don't ever let nothing get you down. Don't be afraid or ashamed to love, or to grieve when the thing you love is gone. Just don't let it throw you, no matter how much it hurts. If you make it in this wilderness, you got to be strong. Do you understand me?"

"Yes, Pappa, I understand. And I'm sorry I cried for the dogs."

"Don't be. Don't ever be sorry for something like that. There ain't nothing wrong with a man crying. I done it for a week when my mamma died. But when you get done with it, start over again, and don't ever look back. Now go on down to the barn and see to Ishmael. He probably won't let Frog or Bonzo touch him."

"I'll see to him, Pappa. I'll feed him and water him and brush him down too. I ran him pretty hard coming back to the hammock."

Tobias watched him run away, seeing him as a boy again but knowing that such a time was gone forever. He said, "You'll see to it proper, Zech. You always have."

After supper Tobias went to the barn to pen the oxen for the night, leaving Emma and Zech alone in the house. Zech was at the table, still brooding about the dogs in spite of what his father said.

Emma sat beside him, wanting to distract him from such thoughts. She said, "Did you have a good time at the frolic?"

"I guess. But I didn't dance. I don't know how."

"Did you meet someone?"

"Yes ma'am."

"Was she pretty?"

"The prettiest thing I ever seen," Zech responded, knowing he could talk to his mother more frankly about something like this than he could his father. "She had hair as red as a sunset, and she smelled like flowers."

"I smelled like flowers once, but not anymore."

165

"You smell just fine, Mamma," he said, touching her hand, "and you always have."

"Not like flowers anymore. That's for young girls. Did you like her?"

"She rode with me on Ishmael. Her name is Glenda. Glenda Turner. Her daddy owns the store at Fort Drum."

"But did you like her?" she asked again.

"I never been that close to a girl before. I guess I did. She made me dizzy, like I was spinning around and around. She said if I come back she'll teach me to dance."

Emma put her hand on his. "Zech, if you like her, don't stay away too long. Flowers has a way of being plucked by someone, and there's not many nice ones out here in the wilderness. They don't stay in bloom forever."

"Maybe I can go back there after the drive. If I can find the time, I'll go."

"You best make the time. Cows won't ever smell good like flowers. Someday you'll know that."

Zech remembered Frog saying to him, "Cows ain't everything." He said, "Thanks, Mamma. I won't forget what you've told me. I'll go back to Fort Drum first chance I get."

Everyone was in the house at noon the next day, just finishing dinner, when the wagon creaked into the clearing. It looked like a mobile grove, with orange trees crammed into every inch of available space. Skillit stopped just beside the stoop and shouted, "I's back, everybody! I's back! Come and see what I got!"

Tobias expected only trees, and he was surprised like everyone else at the sight of a girl on the wagon seat, perched there like a frightened owl, her eyes wide and blinking.

Skillit said, "This here's Pearlie Mae. Preacher done married us, proper and legal." His face was split by a grin, with only teeth showing.

"So that's what your chore has been!" Tobias exclaimed, still staring. "If you wanted a wife, Skillit, why didn't you just say so?"

"I's over forty years old now, Mistuh Tobias, and if I don't start me a family now, I'll soon be too old to even try. Pearlie Mae be a big help to Missus Emma. She knows how to cook and wash and sew and do most everything. You don't mind I brought her here, do you? She won't be a bother to nobody."

"Of course I don't mind," Tobias responded. "You're most welcome, Pearlie Mae."

Frog started jumping up and down, shouting, "Yew-haw! Yee-haw! Old Skillit's done got him a woman! They's going to be babies all over the hammock, thick as junebugs!"

"Shut up yo' mouth, Frog," Skillit said, "afore I pick you up and sling you into a buzzard's nest where you belong! You scarin' Pearlie Mae. She'll think you crazy."

"He is," Tobias said. "Don't pay no mind to him, Pearlie Mae. He's just jealous. Wouldn't nothing mate up with Frog, not even a wolf."

"One thing for sure," Frog said, "ain't no woman going to get the chance. I'd as soon be in a buzzard's nest as be tied to some woman's apron strings."

"You men hush up now!" Emma exclaimed. "You're chattering on like a bunch of jaybirds drunk on chinaberries." Then she turned to the girl. "You got a fine man, Pearlie Mae, real fine. Come on down off there and let's take a look at you."

The girl climbed down reluctantly, looking as if she might yet bolt and run. She was about twenty, two feet shorter than Skillit, and fifteen pounds overweight for her size. Her head was wrapped in a red bandanna, and a feed-sack dress came down to the top of an oversized pair of brogan shoes.

She managed a feeble smile, and then she said, "I's glad to meet you, Missus Emma. Skillit done tole me all about you an' Mistuh MacIvey an' Zech an' everbody else too. I's glad to be here."

Emma put her arm around the still frightened girl and said, "We're glad to have you in the family, Pearlie Mae. Real glad.

Let's me and you go in the kitchen and have some woman talk and leave the men to themselves. I'll fix us a fresh pot of coffee."

Pearlie Mae seemed to relax as she followed Emma into the house. Skillit said, "Where's the dogs? I wanted to show them to Pearlie Mae right off so they'd be friendly with her. I don't want her comin' on them sudden like and think they wolves."

Tobias glanced at Zech, and then he said, "We'll talk about that later, Skillit. The dogs ain't here just now. We need to set out them trees. Ain't good for them to be out of the ground too long, and I got all the holes dug."

Zech spoke up and said, "While you're doing that, could me and Ishmael go down in the woods, Pappa?"

"Sure, go on. We don't need you with the planting."

As Zech walked toward the barn Skillit said, "Zech don't look too good, Mistuh Tobias. He been sick?"

"I'll tell you about it while we plant the trees."

"The cows need salt, Mistuh Tobias," Skillit said. "They looks poorly. Let's take 'em to that river marsh up north of here where they's salt grass."

"I been thinking about that myself," Tobias replied. "After we graze there for a while we can turn south and cross the river. Go and tell the others to turn north."

The prairie was deep brown, burned by drought, and it would take thirty acres to feed just one cow. There were more than two thousand in the herd, all of them lanky after a winter in the swamps and woods. They moved faster than on past grazing drives, clipping the ground bare and ambling on, leaving behind a dust haze that made riding in the trailing wagon a constant annoyance. Both Emma and Pearlie Mae wore bandannas over their faces to gain what protection they could from the dust.

Sun rays bore down unmercifully from a cloudless sky, creating shimmering heat waves that looked like rolling ocean surf made of smoke. It played tricks on all of them, making distance judgment difficult, sometimes blocking out the horizon. Cypress stands ahead of them moved vertically and then horizontally, disappearing momentarily and then coming back like mystic ships with masts devoid of sails. The entire prairie seemed to be one giant vacuum just waiting to explode.

Men and horses were sapped of strength by mid-afternoon, and Tobias' shirt was soaked with sweat when he rode to the wagon. He said to Emma, "There's a pond fed by a spring at the stand over to the right. Pull on over there and we'll stop for the day. I think everbody needs rest and water."

The cows smelled the pond and turned to it without being

herded, and when the wagon reached the stand the pond was already stomped brown with mud. Emma and Pearlie Mae filled buckets at the spring before the cattle desecrated it too.

Skillit tied his horse to a bush and said, "Lawd have mercy, I ain't never knowed it to be so hot this time of year. That old sun puttin' out heat like a wood stove full of hickory. Way I been sweatin' today, I knows I must stink worse than any polecat ever been born."

"I can smell you from here," Pearlie Mae said, grinning. "You sho' sleep by yoself tonight, else you go in the pond with the cows an' wash up some."

"I think I just do that. Move over cows, I's comin' in."

"Flies seem to like this dry heat," Emma said. "They're as thick here as molasses. I don't know how we'll keep them out of the cooking pot."

Tobias dismounted, took a dipper of water from one bucket and poured it over his head. "If I didn't know better I'd swear the tops of them cabbage palms is smoking," he said. "They look like they're going to catch fire any minute. And if they do, with the prairie so dry, we're all going to be fried blacker than coon meat."

"You think we ought to turn back and put the cows in a swamp?" Skillit asked. "We do that, they could at least keep outen the sun."

"No. We'll move on. A couple days more and we'll make the marsh flat. The grass is bound to be better there. I've never seen that flat go as dry as this place."

Zech rode in and turned Ishmael lose at the spring. He dropped to the ground and put his head under water; then he filled his hat and came back to the wagon. He sat by Emma and put the hat back on, flooding his shirt and the top of his pants. "Feels good," he said.

Tobias said to Zech, "Soon as you get done cooling off a bit, take a limb and keep the cows away from the spring. There's water enough for them in the pond, and we don't want the spring messed up too."

The sinking sun brought no relief from the heat. Emma fixed a supper of beef stew, baked potatoes, and biscuits, and even Frog and Bonzo ate lightly. No one seemed interested in food.

Frog pushed his plate aside and said, "Is my eyes playing tricks on me, or is something peculiar goin' on out yonder?"

"I don't see nothin' but cows an' palmetto," Skillit said.

Frog squinted. "Maybe it's just sweat and dust in my eyes, but I swear I just seen some of them bushes pick up and move. There's something out there besides cows."

"I seen it too," Zech said. "Over to the left, about a quarter mile."

They all continued gazing, and then Zech said, "There. You see it then? It's deer."

A herd of a dozen deer stood alert, staring at the cypress stand, then darting behind palmetto clumps and coming out again.

"They act like they want to come to the wagon," Frog said. "You reckon they smell Miz Emma's biscuits?"

"Taint that," Tobias said. "It's the spring. I bet you we done blocked off the only watering hole around here that ain't gone dry. If we have, every varmint on the prairie will be trying to come in here tonight for a drink."

"If'n they do, we'll have more wolves and bears and panthers than cows," Skillit said. "Maybe we ought to move on away from here before it gets dark."

"We could build a whole line of fires around the stand," Frog said. "They sure won't come through that to get in here."

"That wouldn't help the cows," Tobias said. "We can't cram two thousand cows inside a one-acre cypress stand. They'd still be out there in the open, fair game for whatever comes off the prairie."

"If Nip and Tuck were here they could handle it," Zech said.

"They're sorely missed for sure," Tobias said. "I never knew just how much of the work them dogs did till they were gone. But they're not here now, and that's a fact. We can sit here jawin' all night and it won't help matters one bit. We best decide what to do and then do it."

Emma said, "You can't blame the animals. They get thirsty too, and it's their water, same as ours. We can fill the barrel and the buckets and leave. What difference does it make if we camp here or a few miles further on?"

"None at all," Tobias said. "Sometimes you the only one makes sense, Emma. Let's all saddle up and move on, and let them critters out there have their turn. Ain't no use in us starting a war tonight over nothing."

"I'd sure like to be here when all them critters come together at the pond," Zech said. "That'll be a sight to see. I'll bet the fur'll fly thicker than dandelions."

"That's their problem," Tobias said. "Ours is the cows. We'll go a few miles on and stop again."

Just before midnight, when he was relieved from watch by Bonzo, Zech did not return to the camp. Instead, he rode south across the prairie, back toward the cypress stand they abandoned that afternoon.

There was a full moon glowing, and far in the west fingers of dry lightning cut the sky and were followed by dull rumblings. Tobias would be watching this too during his guard duty, watching with concern, hoping the slender fingers from above would not spark a fire in the tinder-dry grass. This was the most feared danger they faced on open prairie, fire that could move as swiftly as deer and destroy all in its path.

A full moon was always magical to Zech, bringing a time of enchantment when all the harshness of sun-burned prairie vanished and was replaced by soft outlines of palm and palmetto. He knew this to be a time of danger, when predators roamed and ruled the countryside, but this reality did not break his thoughts as Ishmael carried him slowly across the quiet plain.

There were many times back in the hammock when he slipped

172

from the house unnoticed and walked alone through the woods and along the river during full moon, seeing and experiencing a totally different world from that of day. There was a warmness about it on winter nights, and a coolness in summer; and always it made him feel as if he were part and parcel of nature and its night creatures, a closeness that dissipated with the coming of the sun.

When he came to within a quarter mile of the stand, he tied Ishmael to a bush and walked on alone, moving slowly and without sound. Then he stopped a hundred yards short of the pond and dropped to the ground beside a palmetto.

The first forms that visited the stand were deer, and they were soon replaced by the smaller vague bodies of foxes and rabbits and raccoons. He lay there in the dry grass and watched a procession come in groups of their own kind: wolves, bears, a mother panther with a litter of cubs, all passing each other without comment, drinking and disappearing again into the night. There were no growls of anger, no warnings to move away, no snarling flashes of superiority—deadly natural enemies seemingly under a truce understood only by themselves, sharing equally a thing they all must have to survive.

Zech watched spellbound, wondering what would happen if Nip and Tuck were with him, if they too would understand and honor this truce, retreat from natural instincts and patiently await their turn; or if they would charge forward and engage in combat to run the others away without sharing. He was glad they were not present at this moment, for he did not want the scene challenged. He knew it was possible he would never again witness it.

Time passed swiftly as the strange parade continued, and he finally realized he should return to the camp lest his mother awaken and find him missing. He got up reluctantly and made his way back to Ishmael.

No one stirred as he tied the horse and unsaddled him. Off to the right, the herd stood motionless, not even the swish of a tail breaking the silence. He wondered if they somehow knew no danger would come their way this night, if they were aware of the ritual taking place a few miles to the south.

He lay on his blanket and used the saddle as a pillow, staring upward at the star-peppered sky, awed by what the night brought him. He was still awake when Tobias rode in from the herd at dawn.

Two days later they reached a low plain that stretched for five miles north and south and three miles eastward from the river. There were no trees here, only unbroken marsh, and the grass was taller than prairie grass and more wiry.

In times past when they brought herds to the salt marsh the ground was soggy, and the imprint of a cow's hoof seeped brackish water. Now there were vast stretches of cracked mud that felt powdery to the step.

They made camp beneath a grove of cabbage palms on higher land overlooking the basin, then they drove the cows into the marsh. In spite of the dryness, the grass was bountiful, and Tobias knew the herd would get salt and minerals here that were unavailable on the prairie. He figured there was sufficient grazing for at least two weeks.

The days and nights settled into a dull routine of eating and sleeping and riding guard, but there was the diversion of going to the river and catching fish that Emma either fried or made into chowder. The river was three feet below its normal level and would be no problem to cross with the wagon when the time came to turn west.

At noon on the fourth day at the marsh, black clouds formed a solid wall in the west, and the wind quickened. Tobias watched hopefully as thunderheads inched upward and closer, and by mid-afternoon the marsh was turned a somber yellow by a sunless sky.

Lightning flashes were followed by sharp, crashing thunder, scattering the egrets and herons from their feeding grounds close by the river. All of the men not on watch cut poles and hurriedly fashioned lean-tos from palmetto fronds.

The wind increased until finally the marsh grass lay flat against the ground; then solid sheets of rain blew in vertically, slashing men, horses and cattle. From the camp the plain became invisible. When they could no longer see the herd, Tobias and Zech abandoned the watch and made their way back to the wagon.

Night came two hours earlier than usual, and the cooking fire hissed and went out before Emma could prepare food. They huddled beneath the lean-tos and ate beef jerky, and soon the pounding rain found its way through the palmetto roofs and drenched them.

The rain stopped just before dawn, and daybreak came once again to a cloudless sky. Tobias stirred and said, "We needed rain real bad, but that one was almost too much. I hope nobody floated away."

He got out of the wagon and walked across the soggy ground, stopping at the rim of the basin. The herd was all there, standing in a sheet of water covering the marsh. It looked as if grass were growing from a lake.

Because the basin was low land and mucky rather than sandy, the water did not run off quickly or become absorbed. Instead, it dropped to a one-inch cover and remained that way, releasing millions upon millions of mosquito eggs attached to the grass, dormant eggs that would incubate quickly in the intense heat and turn into larvae. Each invisible larva would eat and breathe for four days, and after shedding its skin four times, become a pupa. At this stage it discontinued eating and changed rapidly, and in another two days its skin split, allowing an adult mosquito to pull itself out and dry its wings in preparation for flight. No one in the camp was aware of this natural chain of events taking place across the tranquil marsh.

Zech was at the river alone, fishing, when he felt the stinging on his neck and arms. He slapped vigorously, then he waved his hand back and forth across his face. "Skeeters," he mumbled as he threw down the cane pole and then mounted Ishmael.

Tobias and Skillit were with the herd, puzzled by the faint humming sound drifting across the marsh from the north. Then they saw it, a solid black cloud extending from the ground thirty feet upward, moving toward them. As they watched, other clouds formed in the west and in the south.

Skillit said, "What is it, Mistuh Tobias? Is it locusts? I've heard of a locust swarm but I've never seen one."

"Whatever it is, I got a feeling it ain't good. We might need some help with the cows."

Tobias glanced toward the river and saw Zech enter a cloud and disappear momentarily, then emerge in a full gallop. He said "I don't know what's happening, Skillit, but I think we best get out of here."

Before they could turn the horses, the stinging came, setting their bodies on fire. Tobias looked down and his legs were covered solidly by mosquitoes. His horse bolted straight upward and crashed down on its side, struggling and kicking, trying to regain its footing.

Tobias felt the breath go out of his lungs, and for a moment he couldn't move. He brushed feebly at his body as he heard Skillit's horse whinny loudly and start bucking. He also heard frantic bellowing come from the herd.

Cows were bucking, kicking, and falling all around him as Zech raced across the marsh. As soon as a cow hit the ground mosquitoes swarmed over it and formed a solid mass in its mouth and nose, blocking air from its lungs, causing the cow's eyes to pop out as it tried to bellow but could not do so.

Tobias finally jumped to his feet, grabbed the horse and mounted. The horse spun around and around, snorting, trying to force the obstruction from its nose; then it gained control if itself and ran blindly.

Emma and Pearlie Mae were frozen with fear as they looked out over the marsh and watched the cows running wildly in circles, jumping and falling, repeating the frenzied cycle again and again. Emma saw Tobias go down and become engulfed in blackness. She screamed at Frog, "What's happening out there? What is it?"

Frog slapped his arms and legs, and then he said, "It's skeeters, Miz Emma! Solid skeeters! We got to leave here right away! Run for the prairie! Go as fast as you can! I'll bring the horses and the oxen!"

Zech pounded his boots into Ishmael's side, forcing him to run through the swarming mass as swiftly as possible, feeling mosquitoes pound into his face like rain. He could not see ahead and only hoped he was heading in the direction of the prairie.

Skillit stopped briefly and looked back at the spot where Tobias went down, seeing nothing. He scooped a handful of the humming bodies from his left arm, crushed them and released them, and the bloody pulp poured downward like wild honey. His horse stumbled but didn't go down; then he galloped full speed to the east.

Pearlie Mae fell constantly, her short, overweight body crashing into the bushes, and each time she could hear Emma scream, "Get up and run, Pearlie Mae! You have to!"

The mosquitoes followed them two miles into the prairie until a brisk east wind blew them back toward the marsh. No one was together except Emma and Pearlie Mae, and their bodies were stinging too badly for them to even wonder about the others. They sat on the ground rubbing themselves, scratching the welts and making them itch even worse. Emma's eyes were almost swollen shut when she heard Tobias' voice above her, "Emma. Are you all right? Have you seen any of the others?"

He then sat with her as everyone gradually came together, mutually miserable, their bodies angry red, the horses wild-eyed and still bucking but alive. All of them were dazed, and they huddled together silently until Tobias finally said, "Don't nobody go back there. We'll stay the night here. Then I'll go in the morning and see if it's safe."

"What about food?" Emma asked.

"We'll do without."

Zech climbed down from his horse and retched violently. Emma looked to him and said, "I'm sorry, Zech. There's nothing I can do to help you."

"It ain't nothing, Mamma," Zech said. "I'll be fine in a few minutes. I just got a belly full of skeeters and they ain't sittin' well. I must have swallowed a gallon of 'em."

"Don't worry none about vittles, Miz Emma," Frog said. "I couldn't work my jaws even for soup. Feels like ever bone in my body is broke and on fire."

"The cows," Tobias said, scratching continuously. "Ain't no way they could run away from it as fast as the horses, and the horses almost didn't make it. I purely hate to see what's happened to them."

"Maybe they got away," Skillit said. "But if they did, they'll be scattered all over. We'll have to start the roundup all over again."

Tobias went back to the wagon alone at daybreak, taking each step apprehensively, dreading what he might find. When he reached the marsh he saw that he no longer had a herd as such. Cows were scattered across the marsh as far as he could see, and there were many lifeless forms. Mosquitoes were still there, but not in mass as the day before.

He returned to the prairie and led the others back; then the men rode into the basin while Emma and Pearlie Mae prepared food. They counted seventy-three dead cows, and there were also bodies of rabbits, raccoons, and foxes. The swift deer seemed to have escaped the death cloud.

Tobias looked sadly at the carnage, and then he said, "It don't seem to be no end to the pestilence this land can bring. Sometimes I think the Lord is warning us to go away."

"We been through worse than this," Skillit said, "and come out of it on our feet. And I don't think the Lord would turn skeeters loose on a bunch of po' cows. It must 'a been the devil instead."

"Somebody did, and the Book says everthing is the work of the Lord. If it is, I hope He gets done soon with punishing us. I don't even know what we done to make Him so mad."

"I don't either," Skillit said, "but I knows one thing. The Lord ain't going to help us round up the cows. We'll have to see to it ourselves."

Tobias looked up and watched the flights of buzzards that already circled the marsh. He said, "Soon as the sun gets to boring down real good, this whole place is going to smell pure awful. We better work fast and get away from here as quick as we can."

*I*t took them two days to bring the herd together again. Some of the cows had run as far as five miles, and all of them remained spooked and jittery. The loss of blood also made them sluggish, and some had mouths swollen so badly they couldn't eat.

When they crossed the river and headed away from the salt marsh, the path for three miles was littered with the bloodless bodies of small animals. Buzzards were everywhere, flapping off in protest as the cows passed, then returning immediately.

Tobias knew it would take time and grass for the cows to regain their strength, so they let them wander slowly. The rain caused the prairie grass to come back to life and flourish, and they found good grazing. Day by day they drifted across the land lazily, like a summer cloud; and soon the welts and the memories faded away.

The two riders first appeared as black specks on the horizon. They were moving north, and then they turned west toward the herd. They rode marshtackies like Ishmael, but used no saddles.

Skillit was on the left flank of the herd, and they reached him first. Both of them were boys, ages fifteen and seventeen, and were Seminoles. Each carried a lancewood spear.

One of them said, "We are looking for a man named Tobias MacIvey. Could this be his herd?"

"You've found him," Skillit said, wondering why they would be out on the vast prairie on such a search. "He's the man right over yonder, just in front of the wagon. How long you boys been lookin' for him?"

"We went first to his hammock," the older boy said, "and no one was there. Since then we have been riding for two weeks. We thought he would be somewhere grazing a herd."

"You just lucky," Skillit said. "This is a mighty big place. You could have rode them hosses till winter and not found us. How come you lookin' for him?"

"We were sent by my grandfather. But it is not so hard as you think to find a herd. It is not like looking for just one cow. We have crossed the prairies many times and know them well, and we have also been at the MacIvey hammock once before."

"If you say so." As they turned the horses and rode away Skillit muttered, "Now when was them Indian boys ever at Mistuh Tobias' place?"

When they reached Tobias, the older boy said, "Tobias MacIvey?"

"Yes, that's me," Tobias replied, wondering also why the boys were out on the prairie.

"I am James Tiger, and this is Willie Cypress. We were sent to find you by my grandfather, Keith Tiger."

"Sure, I know Keith Tiger. I haven't seen him for a while now. How is he?"

"Not too good. That is why we are here. The long drought has dried up many ponds and streams, and most of the animals have died or gone away. We have no hides to use in trade. We also have no bullets left for the rifle, and there is little food in our village. My grandfather wishes to buy a few cows from you. He has no money now, but he will pay you as soon as he can."

"I don't care about the pay," Tobias said. "I'm just sorry to hear you're in such a fix. How many cows you want?"

"Just a few to get us by until the animals return. Whatever you can spare."

"How about a dozen? Will that be enough?"

"We did not expect so much," the boy said, surprised by the generous offer. "We were thinking of maybe four at the most. A dozen would be more than my people hoped for."

"Twelve cows ain't nothing," Tobias said. "Let's ride over there and I'll get Skillit and Frog to cut out a dozen of the best ones we got. We had some trouble a few weeks back and the cows ain't as fat as they ought to be. But they're coming along fine now."

"This will be a real help for my people, and my grandfather will be pleased. But there is one thing you must know. We do not come to you as beggars. My grandfather will repay you for this."

"Don't worry about it. Whatever he does is fine with me."

They followed Tobias over to Skillit, and after he instructed Skillit what to do, Tobias said, "How long you boys been out here looking for me?"

"Three weeks in all. Two since we left your hammock."

"How you been getting vittles with only them sticks?"

"We have eaten mostly rabbit."

"Then you need some of Emma's cooking. I know how tired a

man can get of eating nothing but coons or rabbits. You can stay with us tonight and fill your bellies and then leave in the morning."

Zech rode up and stopped a few feet away, staring curiously at the marshtackies and the riders. James Tiger looked at Ishmael and said, "Your horse and mine are brothers. The mother is dead now, and the stallion old, but we have others."

"Are you the ones who left Ishmael at the hammock?" Zech asked.

"It was my grandfather, Keith Tiger. But we were with him. Is that the name you gave the horse, Ishmael?"

"Pappa named him. I think he got the name from something your granddaddy once told him about the Indians."

"I know the word." James Tiger then asked, "Do you still have the wolf dogs?"

"No. They're both dead. They was shot by bushwhackers who rustled some cows from us. We named them Nip and Tuck. They were the best dogs I ever seen."

"I'm sorry to hear that. It is a cruel man who would bushwhack dogs. We will give you others to replace them. This time they will be leopard dogs."

"What's that?" Zech asked, his mind bringing forth the vision of a dog shaped like a panther.

"They are part hound and part bulldog, and they fear nothing. I have seen two of them kill a bear."

"Nip and Tuck could do it too. They wasn't afraid of anything. They once ran into a whole pack of wolves and tore one's throat open."

"Yes, wolf dogs are like that. We have no more of that kind. But you will like the leopards. They are fine dogs too."

Tobias said, "You boys could go on jawing with each other all afternoon. Zech, take them to the wagon and get some smoked beef to hold them till supper. And tell Emma to pull up at the next stand. We'll go on and stop for the day so she can fix them a whole washtub of stew."

182

After supper Zech and the Indian boys rode across the prairie, talking constantly about horses and dogs and hunting and the great cypress swamp where the Seminoles lived. Even Ishmael seemed to enjoy the company of the other marshtackies as he pranced lively alongside of them.

Zech said to James Tiger, "If you wanted a few cows, how come you didn't just go out on the prairie and round up some 'stead of coming so far to find us?"

"We are not allowed to do this," Tiger responded. "We are not supposed to even own a cow anymore, and there are men who would do us great harm if we took them off the prairie. They would say we are stealing, although the cows have no marks on them. It is best that we have cows with your mark. That way, no one can say that we stole them."

"It still don't make sense to me," Zech said. "Wild cows are no different from deer. They belong to whoever takes them."

"That is not so in our case. Many of our people have been beaten and even hanged for having just one cow. It is dangerous for us to drive your cows back to the swamp, but we have no choice. Our people suffer from hunger and have great need of the meat."

Zech said, "I'll ask Pappa if I can leave the herd and help you drive the cows to your village. Three of us would be better than two, and nobody would bother us for driving cows with the MacIvey mark."

"I thank you, but we can manage. Your father would have need of you with such a large herd, and we'll be safe once we reach the south shore of Okeechobee. From there our people will help us."

When they returned to the camp Zech lay on his blanket wide awake, thinking of the things James Tiger told him, wondering why anyone would kill an Indian over a few scrub cows when they were numerous everywhere. He could also not comprehend some people denying the Indians the right to even own a cow.

None of it made sense to him, and he felt a deep sympathy for James Tiger and Willie Cypress and all the others who suffered hunger because of what he could only see as gross stupidity and greed. Even the animals were willing to share if it meant survival for all.

He was saddened at dawn when the two Seminoles left, and he watched after them until horses and cows disappeared behind a distant cypress stand. He hoped their paths would cross again someday.

*F*or four more weeks they stayed on the prairie, going wherever there was grass; then Tobias rode ahead and purchased cows that were added to the herd. By the time they reached the Caloosahatchie River the herd numbered over three thousand.

The price this time was twelve dollars per cow, and once again a steamer trunk was purchased to carry the sacks of gold doubloons.

As Tobias was leaving the store, the clerk called to him, "Mister MacIvey, I almost forgot to mention this. We just got in a shipment from New Orleans that might be of interest to you."

"What's that?" Tobias asked.

"Come on in the storeroom and I'll show you. We haven't even put them out yet."

The clerk took a crowbar and pried open a wooden crate; then he removed a rifle and handed it to Tobias. "It's the new Winchester repeater," he said. "You put the bullets in this magazine under the barrel and it'll shoot as fast as you pump the lever."

Tobias turned the rifle over in his hands, examining the octagon barrel; then he sighted it. "How many times will it shoot?"

"Seventeen bullets per load. Most all the cattlemen who've come in lately have heard about it and asked could we get them in stock. They say rustling and bushwhacking is really getting bad everywhere. One man had three drovers killed up south of Arcadia, shot in the back, and a whole herd stole. This rifle ought to could settle a rustler's hash in nothing flat."

"I expect it could," Tobias said, clicking the lever as fast as he could pump it. "I just hope the rustlers don't get ahold of these things first. We done had a little taste of bushwhacking ourselves. They killed both our dogs and winged one of my men. How much do the rifles sell for?"

"Fifty dollars each."

"That's a mite steep, ain't it?"

"Well, not really. If you've got a single shot rifle, owning one of these is like having seventeen single shot guns all loaded and ready to go at once. And you're not paying near as much for this Winchester as you would seventeen single shooters."

"I see what you mean." Tobias counted on his fingers, and then he said, "I'll take seven of them."

"How many?"

"Seven. One for everybody in my crew, including the women. Next time anyone in my bunch gets bushwhacked we'll make some butts sing with guns like this."

"That you will. How much ammunition you want?"

"How does it come?"

"Twenty-four bullets to a box, twelve boxes to a case."

"I'll take four cases. That ought to do us for a while, including practice. We'll have to learn how to operate these things. It sure beats my old one-shooter."

"I'll have everything ready when you come back with the wagon."

Tobias hesitated for a moment, and then he said, "Make that nine rifles instead of seven, and two more cases of bullets. I've got some friends down in Indian country who can make good use of guns like these. You got saddle holsters to fit the Winchesters?"

"Yes, we have them."

"I'll need five. I'll be back with the wagon in about a half hour and pick all this stuff up."

*Z*ech held the rifle proudly, sighting it and then pumping the lever, pulling the trigger and making the hammer click again and again.

Tobias watched him for a moment, and then he said, "You ought not be doing that, Zech. It's bad on the firing pin. Don't ever pull the trigger on an empty gun."

"Can I put some bullets in it?"

"You better wait till we get out of town. That thing could blow a hole in the dock if you accidentally shot it that way. Let's go on out to the camp first and pay everbody off, then you can fire it."

"I wouldn't be afraid to face a whole pack of bears with this rifle," Zech said, putting it into the holster. "It's the purtiest gun I've ever seen. I sure thank you for it, Pappa."

"You just be careful with it," Tobias cautioned. "One of them things can fire as many shots as a whole army squad used to could. It ain't no play toy. You got to handle it like a man."

"I will, Pappa. I'll be real careful. Soon as we get to the camp I'll fire off a few rounds and see how it works."

Emma popped the reins and started the oxen, and the men followed her. Skillit held the Winchester in his hands, pretending to shoot from the saddle.

As they passed one of the holding pens Tobias suddenly froze in the saddle. He stopped his horse and gazed intensely at the herd. Three of the cows closest to him had the mark MCI on their sides. Then he noticed others had the same mark.

He shouted, "Hold up, Emma! Stop for a minute!"

Skillit and Zech came to him, and Zech said, "What's the matter, Pappa?"

186

"Look yonder," Tobias said, pointing. "Look at the brand on them cows."

"It's ourn," Skillit said, puzzled. "How come you reckon they in there? We didn't lose no cows out on the prairie for somebody to find."

"No, we didn't. Let's see what this is all about."

Four men were standing at the gate, and one of them Tobias recognized as a counter for Captain Hendry. The others he had never seen before.

Zech, Skillit, Frog and Bonzo followed Tobias as Emma looked back from the wagon, perplexed by what was happening. Tobias stopped just short of the huddle of men and said, "Who owns this herd?"

"I do," one of the men said. He was the same age as Tobias, lanky too, with a bushy black beard. "How come you want to know?"

"My name's Tobias MacIvey. Captain Hendry knows me well, as do others in Punta Rassa. Some of them cows in there has my mark. Where'd you get 'em?"

"Oh, that," the man said, cautiously eyeing the mounted riders facing him. "Is it the ones with MCI?"

"That's my brand."

"I got a dozen of them. If they're yours, you can have 'em. I ain't got no use for some other man's cows. I just didn't know who they belonged to."

"Where'd you get 'em?" Tobias demanded again.

"Took 'em off some rustlers, over near Okeechobee."

"What kind of rustlers?"

"The worst kind. Indians. Them thieves will steal anything they can get their hands on."

"Were they men or boys?"

"Boys. Seems like they're starting real young nowdays."

"What did you do to the boys?" Tobias then asked apprehensively.

"We hung 'em."

"You what?"

"We hung 'em," the man repeated. "That's the only way you can teach Indians a lesson. If you don't they'll do it over and over again, and there won't be no end to it."

"I gave them the cows!" Tobias roared, his face crimson red, his hands trembling. "They were my cows, and I gave them to them! You killed them boys for nothing!"

Zech leaped from his horse and spilled bullets over the ground as he tried desperately to load the rifle, shouting, "I'll kill 'em, Pappa! I'll shoot every one of them!"

He was on his knees, snatching bullets from the dust, when Skillit grabbed him and threw him back into the saddle, holding the rifle away from him.

Captain Hendry's man started backing away hurriedly, and before any of the men could go for a gun, hammers cocked as Frog and Bonzo aimed Winchesters at them.

Tobias said harshly, "You stay out of this, Zech! I'll handle it! I should of sent someone with the boys 'stead of laying them wide open to vultures like these!"

"What you aim to do?" one of the men asked, backing up against the fence. "How was we to know they didn't steal the cows? They was marked, and we knew it wasn't no mark of a Indian."

"I ain't going to kill you like you done them boys," Tobias said, dismounting, "but I'm going to make you wish I did." He snatched the whip from his saddlebag and unfurled it. "I'm going to rawhide you till you ain't got one piece of skin left on you. Frog, if one of them tries to run away from it, you and Bonzo shoot him right betwix the eyes."

"Yes, sir, Mister MacIvey. We'll do that."

The whip cracked, and the nearest man fell to the ground, cringing. Then it cracked again and again, spraying the air with cloth fiber mixed with blood. Tobias slashed frantically until finally Skillit grabbed his arm and shouted, "That's enough,

Mistuh Tobias! If you wants to kill 'em, do it with a gun, not a whip! They gone suffer plenty from what you done already! I know! It remind me of what happened to me! Shoot 'em, but don't beat 'em to death!"

Tobias stopped, his eyes glazed, his heart pounding, then finally he said, "You're right, Skillit. I done enough. Go in there and cut out our cows. I'll go to the wagon and wait. I don't want to even look at this vermin again."

One of the men tried to stand, then he dropped back to his knees, his shirt and trousers in tatters. He said feebly, "We'll get you for this, mister. It ain't ended yet."

"You know my name," Tobias said calmly. "It's MacIvey. And if you're interested, I live over on the Kissimmcee. You're welcome to come to my place anytime you want to, but if I ever lay eyes on you again I'll kill you on sight. That's a promise, not a threat. Just keep that in mind next time you decide to lynch a couple of boys, or come looking for me." With that he mounted and rode to the wagon.

$\mathcal{T}$obias was still trembling with anger as he counted out the coins and handed them to Frog and Bonzo. He said to Skillit, "You want me to leave your share with the rest till we get back to the hammock?"

"That'll be fine. We can split it up then. What we goin' to do with these other cows? You want to sell 'em here or take 'em back with us?"

"Neither. They'll end up where them boys was taking them. I'll drive 'em myself."

Emma was standing nearby, listening, watching Tobias and hoping the anger would subside. She said, "Tobias, you don't even know where the Indians live. How can you hope to find them?"

"I know," Tobias said. "Keith Tiger once told me if I ever have need of them to come to the far side of the Okeechobee and head south. They'll find me, not me find them."

"But you don't even know where the lake is," Emma insisted.

"They said it's so big I can't miss it."

Emma knew that to argue or reason with him was fruitless, that he was determined to do this thing. She said, "At least take someone with you."

Tobias turned to Frog and said, "What you and Bonzo intend to do now? You going to take some time off before going back to the hammock?"

"We'll do whatever you want us to," Frog replied. "Bonzo has been feeling poorly, so we're not going anywhere. When he turns down a drinking spell you know he ain't up to snuff."

"What's the matter with you?" Tobias said to Bonzo.

"I don't know, Mister MacIvey. Sometimes I feel like my bones is all cracked, and I been having some sweating spells. But it ain't nothing to worry about. I'll be O.K. after I rest up a few days."

"Well, you take it easy if you don't feel good. You and Frog best ride on back with the others. I'll take Zech with me."

"I'll go too if you need me," Skillit said.

"Naw, that ain't necessary. Me and Zech can handle it. And besides, if bushwhackers is getting as bad as they say, all of you need to stay close to the wagon."

"How long you think you'll be gone?" Emma asked, relieved that he was at least taking Zech with him.

"It ought not take as much as two weeks. We'll come straight back after we find the Indians. But I purely dread what I'll have to say to Keith Tiger, if he don't already know."

🐂

Rather than setting out blindly, Tobias decided to go into Punta Rassa and talk to Captain Hendry concerning the location of Okeechobee. He was told that the Caloosahatchie flows from the lake's western shore; thus he could follow the river to its source and then turn south toward the great swamp. From this general description of its location, Tobias figured that on one of their grazing drives they had come to within twenty miles or so of the lake's north shore without knowing it.

Captain Hendry also warned him that the land south of the lake was virtually unknown, a wilderness not yet penetrated except by Indians. He thought such a journey as Tobias proposed was foolhardy, but he made no headway in trying to dissuade him.

It was early the next morning when Tobias and Zech departed from the others at the ferry landing. Emma said a fearful good-bye, imploring Tobias to abandon the drive and turn back if the trip became too dangerous. Skillit offered once again to go with them but was refused.

The area along the river was heavily wooded, so they moved outward and chose a path parallel to a marsh, giving them more control over the cattle. This time they did not let the cows set the pace, wandering slowly, but grazed them for an hour at a time and then moved forward at a steady pace.

Zech noticed that several times during the next two days Tobias slumped forward in the saddle as if in pain, and this perplexed and worried him. Always before Tobias had been alert and attentive to the cattle, but sometimes now he seemed to drift along aimlessly without giving his horse directions. When Zech rode to him and questioned him, Tobias snapped back to alertness, assuring him that he had merely dozed for a moment because of the intense heat. Once at night Zech heard him groaning in his sleep, and when he went to him, Tobias was drenched with sweat.

On the fourth day they struck the western shore of Okee-chobee, marveling at the seemingly endless expanse of water before them. The shimmering surface stretched into the horizon and gave no hint of a distant shore. Vast areas of blooming pick-erel weed lined the water's edge, creating a sea of soft blue that merged gently with clumps of willows and little islands of button-bush with its creamy white flowers. Nearby rookeries exploded with birds, great blue herons and snowy egrets, white herons and wood ibises, whooping cranes and anhingas with their wings spread outward to dry them. Cormorants dived beneath the surface and popped up unexpectedly fifty feet away, startling flocks of ducks and coot that peppered the surface. Majestic roseate spoonbills stalked up and down the shallows, swishing their long paddle bills from side to side as they raked the bottom in search of food, their pink feathers catching the sunlight and making them appear even pinker.

Zech insisted they stop for a day or two and let the cattle graze on the abundant grass, but he was more interested in rest for his father than food for the cows. Tobias agreed reluctantly, want-ing to push on immediately, but in his weakened condition he allowed himself to be overruled.

After making camp beneath a thick covering of alders, they walked back to the shore and watched the unfamiliar sights with fascination, seeing an endless parade of nature's creatures. Willows were so loaded with chattering red-winged blackbirds that it seemed the tree limbs would surely break, and fish were so plentiful their fins cut the calm surface with constant ripples.

Zech took his fishing line from the saddlebag, cut a cane pole, and caught crickets for bait; and in only moments he caught more black bass and catfish than they could hope to eat. On the way back to the camp he gathered figs from a thick grove of wild trees, and for supper they had fish roasted over an open fire, followed by the sugary fruit.

That night the eerie call of limpkins blended with the croaking of bullfrogs and the grunting of alligators, forming a strange type of music never heard out on the prairie. Tobias moved closer to the warming fire and said, "I'm glad we stopped here, Zech. I've never seen a place so full of life. Not even back in the scrub. I can see now why some of the Indians that ran off from here hid in the swamps, hoping to come back someday. I hope they can, but I got a notion they won't. When folks find out what's here they'll take it over, and you won't ever again see an Indian on this lake's shore. Maybe someday we can come back and see it all."

"I sure hope so. James Tiger told me there can be waves out there taller than a man, and at some places there's sand dunes like at the ocean. He also told me that the sun sucks water from the lake, and it'll drop down several inches during the day, and then during the night it'll come right back to where it was. I'd sure like to see that too."

"Maybe someday," Tobias said again. "But right now I think I'll sleep. I feel kinda tired all through and through, like a worc-out old ox."

"You ain't old at all, Pappa. But you get some rest. I'll stay up tonight and take care of the cows."

*T*wo days stretched into three, and Tobias gained strength from the fresh fish, wild fruits and berries. On the morning of the third day they broke camp and continued the drive, skirting the rim of the lake, but when they rounded the western shore and attempted to head directly south, they were met by a stretch of sawgrass with blades so sharp it prohibited the entrance of cows, men, and horses.

At this point they turned to the southwest and entered a custard-apple forest, a jungle unlike anything they had ever encountered. Trees were so dense they formed a barrier almost as impenetrable as the sawgrass. The sky was blocked out immediately by leafy branches completely covered by a solid blanket of moon vines, turning a bright noonday sun to dim twilight.

The cows walked single file to make their way through the wall of trunks, and there was no way to drive them in a straight line. They skirted masses of dead limbs long since blown down by hurricanes, and gourd vines looping from branch to branch formed a curtain of green fruit. Trees were peppered with air plants that blossomed with brilliant red and orange flowers, and the ground beneath was totally bare except for lush beds of ferns, some ground level and others as tall as the horses.

The forest also teemed with Carolina parakeets as numerous as were the blackbirds at the lake, and low-hanging limbs were anchored to the ground by giant spiderwebs. Once Zech threw a stick into one of the webs in a useless attempt to break through; it sang like violin strings and held fast, causing the huge brown and yellow spiders to rush forward and examine the captured missile.

Every foot of the way was blocked by something: trunks, tangling vines, webs, grotesque outcroppings of roots. They turned, zigzagged and backtracked, popping the whips and cursing the bewildered cows, moving tortuously through an atmosphere so murky they couldn't determine if they were heading south or north; and in one four-hour stretch they traveled less than a mile.

There was no sunset that afternoon beneath the solid roof of the jungle, only a fleeting moment when twilight turned to instant darkness. Zech built a fire and they huddled together, hearing the chilling cry of sentinel hawks and the mournful song of whippoorwills. Screech owls then joined the chorus, making the cows also come together in a tight circle. Zech suggested time and again they turn back and seek another way, but each time Tobias shook his head in disagreement.

It was impossible to tell when dawn came, and when finally a dim yellow light drifted down through the vines, it could as well have been noon as mid-morning. They moved again, repeating the experience of the previous day, turning, twisting, and probing, mile after mile of the same frustration. Even Tobias now worried about the cows and horses since there was nothing for them to eat but ferns. He hoped the lacy outgrowths were not poisonous.

Another night was spent beneath the canopy, then another morning vainly searching for an escape route. Just when they both became resigned to the fact that they were hopelessly trapped, they broke free at mid-afternoon and entered a marsh. The cows and horses grazed ravenously, and Tobias agreed to stop for the night.

After building a fire Zech walked back to the edge of the forest. He stepped gingerly onto the moon vines and jumped up and down, finding the green carpet to be as solid as a bed. Then he walked upward slowly, a step at a time, until he reached the top of the trees and stood on the jungle's roof.

The vines stretched away as far as he could see, like a verdant plain splotched with blooming white flowers. He walked forward, at first cautiously and then with confidence, traveling a hundred yards before turning back reluctantly, wishing he could retrace the entire distance they had come but knowing he should return to Tobias.

As he made his way down the leafy incline and onto solid ground again, he trembled with excitement, feeling he now had a newfound secret not to be shared, like a baby eagle no longer earthbound, drunk with the exhilaration of its first flight.

The thrill of the experience carried over past supper and into the night, and as they moved away at dawn, Zech looked back with both fear and joy at the giant tent nature had created over forest.

The marsh dissipated rapidly, and then they came to the edge of the place they were seeking: the great cypress swamp. At first the land was peppered with small dwarf cypress and pond

cypress; then suddenly there loomed before them the mighty
virgin bald cypress trees themselves, reaching up to a hundred
and fifty feet into the air, some with bases seventy feet in circum-
ference.

Cypress knees sprang up all around the base of the trees, like
giant mushrooms, some shaped like deformed human heads,
some like birds, others like small animals, creating a wooden
menagerie. Wild orchids clung to every limb, turning the somber
trees into colorbursts of yellow and white and green and purple.
There were also gumbo-limbo trees, lancewoods, cocoplum bushes, oaks festooned with Spanish moss; and the awesome magno-
lias with leaf-covered limbs reaching sixty feet outward and then
downward to the ground, like a mother hen protecting her brood
with a covering of wing feathers. Piercing all of it were royal palms
whose bare trunks towered above some of the bald cypress,
forming little umbrellas of fronds high in the sky.

At first they stopped and stared, comparing the giant bald
cypress to the little matchsticks that formed cypress stands on the
prairie; then they moved forward again.

The ground was dry, but they could see watermarks several
inches up the cypress knees where water normally reached. They
passed easily over dry sloughs that once would have to be forded,
and skirted around ponds covered solidly with lily pads and green
slime. Cottonmouth moccasins scurried away beneath the surface
and left trail marks, and the snouts of alligators poked upward like
dead logs, their eyes open and blank as the intruders passed by.

They were also greeted by hordes of mosquitoes, not a solid
mass like the cloud at the salt marsh, but a constant annoyance.
Zech and Tobias both slapped and scratched, wondering how the
Indians who lived here could stand it.

They could see areas on the bases of the trees where panthers
scratched the bark to shreds sharpening their claws, and the horses stepped around holes rooted out by wild hogs searching for
food. The deeper they penetrated the swamp, the thicker became

the trees and other foliage, until finally they faced obstacles almost as formidable as the custard-apple forest.

Once again they zigzagged and backtracked, searching for open paths, having difficulty controlling the cows. Zech was doubly worried, wondering if there was no end to this alien land, and also noticing Tobias slumping forward in the saddle, sweat pouring from his face and staining his shirt. He did not believe there was even a bare possibility of finding the Indian village in such an overwhelming swamp, that to continue was foolish and useless; but Tobias would not give up and turn back.

For two days they passed no pond or stream where the water looked drinkable, and at night they rationed themselves to one cup from the canteens. Supper was limited to a thin twist of dried beef and rock-hard biscuit.

On the third night in the swamp they were sitting by a fire, hoping the smoke would drive away the mosquitoes, when a man stepped from the shadows and confronted them. He was dressed in a multicolored shirt that came down to his knees, deerskin trousers, moccasins, deerskin leggings, and a crossed finger-woven sash with long fringes. From his neck downward over his chest hung a georgette fashioned from silver coins hammered thin, and on his head he wore a turban crowned by an egret plume.

Both Zech and Tobias were startled, and both scrambled to their feet as the man said, "Do not be frightened. I bear no arms, not even a spear. We have known you were coming this way since you left the custard-apple forest."

Tobias calmed himself, and then he said, "My name is Tobias MacIvey, and this is my son, Zech. We're looking for the village of Keith Tiger."

"I am Tony Cypress, father of Willie Cypress. We know who you are. I will come back at daybreak and lead you to the village. Your cattle would become lost in the darkness if you followed me now."

"How do you know who I am?" Tobias questioned, puzzled.

"We trust no one, and we watch intruders. You were described today to Keith Tiger and he said it would be Tobias MacIvey. He does not understand why you drive cattle into the swamp."

"Do you know what has happened to your son and James Tiger?" Tobias asked cautiously.

"They were sent to find you and buy cattle, but they have not returned. We sent runners searching for them as far as the south shore of Okeechobee but did not find them. Do you have news of them?"

Tobias dared not tell of the hanging to Tony Cypress alone, fearing the reaction. He would feel safer telling the news to a friend. He said, "We have seen them, and we can talk of this tomorrow with you and Keith Tiger. There's no need to discuss it now."

"Do you have food?"

"Not much, but enough to do us for now."

"I will return at daybreak. Watch your cows closely. Since the deer are scarce the panthers are hungry and will attack anything. Do not let your fire go out." The Indian then stepped backward and disappeared into the darkness.

Zech threw more sticks onto the fire and watched as a stream of sparks drifted upward, glowing briefly like fireflies. Then he took the Winchester from his saddle holster and placed it beside his blanket. He said, "Pappa, what are we going to do if they blame us for what happened to James and Willie?"

"I been thinking about that too. Fact is, I thought about it all the way down here and I don't have an answer yet. I just don't really know. We'll have to wait and see what happens. If I were Tony Cypress, and it was you hung instead of Willie, I'm not sure myself what I'd do."

There were a dozen chickees in the village, small open-sided huts constructed of cypress poles with roofs of thatched palmetto fronds and bear grass. Beneath one a black cooking pot was tended by an old woman stirring constantly with a wooden paddle. All of the men were dressed similar to Tony Cypress, and the women wore multicolored ankle-length dresses with a dozen strands of glass beads around their necks. On top of each one's head was a tight ball of hair held fast by black netting.

At the fringe of the clearing there were several clumps of banana trees and a small garden plot containing wilted tomato plants, okra, squash and corn that had turned brown prematurely from lack of rain.

Everyone in the village watched curiously as the cows invaded the clearing and milled about. Tobias and Zech rode in and dismounted and then followed Tony Cypress to one of the chickees.

Keith Tiger was sitting on the ground, and when he looked up and recognized the visitors, he motioned for them to sit with him. He looked older than Tobias remembered, and his hair was now completely white. Tobias said, "It's good to see you again, Keith Tiger."

"And you too, Tobias," he answered, a smile creasing his face. "I am told by Tony Cypress that you bring news of my grandson and Willie Cypress."

"Yes, I do, but first there are other things," Tobias said, wanting to delay the inevitable as long as possible. "The cattle are for your people, and we have brought gifts. Go and get them, Zech."

Zech went to the horses and returned in a moment, placing boxes on the ground and handing two rifles to Tobias. He passed them on to Keith Tiger and said, "These are Winchester repeat-ers, a rifle that shoots seventeen times in one load. We also brought two cases of bullets, enough to last you for a long time."

Tiger examined one of the rifles and passed the other to Tony Cypress. "I have never seen such as this," he said. "How does it work?"

"You just put the bullets in the magazine under the barrel, and when you pull the lever a bullet goes into the chamber. It shoots as fast as you pump the lever till all the bullets are gone. It will bring down a deer easily at a hundred yards and more."

Tiger stroked the stock with his hand, saying, "This will be a great help to us, and I thank you, Tobias. The bow and arrow is almost useless in the swamp. You shoot at a deer and hit vines or trees instead. It is not like hunting on the open prairie. For here we need guns and bullets. This weapon will provide much food."

"Maybe you can shoot skeeters with it too," Tobias said jokingly, pleased by the reaction to the gift. "I don't see how you folks stand it all the time."

"We have grown used to them," Tiger responded. "There are many things we have been forced to learn since hiding here in the swamp. When our people lived on the land that is now Tallahassee, the soil there grew corn and beans and squash and pumpkins in abundance. Here things do not grow so well. It is the same with hunting. When there is no rain the swamp dries up and animals go elsewhere, and when there is great rain it floods, also driving them away or drowning them. There is always something facing us we must overcome. It has been difficult, but we have survived. But tell me now. Why is it that you drive in the cattle instead of James and Willie? What is your news of them?"

Tobias knew he could delay no longer. He spoke slowly, recounting the chain of events in his mind. "They found us on a prairie north of the Caloosahatchie and explained their mission. They spent the night in our camp and left at daybreak the next morning. Zech offered to ride with them and help drive the cattle but was refused. They said they could handle it alone, and that was the last we saw of them.

"It was several weeks before we reached Punta Rassa with the herd. As we left the village I saw cows with my mark on them in another man's herd. I questioned him about this, and he said he took them from rustlers down close to Okeechobee. Then I . . ."

Tiger broke in and asked anxiously, "If someone stole the

cattle from James and Willie, why did they not return here and tell us of this? Where are they now?"

"I asked them who the rustlers were," Tobias responded hesitantly, "and they told me it was two Indian boys. Then I asked what happened to the boys, and the man who owned the herd told me they hung them. They're dead, Keith. I told the men that I had given the cows to the boys and that they had hung them for no reason. Then I beat all of them with my whip, beat them almost to death. I'm real sorry to have to tell you this. Real sorry. I don't know what else to say."

Both Indian men sat stunned, mentally frozen, trying to accept the finality of the words. Keith Tiger's eyes misted as he said, "In my heart I feared this, but it hurts no less hearing it from you now. I hoped that somehow they would return. This is the end for me. They killed my son in the last war, and now my grandson. James was the only one left, and now there is no one to carry on my name. It is ended forever. It would be better if they would come and kill me also. I have no reason now to live."

Tony Cypress said angrily, "Do you know where the men live who did this thing? If you do, we will find them and kill them!"

"I was so mad I didn't even ask their names," Tobias responded. "After I beat them with the whip, they threatened to come after me later. They know where I live, and if they ever come to my place, I'll kill them myself. This I promise. I hope you don't blame me for what happened. If I had known I would have . . ." Tobias' voice trailed off, and he never finished. He stood up suddenly, staggered a few steps and fell.

Zech rushed to him. He shook him and said, "Pappa! Pappa! What is it? What's the matter?"

Tobias shivered as if cold, and sweat poured from his face. He tried to speak but couldn't; then his glazed eyes locked onto Zech's, begging for help.

Zech brushed sweat from his father's forehead; then he looked to Keith Tiger. "Please, somebody do something!"

Keith Tiger said, "When you came into the chickee I thought

201

Tobias looked ill. How long has he been this way?"

"Ever since we left Punta Rassa. I begged him to turn back but he wouldn't. He wanted to bring you the cows. Can you help him? Do you know what's wrong?"

Tiger put his hand on Tobias' forehead. "It is malaria. We have seen it many times." Then he turned to Tony Cypress. "Get the medicine man, and tell Lillie to bring blankets. Quickly! He is very sick."

"Don't let him die," Zech pleaded fearfully. "If I had known he was this sick I would have tied him with ropes and taken him home. Mamma could nurse him."

"Do not blame yourself for this," Tiger said, putting his arm around Zech, trying to calm him. "It would have happened no matter where he was. It is best he is here. The medicine man can help him more than anyone. He knows what to do. We will do all we can to save him."

The medicine man was in his fifties, tall and lean, with gray hair that came down to his shoulders. He wore a knee-length dress only, and around his neck there hung a deerskin pouch, the sacred medicine bag, a symbol of his power.

Zech watched constantly, hovering, asking questions that were ignored, becoming a nuisance, told time and again to move away but refusing to do so. A bubbling pot sat next to the chickee, brewing a deep red liquid made of roots and herbs and the bark of a gumbo-limbo tree. Lillie held the blankets tight around Tobias as the medicine man lifted him up and forced the brew down his throat. Then they packed his forehead with lily pads made cool with pond muck.

For a day and a night Zech circled the chickee like a wolf stalking a herd, until finally Keith Tiger came to him and said, "There is no need for you to do this. It will not help, and soon we will have two sick men instead of one. Go and get food and rest. Leave your father to the medicine man and Lillie. If there is a change we will tell you."

The old woman in the cooking chickee gave Zech a gourd bowl of sofkee. He went to the far side of the clearing and sat on a log alone, absently chewing the hot gruel. He was not aware that someone was beside him until she said, "Don't fret so. They will make your father well again. The medicine man has great power."

Zech put the bowl down and said, "I'm sorry. I didn't know you were here."

The girl was sixteen, slim and firm, with black hair that swirled down to her hips. She had a thin mouth, high cheekbones and oriental eyes, the look of pure Seminole. She said, "I am Tawanda Cypress. Willie was my brother."

Zech flushed with guilt when she said it, feeling uneasy, as if accused without the words being spoken. He said, "I'm sorry. I offered to ride with them but they wouldn't let me. If I had gone anyway, he would be here now."

"You don't know this to be true. It's possible they would have killed you too just for being with James and Willie. I don't judge you as I judge those men who did such a terrible thing."

Zech looked at her closer, noticing she was very pretty. Something was different about her, something he could not at once place, and then he realized what it was. He said, "The night James and Willie spent in our camp we rode the prairie together, and they told me many things about life here. You don't speak like they did or the others."

She smiled. "Does it show so much? I spent three months with a missionary and his wife who are camped west of here, near the ten thousand islands. They were teaching me to read and write, and I suppose I took up some of their ways of speaking. My father says someone among us should learn to write the white man's language, that it could be helpful someday, and he sent me there. They also instructed me in the Christian way, but I'm confused about that. I cannot understand why Christians kill for cattle."

"I can't answer that for you," Zech said. "I don't understand it myself. But not all white people are Christians, and not all white men will kill for a cow. My pappa would never do it, and I wouldn't either. Pappa almost beat those men to death for what they did, and I would have shot them for sure if Skillit hadn't grabbed me and taken my rifle."

"Can you read and write?"

"No. I've never had learning. Mamma can do it some, but Pappa can't. There's no time or use for such things on cattle drives. All you need to know is how to count heads and money."

"I'll go back soon and stay a while longer. Maybe someday I'll be able to teach you. Then we'll both know how."

"How come you're not afraid to stay with strangers?"

"I was at first. But they're very kind people, and they would never harm me. Their camp is also well hidden from others. Father came on it one day while hunting, and became friends."

"I guess I ought to go back now and see about Pappa," Zech said, starting to get up.

"You love him very much, don't you?"

"Yes. We've done things together ever since I can remember. We've seen some bad times, and he brought us through it. I don't know what me and Mamma would do without him."

"You can't help him now by getting in the way of the medicine man and Lillie. Let them do what they must do. Stay here with me for a while longer. I enjoy talking to you."

"I suppose you're right," Zech agreed, "but I can't help it. If we were at the house now Mamma would run me out with a broom. But I've never seen Pappa sick like this. It scares me."

"Would you like to see the great marsh?" she asked, trying to steer his mind to something besides Tobias. "I can show it to you."

"Is that the place James and Willie told me about? They said there is nothing else like it."

"Yes. We call it Pay-Hay-Okee, the River of Grass. It would be a shame for you not to see it while you're here. If we leave now there is time to go there and return before nightfall. I know the way well."

"Then let's do it. I'll stay out of the way for the rest of the afternoon. I think the medicine man wanted to put me in the cooking pot with that stuff he's brewing."

They walked to where Ishmael was tied, and when Zech picked up the saddle she said, "We don't need that. It's better without it."

"I'll put you on first, then get on behind you," Zech said, throwing aside the saddle.

"An Indian woman would never do such a thing," Tawanda said teasingly. "We ride behind the man, not in front."

"If that's the way you want, it's fine with me."

Zech leaped onto the horse, then he took her hand and pulled her up behind him. As they started out of the clearing she held on as tightly as possible. Zech followed her directions, and they rode deeper and deeper into the swamp, skirting islands of ferns taller than Ishmael, passing through myriad knees surrounding the giant trees. When finally they came to a narrow stream she said, "Stop here and tie the horse. We will go on in the canoe."

On the bank there was a long dugout cypress canoe and two thin poles. They pushed the canoe into the water; then Zech stood in front and Tawanda in the rear, and they poled the slim craft down the creek. At first it was tricky for Zech, and he almost lost his balance. Tawanda laughed at him until finally he gained confidence and pushed the canoe with ease.

The stream twisted and turned, sometimes just wide enough for the canoe to pass, and several times it led into small ponds covered with lily pads where turtles and alligators moved away as they glided by. Then suddenly the swamp ended, as if a line had been drawn to separate swamp from marsh, and looming before them was Pay-Hay-Okee, a land so overwhelming in its vastness it caused Zech to blink his eyes in wonderment.

Sawgrass stretched on and on, broken only by small island hammocks of hardwood trees and cabbage palms. Flights of egrets and herons drifted for miles, dwarfing what Zech had seen at

Okeechobee or elsewhere. He continued staring as Tawanda said, "You're one of the few people to ever see this besides an Indian. What do you think of it?"

"It seems like the whole world out there. How far does it go?"

"To the sea in the south. It is many days journey from here to the end of it, and it is very difficult pushing the canoe through the sawgrass. Sometimes the grass is taller than two men. When our people make the journey they push down the grass and sleep on it at night, and sometimes snakes crawl in with you. There are also many alligators out there, and crocodiles too."

"I'd like to cross it someday," Zech said. "Would you go with me and show me the way?"

"I would if you asked, but it is not a good place for women. We'll go a bit further now. Then we should turn back."

As they poled the canoe, Zech watched with interest as an Everglades kite glided over them, its huge wings extended, moving so slowly it seemed to be suspended in midair. Then a flight of small birds swooped in and harassed it, diving and pecking, until finally the kite shot downward into the sawgrass and disappeared.

The canoe sliced like a knife through the dense grass, and when Zech reached out and touched it with curiosity, blood oozed from cuts on his hand. They circled one small island and then returned to the creek.

When they reached the place where Ishmael was tied, they pulled the canoe back onto the bank. Zech said, "I'm glad you brought me here, Tawanda. I'll always remember this place."

He mounted Ishmael and lifted her behind him, and they rode back toward the village. The sun sank rapidly as they approached the village, and already nighthawks swooped about, zigzagging crazily as they chased mosquitoes. She followed him to the chickee and stood beside him as he looked down at his father. There was no change in Tobias. The medicine man and Lillie still hovered over him, paying no heed to Zech and Tawanda. Zech knew it would be useless to question them, so he turned and walked away.

One of the cows had been slaughtered while they were gone, and the smell of roasted beef drifted from the cooking chickee. Tawanda prepared two wooden plates for them; then Zech followed her to the edge of the clearing. They sat on the ground just at the point where fire shadows faded into darkness, eating silently. Tawanda then said, "We're breaking a Seminole rule. An Indian woman does not sit beside a man while eating."

Tawanda got up suddenly and said, "I'd better go to the chickee now before my father comes looking for me."

Zech sat by himself for a while; then he took his blanket and placed it beside the chickee where his father tossed restlessly. The medicine man was gone, but Lillie was still there, changing the pads that cooled Tobias' face.

The next morning Tawanda fixed a breakfast of koonti biscuits and fried beef strips, and he ate eagerly. He returned to the chickee and sat by his father, ignoring her. She understood, and said nothing.

At noon the fever broke, and Tobias sat up and sipped a cup of beef broth. He smiled at Zech, then he lay back down and drifted into a calm sleep. Zech's spirits soared as Keith Tiger said him, "Tobias will be fine now. He has passed the worst of it. In a few days you will be able to take him home. I know your people are worried."

The words caused Zech a new concern that had not come into his mind while Tobias was so ill: his mother would be frantic with worry if they did not return soon. There was no way anyone from the hammock could ever find them here in this small village in the great cypress swamp.

He continued hovering about the chickee, again making a

nuisance of himself until finally Lillie spoke the only words she said in three days, "Go away and let us take care of him. You are worse than a puppy."

Tobias gradually gained strength, getting up and walking a few steps at a time, then eating solid food. He had become even more thin, and his clothes hung on him like sacks. On the morning of the sixth day he said to Zech, "How long have we been here? I don't remember much since the day we arrived."

"Almost a week, Pappa."

"A week? Good heavens! Emma will be worried sick. We'll have to leave in the morning."

"Are you sure you're strong enough to ride, Pappa? I could go to the hammock and tell them you're fine and let you stay here and rest. Then I would come back for you. I couldn't leave while you were so sick."

"No. I'll be fine. We'll go back together."

Keith Tiger spoke up. "You're welcome to stay here as long as you wish, Tobias. But if you leave, you must ride easy and not push yourself. See if you can find quinine at a trading post. It is what the soldiers use for malaria."

"I'll do that. And I truly thank you for what you've done for me."

"It is we who owe you thanks. The cows and rifles will save our people. Is there anything you wish from us in return?"

"My life is enough. But there's something Zech wanted if you can spare it. Dogs. Some rustlers killed the wolf dogs you gave us."

"That is no problem. We have puppies, and you can take your pick."

"No!" Zech said quickly. "James promised me some dogs he called leopards, but if I took them now they'd remind me of him and Willie. I couldn't stand it. I don't want dogs."

"I understand," Keith Tiger said. "It will be as you wish."

"I thank you just the same," Zech said more calmly, not wanting the Indian to think he didn't appreciate the offer.

"What's the name of the medicine man who tended me?"

Tobias asked. "I haven't thanked him yet."

"His name is Miami Billie," Tiger responded. "He is out gathering roots and bark to make medicine for you to take with you on the trip home. He will return soon. Tonight we will have a celebration of your recovery, Tobias. We will roast the tail of an alligator. This afternoon I will test the Winchester against a 'gator's hard skull. You will enjoy the feast."

All of the Indians were in a festive mood as the huge chunk of meat roasted on a spit over the fire. Zech and Tawanda again isolated themselves from the others and ate together, and the alligator was as good to Zech as the first chicken he tasted in Punta Rassa.

Tobias was tired and went to bed immediately after eating, and soon the village became quiet as everyone drifted into the chickees. Zech was almost asleep when Tawanda came silently and lay down beside him. He put his arms around her, absorbing her warmth. She pressed closer, facing him, and sleep came imperceptibly as they clung together. Neither of them was aware when her father came from the shadows and looked at them briefly, seeing them asleep together like children, then turning and going away.

The next morning as they were exchanging final good-byes, Keith Tiger said to Tobias, "Do not go back the way you came. It is too difficult in the custard-apple forest. Go to the east side of Okeechobee, near the ocean. There are pine lands there, and open prairie. It will be easier for you."

Tobias mounted the horse shakily and steadied himself, still weak but determined to ride. Zech and Tawanda glanced at each other, their eyes meeting in a silent understanding that he would return, but no tears came to Tawanda's eyes. To cry at parting would not be the way of an Indian woman.

They looked back and waved as they entered the woods, and

the sight of Tawanda became etched in Zech's mind. She looked small and alone as the early sunlight caught in her raven hair.

Tobias then said, "Let's ride now. We got a long way to go."

They moved slowly, stopping often to let Tobias rest and sip the medicine Miami Billie gave him, and when they rounded the east shore of Okeechobee it was as Keith Tiger said, pine scrub and palmetto prairie.

Days stretched into a week, and soon they came to the marsh where the herd drowned on their first grazing drive. From here they turned northwest, going out of the way toward the trading post at Fort Drum to see if Tobias could purchase quinine.

When they entered the settlement at noon the street was deserted, and there was no one in the store except Turner. Zech hovered in the background as Tobias inquired about quinine and was told they had none but it was on order and should be in soon. He waited until his father started out before going to the counter and saying hesitantly, "Hello, Mister Turner. I'm Zech MacIvey. Is Glenda here?"

"No, she's not. She's up in Jacksonville staying with her aunt so she can go to school." He then looked closely at Zech and said, "I remember you now. You were here last spring during a frolic. Glenda has spoken of you."

Although he wanted to see her, Zech felt relief that Glenda was not there. This would give him time to sort out his feelings for her and for Tawanda before seeing her again. He said, "Will she be coming back soon?"

"She'll be here for the Christmas frolic. Are you coming? I think she expects you."

"Well, I don't know, Mister Turner, but I'll try. Next time you write Glenda would you tell her I came by to see her?"

"Why don't you write yourself? I can give you the address. I know she'd be glad to hear from you."

"No, you tell her for me if you will," Zech responded, not wanting to admit he couldn't write. "I don't know when I'll be back here to post a letter. I better go now. Pappa is waiting outside."

Turner was amused by Zech's awkwardness as he almost fell over a pickle barrel while walking rapidly from the store.

Emma ran to them immediately when they entered the clearing, her cries of "Tobias! Tobias!" bringing the others outside.

Tobias dismounted quickly and hugged her, and then she said, "You've been gone so long. I was worried about you. But I'm glad you're back now. We had a bad thing happen while you were gone."

"What's that?" Tobias asked anxiously, alarmed by the gravity in her voice.

Frog spoke up first, "Bonzo died, Mister MacIvey. He took real sick on the way back from Punta Rassa. It was malaria. We done everything we could for him, and for a while it seemed he got better, but on the first night back here he just up and went away."

"That's too bad," Tobias said regretfully. "I'm real sorry to hear it. I wish I could have at least been here for the funeral."

"He's down by the river," Frog said. "Miz Emma said words, and it was a proper burial. It surprised us all, and I sure hated it. Me an' ole Bonzo went through a lot together."

Zech said, "Pappa had it too, and that's why we're so late getting home. He was so sick he like to have died. The medicine man cured him!"

"Tobias!" Emma exclaimed, grabbing his arm. "You had it too? I should have been there with you!"

"There's nothing to fret about now," he assured her. "The Indians looked after me real good. I still got some medicine Miami Billie made for me, and they're getting in some quinine at Fort Drum. All I need is a few days rest and I'll be fine."

"Did you have trouble findin' the Indians?" Skillit asked. "We all figured you'd end up down in Cuba."

"It wasn't easy," Tobias said. "There were times I didn't think we'd make it."

"We seen things you won't believe," Zech said excitedly. "I walked on vines right over the top of the woods, and the cypress trees down there are so big they make everthing here look like nothing. And I went to Pay-Hay-Okee."

"What's Pay-Hay-Okee?" Emma asked curiously.

"It's a place like nowhere else. We went there in a dugout canoe. Tawanda took me."

Emma said, "Let's go in the house and I'll fix something to eat. Then I want to hear all about your trip and everything you saw."

The entire group followed Tobias and Zech inside.

✠

A cold December wind stung his face as Zech rode alone across the prairie. There had been no change of seasons here, no brilliant colors to signal the coming of fall, no bare trees surrounded by decaying leaves to herald winter, no ice-covered bushes or frozen ponds. The cabbage palms and palmetto clumps and cypress stands looked the same and stayed the same, and the biting wind was the only indication of the dormant season.

Zech shivered as he pulled the jacket collar tighter around his neck; then he put Ishmael into a canter, hurrying along because the days were now shorter and sundown would come two hours earlier than usual. Mile after mile of brown prairie all looked the same as he headed for Fort Drum and the Christmas frolic.

The sun was not brilliant as in summer, and there was a desolate yellow glow across the land, a mid-afternoon twilight made even dimmer by an overcast gray sky. There were no long flights of birds winging their way casually toward distant feeding grounds, and the cypress stands were flooded with white and gray specks as egrets and herons sought refuge from the wind and cold.

It was three days before Christmas, a festive time Zech had never really known. Emma always tried to fix something special for Christmas dinner, baking sweet potato pies covered with wild honey, a turkey if Tobias could kill one, or whatever else was available to mark this one day from all the others. But there had been no gaily decorated tree, no exchange of colorfully wrapped gifts, no frolic or church services. When they lived in the scrub the only gifts he received were made with Tobias' hands, a chinaberry slingshot or a little windmill or a toy gun carved at night while he was sleeping. For the past three years Tobias purchased things at a trading post, hiding them in the barn loft until Christmas morning: a bolt of cloth or a bonnet for Emma, a hunting knife or a canteen for Zech; but there was no gathering of a family clan with joyous singing and a yard full of excited children.

Several coins jingled in Zech's pocket, and he wanted to reach the settlement in time to purchase gifts before attending the frolic. For his mother he wanted lilac water, remembering when she said she once smelled like flowers but no more; and for his father a pocket watch with a long chain, something he had seen men wearing in Punta Rassa.

As he drew nearer to Fort Drum, Zech's spirits rose and fell as unpredictably as winter weather—high and soaring one moment, downcast the next; excited by the reality of seeing Glenda again, but remembering Tawanda. Each one took turns occupying his thoughts, and to him each was as different as marsh land from prairie. He couldn't picture Tawanda at a Christmas frolic, or Glenda in a chickee. Both were equally fascinating yet so very far apart, in totally different worlds.

Night beat him to the trading post, and the glow of coal oil lamps spilled from the old building when he rode up and hitched Ishmael. The frolic would not be held in the open this time since the barnlike meeting hall was now completed.

Turner was starting for the door to lock up as Zech entered. He said, "Hello, Mister Turner. Looks like I just made it in time. I need to buy a few things before you close up."

"Sure, Zech. I was just leaving to get ready for the frolic. What you got in mind?"

"Lilac water if you have it. If you don't, something else that smells good, like flowers. It's for Mamma."

"I got something better than lilac. It has the scent of peach blossoms. What size bottle you want?"

"The biggest you got. And I want a pocket watch too, one with a chain."

Turner took the items from a case beside the counter and put them into a brown paper sack. "Is that it?"

"I need to get a little something for Skillit and Pearlie Mae and Frog. Maybe a couple of pipes and tobacco, and a sunbonnet. And I need a bundle of red ribbon."

Turner added these to the sack, his interest raised by the strange names. "Be anything else?"

"A dozen apples. Ishmael needs a Christmas treat too."

"Ishmael? Who's that?" he asked, his curiosity getting the best of him.

"My horse."

"Oh. That's mighty thoughtful of you. Wouldn't many men spend money buying a Christmas gift for a horse. That'll be a total of twelve dollars."

Zech put money on the counter, picked up the packages and turned to leave. Turner said, "I'm glad you made it for the frolic, Zech. It ought to be starting about now. I'll be a bit late, but Glenda's already over there."

Zech went outside and put one package in the saddlebag, and then he started feeding apples to Ishmael. He watched as Turner walked away down the dark street; then it dawned on him he should have purchased something for Glenda.

Ishmael had eaten four apples when the sound of fiddles drifted from a nearby building. Zech put the remainder in the saddlebag and walked slowly to the meeting hall. When he entered and looked about, he felt embarrassment. He was dressed in faded jeans, dusty boots and denim jacket, and all the other men and boys wore black suits, starched white shirts and string ties.

Chairs were lined against the two walls, and the fiddle players were on a raised platform in the rear of the room. Adjacent to that a table covered with a white cloth held a large punch bowl and glass cups.

Glenda was behind the table, her red hair standing out like a flag. She wore a blue dress decorated with white lace, with a blue ribbon in her hair. When she glanced toward the door and noticed

Zech she waved at him. He stared, seeing her almost as a stranger, even more beautiful than he remembered.

For a moment Zech hesitated, feeling the urge to walk backward to the door and run for Ishmael, then retreat to the prairie where he belonged. Had he known about Christmas frolics he could have purchased suitable clothes somewhere, but no one told him. He had never seen his father in a suit or his mother in a blue dress with lace, and because of this he blamed them for his present situation and felt anger at them for allowing him to come to the frolic dressed as he was. Then it came to him they wouldn't know either. Perhaps they once did, but that was too long ago in the past. In his memory he knew there had been no Christmas frolic in Florida for his mother and father and none now, and the sudden anger at them for something beyond their knowledge shamed him.

His embarrassment was his alone, for no one paid him even the slightest attention for the way he was dressed. The black suits in the room were worn only for funerals and weddings and the Christmas frolic, and by morning every man and boy would become a duplicate of Zech. If he had looked closer he would have seen moth holes, torn seams and frayed collars and cuffs, outgrown pants four inches short, missing buttons, and coat sleeves that came halfway to the elbow when an arm was bent.

A pot-bellied stove at the left of the door grew ripe and turned red, overheating Zech and causing him to move away. He walked across the open floor to the table. One of the ladies in attendance said, "Would you like punch?"

"I'll serve it," Glenda said. She poured a cup, came around the end of the table and handed it to Zech. "I'm sorry I haven't come to you sooner. I had to help mother. It's really good to see you again. I've thought about you often and hoped you'd be here tonight."

"I came by the store this fall to see you."

"Yes, I know. Daddy told me. I wish I'd been here. I like Jacksonville, but it's good to be home."

"You like it better than here?"

"Not better, but there are a lot of things to do there that we don't have here. They have cafés and little parks and theaters. Every Saturday night there's a dance, and on Sunday afternoon people dress up and ride in their carriages. It's all a lot of fun for a change, but I like Fort Drum too."

"We go to a café in Punta Rassa. They make good fried chicken and fish. But there's not much else to do there. It's just a place to ship cattle to Cuba. We own a hundred and fifty acres on the Caloosahatchie, and someday I'm going to build a cabin on it so we won't have to camp out ever time we take cows there."

"That would be nice. Maybe someday you can take me with you. I'd like to see Punta Rassa. It's such a lovely name."

"You'd be disappointed. Like I say, it's just a cowtown. Wouldn't be nothing like Jacksonville."

The music started again, and soon the room thundered with the sound of leather pounding the wooden floor. Glenda said, "Would you like to dance with me?"

"You know I don't know how."

She grabbed his arm. "I'll teach you!"

Zech pulled away. "I'm not dressed right, Glenda. You can see that. I ought not even be here, much less out on the dance floor. If I'd known everbody else had on a suit but me, I wouldn't have come inside."

"Oh pooh!" she said, taking his arm again. "You look fine. Mother has to practically hog-tie Daddy to get him in a suit, and he'll probably show up tonight dressed just like you are. And besides that, every girl here has her eye on you and would stand in line to dance with you. I know I would, and I'm sure not going to let them. You're not going to get away from me that easy, Zech MacIvey!"

"Well, O.K.," he agreed reluctantly. "But if it don't work out, let's quit."

Zech tried vainly to imitate the others, watching constantly and as stiff as a cypress pole, kicking when they kicked and turning when they turned. He was beginning to get the hang of it until they changed partners and swung down the line; then his boots grew as large as a wild steer's horns, tripping him up and staggering him sideways. He righted himself clumsily and retired from the floor.

Glenda continued the dance, and Zech watched from the sideline as she skipped from partner to partner, floating down the line as light as a feather. She glanced at him as she passed by, motioning for him to come back, but he backed further away and leaned against the wall.

When the music stopped she came to him immediately. He said, "I'm sorry. I must have looked plumb awful out there."

"You didn't either. You were doing real good, better than most people when they first try."

"I guess dancin' isn't my strong suit. Maybe I better stick to horses."

"You can learn. And I'll bet you didn't know how to ride a horse first time you got on one. We'll try again in a little while. Would you like more punch?"

He said, "Maybe that would help clear my throat. That scared me out there worse than a pack of wolves."

Glenda sensed he was more shamed by his performance than he would admit. She said, "Let's go outside for some fresh air. We can have punch later."

The cold wind struck them as they left the building and started up the street. They walked silently until Glenda said, "It's cold! Put your arm around me."

He put his arm around her waist as they continued, and then he said, "It's going to be bad out on the prairie tonight. I'll have to build a big fire to stay warm."

"The prairie?" she exclaimed, stopping and facing him. "What do you mean? You're not going home this late at night, are you?"

"Yes. Soon as we get back to the hall. I'll go out a ways and make camp, then go on in the morning."

"Zech! You can't do that! It's too cold, and there's no need of it.

You can stay at my house tonight. We have an extra room."

"Your house?" he questioned, not sure he understood the invitation. "Your daddy would probably take a whip to me if I even showed up there."

"He wouldn't either! He wouldn't mind at all. I've told my mother and father how I feel about you."

"Told them what?"

"That I love you, more than anything. They know about us."

Zech gulped. "I'd like to stay, Glenda, I really would, but I just can't. It just don't seem right."

"It would if we were promised."

"Promised? What's that?"

"You know, going steady. Promised to each other."

"How can we go steady with you up in Jacksonville?"

"I won't be there forever. School ends in May. And if I'm promised to you I won't even look at another boy. Will you do it?"

"I guess," he agreed reluctantly, still not sure what it meant; and then he said with more fervor, "Yes, I'd like to. But you'll have to tell me what to do."

"You can start by kissing me."

He kissed her and then said, "Don't be mad at me, Glenda, but I can't stay at your house tonight. Pappa needs me to help him with something, and we have to be in Kissimmee before noon tomorrow."

"Well, I guess if you have to, you have to," she said, disappointed. "But don't you forget we're promised! You hear? I mean it, Zech MacIvey! You're promised to me now!"

"I won't forget. I could never forget something like that."

"You can kiss me again if you want to."

"I want to," he said, pulling her back to him, once again overwhelmed by the smell of lilacs.

A full moon could be seen fleetingly as clouds raced across the sky. Zech galloped Ishmael during brief moments of light, then slowed to a walk when darkness rushed back in. He was ten miles out of the settlement when he stopped at a cypress stand and built a fire.

He searched himself for a reason why he lied about his father needing him, why he refused to stay in Fort Drum with Glenda. Other things also bothered him, his ease with Tawanda and his shyness with Glenda. He wondered if his father had ever been so tormented by girls, or if this anguish was his alone.

He liked Glenda very much, this he knew; but it puzzled him why she had chosen him so quickly over boys in Jacksonville who could make him look like nothing more than the prairie hick he took himself to be. She was the most beautiful girl he had ever seen, or probably would see, and he should be overjoyed by her love; yet he couldn't comprehend her choice of him, which made accepting it more difficult.

He got up and fed Ishmael an apple, and then he said, "I like you best of all, Ishmael. We go where we want to go, and there's no fuss about what to wear or where we're going to sleep or nothing else. Maybe I best stick with you and let the rest of it go. It just ain't worth it." The horse whinnied and nudged him, wanting another apple.

He lay close to the fire and rolled himself in his blanket, shivering as the wind sang through the cypress trees.

No one was in the house but Emma when Zech rode in. As soon as he entered she said, "I'll bet you haven't eaten a thing since you left Fort Drum. Sit at the table and I'll fix something for you."

She noticed he seemed agitated, and she watched him closely while fiddling with a spoon, stirring a pot unnecessarily. Finally she said, "Did you have a good time?"

"Yes, Mamma. It was real nice."

"Maybe when your father gets to feeling better we can go to the next frolic with you."

Zech toyed with the food, and then he said, "Mamma, do you know what it means to be promised?"

"Yes, I know. Your father and I were promised. It means you intend to get married someday, and you're not supposed to be seeing anyone else."

"I bought you a Christmas gift! You'll like it!"

"Let's see! Let me see what it is!"

"Oh no! You'll have to wait. It's a surprise for Christmas morning."

Emma put her arms around him and said, "I love you, Zech, and I can see why any girl would want you. Girls want a man, not some fancy dancer who couldn't skin a rabbit if his family was starving. You don't understand this, but girls do. That's why I chose Tobias. You've got strength like your father, and that's what girls look for in a mate. Glenda has more sense than you give her credit for. She knows what she's doing."

Zech suddenly realized something he should have known all along: there is more to life and survival than frolics or black suits or bowls full of punch. The Kissimmee and the Caloosahatchie and all the prairies and swamps between are not Jacksonville with its parks and cafés and theaters, and never will be; and someone must round up the cows and blaze the trails and fight the wolves and bears and plant the orange trees like his father had done. He was schooled not in reading and writing but in survival, and this was not something he should be ashamed of. His teachers were the best, and he loved them for it. He vowed he would never again make excuses to himself or to anyone for what he was or who he was. He was a MacIvey, and proud of it.

He jumped up suddenly and said, "I think I'll go down in the woods and see can I shoot a turkey; then I'll cut us a tree. I bought a big bundle of ribbon at the store to decorate it. We've never had a Christmas tree, and it's about time we did."

✝

February
1880

"Emma! Emma! Come and see! You got to see!"

Tobias was running through the woods as fast as his lanky legs would carry him, shouting again, "They're blooming, Emma! They're blooming!"

Emma rushed from the house and said, "What on earth is the matter with you, Tobias? The way you're hollering you'll scare the life out of everybody in Kissimmee!"

"The orange trees . . ." Tobias panted, "they're in bloom! They finally done it! Millions of buds, bustin' out all over! And the smell . . . Lordy, the smell! You got to see it!"

"You know you ought not get so worked up," Emma admonished. "If you don't calm yourself you'll have another spell."

The shouting attracted the attention of everyone else, and they poured from the barn and the cabins. Pearlie Mae had given birth to three boys in three years and gained an additional thirty pounds in the process, and she waddled like a duck as her brood followed close behind her. Skillit scooped up two of the toddlers and put them on his shoulders as he ran for the sound of the commotion.

Three more times Tobias had replanted the orange trees and expanded the plot, and now there were one hundred acres inside the fenced area. He said to the assemblage, "We gone have enough to fill a whole schooner at Fort Pierce! It'll take ten wagons to haul 'em there. That's what the future is—oranges! We don't have to round 'em up or brand 'em or do nothin' but pluck 'em off the trees!"

"Calm yourself, Tobias!" Emma cautioned again. "Let's all go and see before he gives himself a stroke."

Tobias took the lead, stepping lively, and halfway through the woods it came to them, seeping from the grove a quarter-mile distant, an overpowering fragrance. They all stopped, feeling intoxicated by what hit them. Emma breathed deeply and said, "Oh my! Oh my, Tobias! I've never smelled anything like it in all my life. It's like the Lord has turned the rain to perfume and it's come down over everything. I wish I could figure out a way to put it in a bottle."

When they left the woods and came into an open area, they were greeted by a sea of white blossoms, row upon row of trees that seemed to be covered with snow. There was a steady drone as bees darted from blossom to blossom, gorging themselves on nectar.

Skillit said, "Lordy me, Mistuh Tobias. It sure is a sight. Will all them little flowers turn into oranges?"

"They surely will. I done told all of you! There's as much gold on them trees as a whole herd of cows."

"We ought to build some bee hives," Zech said. "We could get lots of honey out of here."

"If it would taste as good as the blossoms smell," Emma said, "it would be a gift of the Lord. Orange blossom honey. It even sounds pretty. I'm real proud of you, Tobias. You stuck with it all this time, and now it's finally happened."

"There's been times I wanted to quit and give it up," Tobias said, "especially when the cows kept eating the trees. But they can't do it no more 'less they can fly. And that's thanks to you,

Emma. I wouldn't have ever bought taller trees if you hadn't told me to. I'd a just gone on forever planting cow fodder."

"I could stand here the rest of my life and just sniff," Emma said. "I hope heaven smells like this. But I've got things to do at the house. I'm just getting started with my dress and the wedding is almost here."

"I'll bet ole Ishmael'll be glad when that wedding is over," Frog said teasingly. "Mister Zech done wore that pore hoss out runnin' him from here to Fort Drum."

"Ah, shut up, Frog!" Zech said. "I haven't been over there that much and you know it. You just running on like you did when Skillit got married."

Zech and Glenda had finally set their wedding for the last week in February, having honored her father's request that they wait until she finished four years of schooling in Jacksonville. She now helped her father in the store and tutored area children in English and math.

Skillit and Frog followed Tobias into the grove for a closer look as the others went back to the clearing. As soon as they were in the house, Zech said, "Mamma, I'm glad to see Pappa so happy with his grove, but there's something about it that worries me real bad."

"What's that?"

"He's worked so hard all these years and finally it's about to pay off. But somebody could come along and take it all away from him, even the house and everything. We don't own this land."

"That worries me too. Tobias thinks it's ours because we live on it, but I know it isn't. If somebody did take the grove it would just about kill him. The malaria spells are coming so often now he can't go on riding herd much longer. Sometimes when he walks down to the garden he comes back panting like a horse that's been run. He needs something like the grove to stay here and look after."

"We've got to own this land and a bunch more too," Zech said. "It's getting harder all the time to find wild cows, and if we stay in the cattle business we'll have to start raising our own or buy them off other folks and fatten them up. Somebody has bought a big piece of land up north of here and built a house on it, and if they want to, they got a legal right to stop us from grazing there anymore. And it's soon going to be the same everywhere."

"You want me to talk to Tobias again?"

"It wouldn't do any good. I'm going to handle it myself. Last time I was in Kissimmee I went to the land office and inquired about this place. All the land here was once owned by a timber company that never did anything with it. It was too much prairie and not enough trees, so they let it go back for taxes. I can buy it now for twenty cents an acre. I'll tell Pappa I'm going to Kissimmee for supplies. Then I'll take the buckboard and some of the money in those trunks and buy the land. Pappa won't know the money is gone. He hasn't looked in those trunks in years."

"Just go ahead and do what you need to do. I'll never tell him."

"While he's at the grove, I'll take the money down to the barn and hide it. Then tomorrow morning I'll set out for Kissimmee. I know it would break Pappa's heart if somebody took his grove, and that's sure to happen sooner or later if I don't do something about it."

"You're doing the right thing, Zech, and don't ever let it bother you because your pappa doesn't know. It's not like you're going behind his back for something you want. It's for his sake. And money isn't the reason why Tobias hasn't bought the land himself. He's just too stubborn to admit he's wrong, and he is wrong about this. He thinks the land is a gift from the Lord for everybody's use and it's not right for anybody to lay claim to it. Maybe it ought to be that way, but it's not. You go on now and hide that money before he gets back. Someday he'll be thankful you did this."

"I hope so, Mamma. I don't want to see him hurt, and there's nothing the Lord can do if somebody shows up here with a deed. That would be the end of it."

*Z*ech came from the land office smiling, clutching the deed firmly as if it might fly away. The title was in three names, his and Tobias' and Emma's, and later he would add Glenda's name after she became a MacIvey.

He unhitched the horse and drove the buckboard down the street, overwhelmed by the fact they were now landowners. He felt like shouting it for all to hear, MacIvey land, cattle and oranges. They were no longer squatters but rightful owners, free and clear with no debt owed.

He stopped at one of the mercantile stores and went inside, telling the clerk he was interested in a black suit. There was a rack of them, all identical, double-breasted and scratchy looking, large mother-of-pearl buttons and baggy pants. He held one in front of him and looked in a mirror, thinking that a man would have to be crazy to wear such an outfit except for absolute necessity. For Glenda, he would do it, but he would not suffer alone. He also purchased one for his father, surmising they would all have to hold Tobias down and force it on him, like saddling a wild horse. He also bought white shirts and string ties and a tin of boot polish.

There was a rack of dresses next to the men's department, and he examined them reluctantly, hoping no one would come in and see him in the ladies' section. The rack was next to a counter piled high with corsets and bloomers and brassieres, and he glanced at them warily and at the female clerk who watched him with amusement. He finally selected a dress he thought would fit Emma. It was pale blue, like the one Glenda had worn at the Christmas frolic, and it was decorated with white lace.

He put the packages in the buckboard and started down the street, wanting to hurry home and show the deed to Emma, and surprise her with the dress. At first he just glanced at it as it glinted in the sunlight, strapped to the saddle as a man rode past; and then it dawned on him what he had seen, a double-barreled ten-gauge shotgun, half the length of the horse, its weight pulling the saddle sideways. He stopped the buckboard abruptly, turned and followed the rider until he hitched the horse in front of a saloon.

Zech reached beneath the seat, picked up the Winchester and pumped a bullet into the chamber; then he walked quickly to the man and shoved the barrel into his back, saying, "Mister, if you so much as breathe, I'll blow the backbone slam out of you."

"What. . . ?"

"The shotgun . . . I want to see the stock. Just ease over there with me and don't make any sudden moves."

Zech turned the shotgun over with his left hand, and there it was, carved into the wood, MCI. He said, "That's my pappa's mark. This gun was stole from him a long time ago. Are you the one who took it?"

"I don't know what this is all about, but I didn't steal no gun. I bought that thing early this morning and paid fifteen dollars for it. The man who sold it to me said he was tired of hauling it around 'cause it's so heavy. He had a new Winchester, one like you got there."

"Don't you lie to me!" Zech said, shoving the rifle harder. "Can you prove you bought it?"

"Naw, I can't prove it! Can you prove you bought that buckboard? I paid cash money, and that's all I can say. I got a place just north of here, and everybody in Kissimmee knows me. They also know I ain't the kind to steal a gun or nothing else. Only reason I bought that blunderbuss is to shoot wild hogs that keeps tearing up my pasture. If it belongs to your daddy you can have it. Just take that rifle away before you bust my ribs with it."

Zech lowered the rifle and said, "You don't seem like a bushwhacking rustler, so I'll take your word for it. But I'd sure be interested to know where the man is who sold you the gun."

"They was camped three miles east of here, down by Panther Creek. But if I was you, I wouldn't go there alone look'n for a fight. There was nine of 'em, the meanest lookin' bunch I ever seen. I was scared myself till I rode away. I thought for sure they was going to rob me."

"Maybe I'll shoot them in the back, like they're prone to do with men and dogs."

"Fella, I ain't joshin'. I wouldn't go after that bunch 'less I had a army with me."

Zech took a doubloon from his pocket, handed it to the man and said, "Here's your money back. I want the gun. It used to mean a lot to my pappa. And I'm sorry if I scared you."

"Well, you sure did! I'm not used to having a Winchester shoved in my back. I'll just go on in here now and drink myself fifteen dollars worth of whiskey to settle my nerves."

Zech put the shotgun in the buckboard. "Which way is it to Panther Creek where they were camped?"

"About three miles out along the main east road there's a trail that goes off to the south into some thick woods. That's where they was early this morning. But you're a fool if you go there."

"Much obliged for the directions," Zech said as he drove off.

"Didn't need that cannon noway," the man muttered as he went into the saloon.

Zech trotted the horse until he found the trail; then he tied Ishmael to a bush and walked into the woods, the rifle in his hands. He stayed to the left of the path, moving slowly from tree to tree, listening for any sound that might indicate the men's presence. Nine to one was bad odds even for a Winchester, and he wished Frog and Skillit were with him. But if he could slip up on them undetected, he could draw down before they had a chance to go for their guns. What he would do next he didn't know.

He covered a hundred yards and then came to the remains of a camp beneath a live oak. Empty bean cans were scattered about, and the fire coals were still warm. An empty gallon jug with a corn cob stopper lay at the base of the tree. He kicked the jug and watched as it tumbled over the ground, down the bank and into the creek. He said, "I'll catch up with you someday!" Then he turned and went back to the buckboard.

Tobias was at the grove when Zech drove in, and Emma was in the house. When he saw that she was alone, he grinned and waved the deed; then he hugged her and said, "It's done, Mamma!"

"How much did you buy?" she asked curiously.

"Twenty thousand acres."

"Twenty thousand? That's an awful lot, isn't it, Zech? Will we ever have need of so much?"

"Mamma, at twenty cents an acre, it was only eight sacks of coins. It didn't even make a dent in one trunk, and that gold's not doing anything but gathering dust."

"Well, it's for sure Tobias will never know the difference."

"The land is ours now, clear and legal. Nobody can ever come along and take it from us."

"I'll sleep better knowing that."

"Where's Pappa?" Zech then asked. "I've got a real surprise for him in the buckboard."

"He's been up at the grove all day, just sitting and looking. I think he expects to see oranges pop out right before his eyes. What did you get him?"

"His old shotgun."

"Really? How on earth did you do that?"

"I saw a man with it, and sure enough, it had Pappa's mark on the stock. He bought it off another man, and I gave him his money back and took it. I went looking for the man who sold it but he was already gone."

"It's a good thing he was. You ought not be around folks like that. You could get yourself killed. It's best you forget things that happened a long time ago and let it be."

"I don't forget easy, Mamma. Just don't worry about it. When the time comes I'll handle it. I got Pappa another surprise too. I bought both of us a suit for the wedding."

"That'll be a sight to see," Emma snorted. "It'll take a team of oxen to drag him into it. Only time I figure to see your daddy in a suit is at his funeral, and then he'll probably pop up in the casket and put on his overalls."

"I got something for you too," Zech said, smiling. "I'll bring it in now."

He went to the buckboard and returned with a brown paper bag. He held it behind him and teased, "Guess what it is and you can have it. Guess wrong and it goes to Pearlie Mae."

She snatched at his arms but he backed away. "You've got to guess first, Mamma."

"Oh, Zech, what is it? You're too big for me to spank anymore. Stop teasing and let me see!"

He handed her the bag, and when the dress came tumbling out she said, "Oh, Zech! It's the prettiest thing I've ever seen! I love it! Oh, it's so pretty!" Then she sat at the table and cried, the dress held gently in her lap.

Zech was startled. He said anxiously, "What's the matter, Mamma! What is it?"

She looked at him through misted eyes; then she took his hands in hers and said, "Oh, Zech, you've got a lot to learn about women, and you about to marry one. A woman cries when her heart is filled with joy, and that's the kind of crying I'm doing now. You've made me so happy! I've never had a dress like this. I'll wear it proudly at your wedding."

"Put it on and let's see how it looks," he said, relieved. "And don't scare me like that again. I sure hope Glenda doesn't cry when she's happy."

"She will. And when she's sad too. It's a woman's way. You might as well get used to it."

Emma took the dress into the bedroom, and when she returned Zech stared at her, seeing someone other than his mother. He exclaimed, "Mamma! You're the purtiest woman I've ever seen! You look even better than Glenda did when she wore a dress like that at the frolic. Pappa's got to see too! I'll go bring him back to the house. You hide behind a door and step out in front of him.

I'll bet his eyeballs pop out and roll around on the floor. I'll run get him now."

Emma stepped out on the stoop and watched as he dashed away through the woods. Then she ran her fingers over the dainty lace and cried again.

CHAPTER TWENTY-THREE

♉

"Tobias MacIvey! You put on that suit! If you don't, I'll never cook another bite of food as long as I live."

"Well now. That would be bad, wouldn't it? I guess I'll just have to learn to make stew."

"For God's sake, Mistuh MacIvey, put it on!" Frog urged. "You heard what Miz Emma said. You want us all to suffer because you so stubborn.?"

"I'll hold him down," Skillit said, "and you jerk off them overalls. Then we'll hang him by his feet in a tree, like a hawg at scrapin' time, and dress him up real purty."

Tobias backed away as the two of them came toward him threateningly. He said, "All right! All right! I'll do it this once, but I still don't see why a man's got to dress up like a circus clown to go to a wedding. Back off now! I'll do it myself."

"That's better," Emma said. "And as soon as you get done in the wagon I'll put on my dress."

They were camped three miles west of Fort Drum. Zech had insisted that everyone come to the ceremony, including Pearlie Mae and the three boys. It was to take place at high noon that day in the town meeting hall.

Zech stood off to one side alone, watching and grinning, remembering what his mother said about Tobias and the suit and a team of oxen. He had been up since dawn, shaved twice, and slicked down his tousled sandy hair. His broad shoulders and muscled arms filled out the suit to perfection, and he was quite pleased with himself, although the rough wool made his legs itch, causing him to scratch constantly. When Frog laughed at him he threatened him with a hickory club; then all the attention was shifted to Tobias.

Tobias finally came from the wagon, scratching also, and Frog put his hand over his mouth to suppress a giggle. Emma said, "You look pure handsome, Tobias. I don't see why you made such a fuss over it. And all you men stop this foolish joshing! This is Zech's wedding day, and you're all acting like a bunch of silly children. Now stop it, you hear!"

Frog's grin vanished quickly as Emma went into the wagon, and when she came out wearing the blue dress they all gasped in admiration. Pearlie Mae said, "Lawsy me, Missus Emma, you sho' a sight to see! Everbody at the wedding going to stare at you."

Tobias was seeing Emma in blue for the second time and with just as much excitement as the first. He said, "You look so purty, Emma. It seems more fittin' for you and me to be getting married today instead of Zech. Maybe we'll just take that honeymoon trip for them and let them go on back to the hammock."

"Hush up, Tobias!" Emma said, feeling radiant from the compliments. "We're too old to even think of such a thing. This is Zech and Glenda's day, not ours. Now let's get started! We surely don't want to be late."

The procession then set forth, Tobias and Emma leading with the buckboard, followed by Skillit and his brood in the ox wagon and Frog and Zech on horseback. After the wedding Zech and Glenda would take the buckboard and the others would return to the hammock in the wagon.

As a wedding gift Glenda's father had purchased round-trip passage for them on an inland schooner from Fort Pierce to Jacksonville, and they were to leave the buckboard at a livery stable in Fort Pierce.

They arrived in the settlement a half hour before noon and found the street deserted. The store was closed, and tacked to the door there was a wreath of white flowers. They went directly to the meeting hall since Emma cautioned Zech not to go to the Turner house beforehand and see Glenda prior to the ceremony for it would bring bad luck.

Horses, oxen, and wagons were hitched in front of the building, and when they entered they were confronted by the same moth-eaten black suits Zech saw at the frolic. Most of the women had on hats topped with artificial fruit and flowers. Every head turned and stared as the MacIvey clan marched single file up the center aisle and filled the seats at the front of the room. Pearlie Mae whispered, "Now the fust one of you youngens so much as open yo' mouth, I'll blister yo' hiney good when this over."

All of the bodies were overheating the room, and Zech was sweating profusely when a fat woman in a pink dress stood up and started singing. The ceremony was to be performed by an itinerant preacher who conducted services in the meeting hall once a month. As soon as the song was finished, the preacher came up the aisle and motioned for Zech to come forward and stand to his left. An usher conducted Glenda's mother to a front seat; then there was a commotion in the rear as Glenda and her father entered, causing another bout of neck-stretching and staring.

Zech stared wide-eyed, seeing Glenda in a flowing white dress, her red hair covered by a veil of white lace. She floated up the aisle, her face beaming, her eyes sparkling and transfixed on Zech as her father guided her to his side. Blood pumped through him so vigorously his face turned white and then crimson, flushing back and forth, and his legs wobbled as if he would pitch forward and fall flat.

The ceremony was a blur, incomprehensible words flowing from the wool-draped preacher, sweating and scratching, all of it unreal until he felt himself slipping the ring on her finger, a simple gold band made from a Spanish doubloon. Then the veil came up and he was aware of kissing her, a flood of people pressing them, pumping his hand and hugging Glenda, then a loud wail as Pearlie Mae's hand struck flesh.

Zech followed Glenda outside where they were greeted by a spring day come early, a pale blue sky, emerald trees flooded with soft sunlight. She took his arm and clung to him as they led the gathering down a dirt street, stirring up puffs of dust, heading to the Turner house for punch and cake.

Once again there was hand pumping, back slapping, and hugging, until finally he said to himself, "Please Lord, no more. Let it end." He was not aware Glenda was gone and was surprised when she came from the bedroom wearing a pink cotton dress and white ribbon in her hair. She took his hand and whispered, "It's time now, Zech. We can go."

He picked up her bag in the hallway; then everybody spilled from the house to watch as they headed for the buckboard. He lifted her to the seat, jumped in, and slapped the reins, causing the horse to bolt forward. Glenda looked back and waved, but all Zech could see was the wreath on the store front as it flashed by.

Continued in Volume 2.

In Volume 2, with the birth of Zech and Glenda's son, Solomon, a new generation of MacIveys learns to ride horses, drive cattle, and teach rustlers a thing or two. Sol and his family earn more and more gold doubloons from cattle sales, as well as dollars from their orange groves. They invest it in buying land, once free to all, now owned and fenced and increasingly populated, until it becomes just a land remembered.

If you enjoyed reading this book, here are some other books from Pineapple Press on related topics. Ask your local bookseller for our books. For a complete catalog, write to Pineapple Press, P.O. Box 3889, Sarasota, FL 34230 or call 1-800-PINEAPL (746-3275). Or visit our website at www.pineapplepress.com.

A Land Remembered is available in a version for adults. Tell your adult friends and relatives what a great story it is.

FICTION
Blood Moon Rider by Zack C. Waters. When his Marine father is killed in WWII, young Harley Wallace is exiled to the Florida cattle ranch of his bitter, badly scarred grandfather. The murder of a cowman and the disappearance of Grandfather Wallace leads Harley and his new friend Beth on a wild ride through the swamps and into the midst of a conspiracy of evil. Ages 9–14.

Escape to the Everglades by Edwina Raffa and Annelle Rigsby. Based on historical fact, this young adult novel tells the story of Will Cypress, a half-Seminole boy living among his mother's people during the Second Seminole War. He meets Chief Osceola and travels with him to St. Augustine. Ages 9–12.

Solomon by Marilyn Bishop Shaw. Young Solomon Freeman, and his parents, Moses and Lela, survive the Civil War, gain their freedom, and gamble their dreams, risking their very existence, on a homestead in the remote environs of north central Florida. Ages 9–14.

The Spy Who Came In from the Sea by Peggy Nolan. Teenager Frank Hollahan moves to Florida in 1943 at the height of WWII. He soon becomes entangled in a mystery involving a German spy that ends up teaching him valuable lessons about friendship, perseverance, and the power of the truth. Ages 8–14.

Cracker Westerns:
Bridger's Run by John Wilson. Hot-tempered Tom Bridger travels across Florida's frontier in search of his long-lost uncle and a hidden treasure.

Ghosts of the Green Swamp by Lee Gramling. Saddle up your easy chair and kick back for a Cracker Western featuring that rough-and-ready but soft-hearted Florida cowboy, Tate Barkley, introduced in Riders of the Suwannee.

Guns of the Palmetto Plains by Rick Tonyan. As the Civil War explodes over Florida, Tree Hooker dodges Union soldiers and Florida outlaws to drive cattle to feed the starving Confederacy.

Ninety-Mile Prairie by Lee Gramling. Young cowhand Peek Tillman and fierce Florida frontiersman Chekita Joe work to protect a Yankee couple from greedy outlaws.

Riders of the Suwannee by Lee Gramling. Tate Barkley returns to 1870s' Florida just in time to come to the aid of a young widow and her children as they fight to save their homestead from outlaws.

Thunder on the St. Johns by Lee Gramling. Riverboat gambler Chance Ramsay teams up with the family of young Josh Carpenter and the trapper's daughter Abby Macklin to combat a slew of greedy outlaws seeking to destroy the dreams of honest homesteaders.

Trail from St. Augustine by Lee Gramling. A young trapper, a crusty ex-sailor, and an indentured servant girl fleeing a cruel master join forces to cross the Florida wilderness in search of buried treasure and a new life.

NONFICTION

A Land Remembered Goes to School by Tillie Newhart and Mary Lee Powell. An elementary school teacher's manual, using A Land Remembered to teach language arts, social studies, and science, coordinated with the Sunshine State Standards of the Florida Department of Education.

Middle School Teacher Plans and Resources for A Land Remembered: Student Edition by Margaret Paschal. The vocabulary lists, comprehension questions, and post-reading activities for each chapter in A Land Remembered: Student Edition make this teacher's manual a valuable resource. The activities aid in teaching social studies, science, and language arts coordinated with the Sunshine State Standards.

African Americans in Florida by Maxine D. Jones and Kevin M. McCarthy. Profiles African Americans during four centuries of Florida history in brief essays. Ages 10 and up.

Drawing Florida Wildlife by Frank Lohan. The clearest, easiest method yet for learning to draw Florida's birds, reptiles, amphibians, and mammals. All ages.

The Gopher Tortoise: A Life History by Patricia Sawyer Ashton and Ray E. Ashton Jr. With hundreds of color photos and easy text, this book offers children and adults a first-rate explanation of the critical role this fascinating tortoise plays in shaping upland Florida and the Southeast. Ages 10 and up.

Hunted Like a Wolf: The Story of the Seminole War by Milton Meltzer. Offers a look at the events, players, and political motives leading to the Seminole War and the near extermination of a people. Ages 12 and up.

Native Americans in Florida by Kevin M. McCarthy. Teaches about the many diverse Indian tribes in Florida from prehistoric times to the present. Also includes information about archaeology, an extensive glossary, and legends that teach moral lessons. Ages 10 and up.

Patchwork: Seminole and Miccosukee Art and Activities by Dorothy Downs. Learn about the history of the Seminole and Miccosukee people, and how they do their crafts. Make your very own patchwork and doll, just like the Seminoles and Miccosukees—using colored paper and glue instead of fabric and a sewing machine. Ages 9–12.

Those Outrageous Owls by Laura Wyatt. Those Terrific Turtles by Sarah Cussen. Those Amazing Alligators by Kathy Feeney. Those Excellent Eagles by Jan Lee Wicker. Those Peculiar Pelicans by Sarah Cussen. Those Funny Flamingos by Jan Lee Wicker. Each of these books contains 20 questions and answers about these fascinating creatures. Illustrated by Steve Weaver. Ages 5–9.

Young Naturalist's Guide to Florida, 2nd Edition by Peggy Sias Lantz and Wendy A. Hale. This enticing book for young readers is now available in a newly designed and updated edition. This new edition provides up-to-date information about Florida's wonderful natural places and the plants and creatures that live here—many of which are found nowhere else in the United States. Ages 10–14.